WALKER

CHAINS AND DAMES BOOK ONE

E.M. RAEGAN

DEAR READER,

This page is for you.
Thank you for reading.
Books inspire us. They bring us joy and allow us to escape for a
little while.
I hope you find that with mine.
Thank you for taking the time out of your lives to read my hard
work.
It means the world,
Erin.

WALKER

Walker Lawson had me before he even knew my name and he knew it. Reveled in it.

I left home to tour the world with a rock band.

I was out of my comfort zone and rolling through the lifestyle with a deep-seated need to find my own independence.

To prove to myself that I was capable of finding my own way.

To prove that I was more than a burden.

Keep my head down.

Focus on my health.

Those were my only two goals.

And then eyes the color of a brewing storm met mine.

Johnnie Walker Lawson.

Famous Drummer.

Sexy Rock Star.

Quiet, pensive, brooding—he was the opposite of everything I thought he would be.

Opposite of everything I thought he could be.

I hadn't been prepared for him. For just how far he would go to catch my attention and keep it.

But now that he had it—had me—I was terrified of losing him along with everything else I'd gained. He was quickly becoming everything I could have ever wanted. Everything I had been searching for.

Secrets have a way of burrowing themselves inside you. But they never stay quiet.

They'll come crawling their way out no matter what you do or what you have to lose.

.

For my mother.
Happy Birthday!

My uncle Varian increased his pace, his expensive glossy black shoes clicking on the sparkling marble floors. I heaved my bags higher up on my shoulder, trailing behind him. The worn-down traction of my own ratty sneakers was mocking me, my feet slipping back with every quick step.

"Catch up, Shy," he ordered me with a clipped tone.

I took wide strides to keep up with my uncle, almost losing him in the airport's crowded halls. My bags and his were weighing me down and my shoulders were aching, but I was determined to prove to him that I could handle this new job.

My parents had to nearly beg him to take me on. *Poor little Shiloh*, they likely told him. *She can't keep a job.*

Give her a chance, my mother had tearfully begged over the phone. I was both humiliated and grateful he agreed. As much as it hurt to admit, I *couldn't* hold down a job. Twenty-two years old and my future was looking pretty bleak. That wasn't how it was supposed to go. Three grueling years in college that amounted to nothing.

My parents had tried to understand, they really did, but how could they when I didn't understand it myself?

I had been born premature, eight weeks early. That had been what started it all for me. As a child, l required speech therapy, occupational therapy, and the extra help at school. My parents tried hard to help me stay with the kids my age. But by second grade, I was held back. If I hadn't been, school would've been an even greater struggle for me later in life.

By my first year in high school, I was diagnosed with Crohn's disease. To say that had derailed me would be a massive under-statement. I didn't get to graduate high school until I was nine-teen years old. I had been so damn grateful after everything that I'd finished and was finally going to college.

At first, I couldn't decide what I wanted to do with my life. I had no direction. After trying so many different majors in school it became clear that even if I could've decided, I didn't have the ability or desire to actually compete with the other students.

I had learned just how hard college was on me when I had a flare-up, or my medicines were adjusted. When I had a treat-ment, it would take me at least a week to recover and so during that time, I'd accomplish nothing.

My health, coupled with my developing depression and severe anxiety, had forced me to make the decision to drop out. My parents, instead of being angry or disappointed, were relieved to have me back home where they could hover over me at all hours of the day.

I'd looked for jobs, trying to afford my own place. But without experience, apart from babysitting, I was stuck as a cashier at the local market. The first time I had a flare-up, I lost that job. Next, it was the local coffee shop. My boss there had at least stuck it out with me for a few months before solemnly informing me they had to let me go but they wished me all the best.

With no job following, my music agent uncle was my last resort. He at least knew what I was battling. He knew I might need a week—or several—off work if my body decided to shut down on me. That my diet was very limited and important to my health as well as the medications and vitamins I took daily. He was willing to work with me and give me an opportunity to provide for myself. Even if it was a handout, I wasn't in a position to be stubborn or prideful.

I was to be his assistant. Not in the way Julie was his assistant, keeping his calendar and contacts, but following him and the band around, getting them every small thing they might need. I was an errand girl, and that was fine with me.

If I was lucky, he may even allow me to take some photos for the band's social media accounts. The unknown had me nervous. But I was also excited.

And very out of shape.

Struggling to keep up, I focused on the security crew as they escorted us with the rest of Uncle Varian's team out to the tarmac where a private jet was waiting. The band's music label, Farryn Records, was painted in black down the side in elegant script.

The place was crawling with security that were keeping photographers, journalists and fans at bay near the gates, waiting for the band to arrive. I was unused to having so many eyes on me and though I wasn't who they were all there to see, it felt strange to be on the other side of that gate, no longer looking in on the mysterious world of the rich and famous, but instead experiencing it. At least a small part of it, anyway.

I jogged up the narrow steps into the plane, my chest heaving from exertion. Cream colored walls and leather seating in the cabin, it looked more like a luxurious hotel than an airplane. In search of a seat, I maneuvered my way past a few women and men in business attire and casual clothes trying my best to keep from hitting them with the luggage I was carrying. I couldn't tell any of them apart or what they were here for, other than the obvious—the band. Everyone was here for the band in some capacity, including now myself.

My presence went completely unnoticed. Not a single person greeted me or looked my way. I was invisible and that was fine with me. I preferred to remain that way. The less attention I drew to myself the better. I didn't handle attention very well. Not since high school, when I was known more as *that sick girl* rather than a real person.

"Shiloh," my uncle called out.

I jumped, startled, and rushed to catch up to him at the back of the plane.

He looked me over as I made my way to him, his face softening when he saw me struggling with the bags. I didn't know what he had in all of them but apparently one carry-on per person was not upheld when you flew on a fancy plane owned by a multi-billion-dollar record label.

He stood up, taking all the bags except for my carry-on from me. My shoulders dropped in instant relief. "Settle in back here. I'll check on you shortly."

I nodded, slumping into the nearest seat as he took his bags to the front of the plane.

I'd been on a few planes in my life. The rare trips when my uncle would invite us out to his home in California or the one time my parents and I took a trip from our home in Montana to Florida to see my grandparents. This was so much different than any of those planes. This time my bottom sank into the soft seats, which felt like clouds compared to the stiff boards on a commercial flight. I had so much more leg room, even if I didn't have the height to fully appreciate it, and it smelled fantastic. There was no musky stench my mother had complained about every time we flew.

I pulled my backpack onto my lap and opened it to check my camera over. I hadn't packed it in my suitcase, which was probably in the belly of the plane by now, worried it might get damaged. However, it was safely tucked inside my carry-on along with a few books I'd chosen for the flight. I fetched one out, the pages dog-eared at my favorite parts, and cracked it open.

With the chatter on the plane, the energy anxious and buzzing, I couldn't bring myself to read any of it. Instead, I scooted to the window seat and lifted the shade. The evening sun cast a pink glow across the horizon. California was so unlike Montana. I'd only been here three days and I was missing home already. Missing the chill in the air and the quiet atmosphere. In several hours, I would be even farther away.

We were headed to New York first. I'd never been but, already homesick, I wasn't looking forward to it as much as my mother and I had thought, gossiping over all the things I was going to see on tour.

I pulled my phone out, re-reading her last text:

I'm so proud of you! We love you so much! Call us when you get there!

Then my dad's:

Don't fall in love with any rock stars.

A smile tugged at my lips.

I missed them both so much. My mom was so excited for me, and so thankful I was out and doing something adventurous. My dad was a harder sell. He was grateful to my uncle, but he wasn't happy about who I was going to be spending my time with.

He needn't have worried. My uncle made it clear that I wouldn't have much interaction with the band. At least not alone.

Even so, I wasn't even a blip on their radar. I knew all about the band, *Chains and Dames*.

I doubted there was a person in the world who hadn't heard of them. Their music, biting, melodic, and hypnotizing, was all over the radio. They'd won award after award this past year. They were brand new in the mainstream. Up and coming, taking the world by storm. But as amazing as their music was, it was the brothers that put them on the map.

The Lawson brothers. The two had started the band over a decade ago when they were only kids. They'd likely have made it big a long time ago had it not been for the eldest brother's stint in prison. The band and the label were pretty tight-lipped about what had exactly happened, but the media was a dog with a bone, and it hadn't been long before the world found out that the famous drummer had been put away when he was only eighteen for beating a man so badly he was hospitalized.

His younger sister had died from a drug overdose only three days before the incident that put him in jail. Their mother died of cancer only a year before his sister.

I squinted into the sun, gnawing on the inside of my cheek. My uncle said he wasn't dangerous. He'd told my parents he'd gotten a raw deal. That there was more to the story than you could see on the surface. But my father disagreed. The massive drummer was frightening to look at, an enigma. He'd gone away a teen and had grown into a man hardened to the world.

I watched the limo pull up beside the plane, a tight feeling of anticipation in my chest. The media at the far back of the tarmac was already screaming for their attention.

Brooks—Blonde Beard—Jackson, the bassist, climbed out first. He smoothed back his short-cropped hair with his hand before scratching at the full beard along his jawline. He marched to the steps of the plane, his wide shoulders thrown back. Right behind him walked Lake Winter, the band's guitarist. The leaner man had lighter blonde hair that was long and disheveled, flying in the wind around his shoulders.

Then it was the Lawson brothers. Their father, Harrison Finley Lawson— who was famous for his music as much as his battle with alcohol—without an ounce of shame named both of his sons after his choice of drink during tours around the time of each of their conceptions.

My breath caught as I watched Jameson Lawson, the younger Lawson brother, climb out behind Lake. He was the band's front man. His voice was raspy and silky, and just as captivating as his father's. Jameson may not have lived with the stain of hurting another human but he carried the same dark weight as his older brother since their sister died. Both brooding and menacing, beautiful and covered in tattoos, they drove their female fans to extreme stages of excitement. Jameson was in the headlines nearly daily with a new woman on his arm, eating up the attention, while his older brother was dragged through the mud in the media and didn't give a lick of attention to the women throwing themselves at him.

Jameson's long dark hair was pulled back into a ponytail which hung down to the middle of his back. He wore tight jeans and a tighter white T-shirt, and jewelry on his fingers and wrists.

Several delicate chain necklaces dangled down the center of his lean chest. He was tall—taller than the other two members of the band, but then so was his brother.

Johnnie Walker Lawson—Harrison's first born and known only as Walker— was the last to exit the limo. His hair was as dark as his younger brother's but buzzed short at the sides and slightly longer at the top in a military style cut. Both of them were beautiful, but Walker held an air about him that dared anyone to define him as such. His face was harsh, lined with a darkness that warned you away from looking too closely, and he wore a dark, long-sleeved shirt, covering up the colorful tattoos he had on his muscular arms. Powerfully built to support the endless hours he spent pounding away on the drums.

He shook hands with the pilots and the flight attendant at the stairs. Sunglasses shielded his eyes, but he glanced to his brother to see him flipping off the media standing outside the line of security. Walker's heavy hand dropped down on his brother's shoulder and gave it a push, urging him up the stairs. Jameson's head tipped back and he laughed but ducked into the plane.

I relaxed back in my seat and leaned to the side to see past the line of people crowding the aisle watching them board. Lake and Brooks sat at the front of the plane, conversing with several people.

Jameson continued to duck as he moved through the plane to save himself from the low ceiling. He headed to the nearest seat and dropped down into it. With a sly grin, he exchanged a few words with my uncle who was standing close by. I couldn't hear with all the chatter filling the plane but my uncle shook his head, a stern yet reluctantly amused smile on his lips.

The smile fell clean off as Walker climbed up. My uncle said something low to Walker, his hand touching his shoulder and giving it a squeeze. Walker nodded without looking at him and walked down the center of the plane, his head also ducked to avoid hitting the ceiling.

He pushed his sunglasses to the top of his head, revealing over-cast grey eyes, the color of a storm, that drifted over the available seating. He slowly sauntered in my direction and I hunched down when his eyes neared my seat. My face was flushed and I rummaged through my bag in an attempt to hide my nerves.

I wasn't afraid of him. My uncle had assured me he was not violent despite his past and I trusted Uncle V more than most people in my world. He wouldn't have me working with the band if he thought Walker was dangerous. But Walker was handsome, and I was a woman who could appreciate a good-looking man.

My body involuntarily tightened with his every step. I felt him pause, and the hairs on the back of my neck stood on end. He sat two seats ahead of me and I let out a relieved breath.

I was sweating, my tummy doing summersaults as I slumped into my seat. I knew I would be seeing them. Seeing Walker. But I hadn't been prepared for his magnetism. I hadn't been prepared for the draw.

Women all over the world screamed and cried their names. Obsessed and madly in love with them. They knew nothing about them apart from how beautiful and unobtainable they were. But it was enough. Enough to have the world at their feet.

I was no starstruck groupie. I loved their music as did most people in the world, but I wasn't interested in getting a piece of them. I had my own problems without adding lust and infatuation into the mix.

Still, I couldn't deny the pull they had on the female population. I was still a woman after all. It would've been a blatant lie to not acknowledge it myself. With my eyes on the dark head two seats ahead of me, I pushed the butterflies as far down into my belly as I could get them. I was determined to not let them overtake me.

♪♫

I SAW IT COMING. BILE RISING IN MY THROAT AS MY UNCLE was giving us a quick rundown of the itinerary for the first stop on the band's first world tour. I watched my uncle's eyes shift to me mid speech and I hunched into myself, my eyes wide and begging him not to single me out.

He ignored my desperation completely.

"As some of you may have noticed," he said. "We have a new recruit with us." His hand lifted and he gestured toward me at the back of the plane. I felt every single eye on me like a hot brand. "Shiloh, my niece, will be working with me for the first leg of the tour."

There were a couple murmurs, some people stood to look over the seats. Everyone was staring at me.

"Shiloh." He broke the awkward silence that had crept in. "Please stand up."

My wide eyes were locked onto his stern ones and my knees almost buckled under me as I rose to my feet. I waved, squeaking a "hi" which earned a few chuckles.

"She is new to the industry so please make her feel welcome."

A chorus of agreements from everyone resonated through the plane.

"Okay, okay! Let's get this show on the road." My uncle finished up and I was no longer the focus as the band and team reverted to conversations they were having beforehand.

I let out a sigh, flopping down into my seat.

As the pilot made an announcement over the intercom before takeoff, I noticed a dark head of hair turned my way.

Grey eyes met mine. Dark, stormy and devoid of any emotion.

Air caught in the back of my throat and I couldn't look away.

For one long, blistering moment in time, neither of us blinked.

Then it was over all too fast and Walker Lawson turned back around, glancing down at the book in his hand. I immediately felt bereft and cold without his eyes on mine. But also strangely like I'd narrowly avoided a speeding train.

It was much longer before I could force myself to look away from him.

2

No one spoke to me during the flight which didn't bother me. I was quietly tucked away in the back of the plane, listening to my favorite music while reading a book about a pirate and the maiden he rescued from a wrecked ship.

I'd seen my uncle try and make his way back to me a few times, but there was always someone calling for his attention either with endless questions or Julie going over the things she kept track of on a daily log on her tablet. He'd already had a few brief conversations with me on what was expected of me, but it was nice of him to want to check on me.

In my family, I was the one everyone looked out for. A burden to my parents financially, emotionally, and with their time. They claimed they never thought of me that way, but I couldn't help but feel like that was exactly what I was—a burden. Something to be managed.

Doctors' appointments and therapies were a regular part of their lives before I went off to college. Learning to manage those things on my own while in college had given me just enough independence for them to learn to trust me. I knew it was the only reason they'd allowed me to go with my uncle on this tour. My mother kept trying to convince herself that it was an amazing opportunity. It was her idea after all, but only because she'd worried about my growing depression. She knew it would be good for me, but I was still her baby and her only child, and so I knew she would be hounding me for every last detail. Every little thing she was missing. I was expecting a slew of messages from her when I landed.

As the plane began to descend over New York, I leaned my head against the window and admired the city down below. All the lights blazed like little twinkling stars.

We would only be in the city that never sleeps for two days. Tonight, we'd have a few hours to rest in a fancy hotel before meeting with their record label in the morning, followed by the show, then boarding buses to tour the United States for three months. From there we were headed overseas.

I was going to Australia with them, from there, my uncle told me I could decide if I wanted to finish the tour out in Europe or head home. But he made me promise I would give the tour at least a few months of my time to really get acquainted with the life before I made that decision.

Touring was a hard life, my uncle had warned me. Fast and thrilling nights followed by endless strenuous days of travel.

Exhaustion would soon be my faithful companion. My uncle loved every minute of it. Though he was on blood pressure medication, he was a firm believer in meditation and yoga. His job was demanding, but he wouldn't give it up for anything. Not even his health. My father had been worried about him for as long as I could remember.

My uncle Varian had been an agent in the music industry since before I was born. As was his father. Their name was well known in those circles but my father had never wanted any part of it, not even for the money. Varian represented some of the most famous music artists in the industry but when he'd told us last year he'd taken on Chains and Dames, I'd never seen him so animated or motivated. He'd handed over most of his other clients to others in the company to look after while he accompanied the band on their first world tour. Traveling so much wasn't normally part of his routine. He would tour but only for short periods of time, and though this time I knew he would be often flying off to handle other responsibilities and attending meetings, for the majority of this tour he would be sticking by the band's side.

His attention to his clients and love for the music was why he was so highly regarded in the industry. The money was why he got into the business, but the life and music was why he stayed. His clients loved him for it and his colleagues respected him for what he was able to accomplish.

I was fulfilling a paid intern position and I felt guilty for taking it from someone I knew would have been desperate to be in my position. I'd never shown an interest and I felt like I was taking away someone's dream who would have been far more deserving. The only thing that comforted me was how picky I knew my uncle was— he hadn't filled the position even after dozens of interviews, and Julie had been worried it wouldn't be filled at all before he gave it to me. Still, I'd made Julie promise me that she would let me know if I wasn't doing my job adequately because I knew my uncle likely would not. My mother may have had to push him into the idea of me coming along, but my uncle's only reservation was my health. He worried it would be hard on me.

Uncle V was a hard man by nature, stoic and demanding, but he loved me like a daughter and he would put up with my shortfalls silently for that reason alone.

I sat still as the plane started to empty. My eyes fixed on the dark head in front of me. When only a handful of people remained, I squirmed anxiously, unsure if I should leave ahead of him. Walker sat so still, I wasn't certain if he was even awake.

My uncle walked toward the back of the plane, his eyes on the statue still man. "Walker?" He put his hand on Walker's shoulder, leaning down to say something quietly. Walker nodded, his hands coming up to scrub roughly at his face.

After Walker stood, my uncle looked at me questioningly and I jumped up, pulling my bag onto my shoulder.

"Tired?" My uncle asked me.

"Not really," I lied. Was it even possible to sleep on a plane with four mega stars so close to you? The five-hour flight was exhausting. My eyelids felt heavy and I was ready to crash. I'd never looked forward to jumping into bed as much as I did at that moment. I couldn't wait to get to the hotel.

"You feelin' okay?" He asked quieter this time.

I sighed, this was not going to be the first time I would hear that question uttered from him and more than likely also Julie during my time with the band. He loved me. I loved him. He would be worried. I was just going to have to prove to him that I was fine. "I feel great."

I even tacked on a wide smile to prove it. He narrowed his eyes on me but faced forward to shake hands with the pilots and flight attendant before going down the stairs out onto the tarmac.

I should've been prepared. I'd seen paparazzi and fans at the last airport, but I was taken off guard by the sheer size and excitement of the crowd waiting outside. Why they even allowed them this close on the tarmac—on the tarmac at all—was baffling. But my uncle went along with it, so it was likely good for publicity or something along those line.

Cameras were flashing, nearly blinding me as I made my way toward the limo. I stumbled forward, and Walker grabbed me before I hit the ground. He was holding my arms—his grip firm—and I straightened up as my heart raced.

I froze, glancing over my shoulder. Our eyes met for the third time in so many hours and it was just as arresting this time as every time before.

"Thanks," I told him quietly, my voice barely above a whisper. He frowned down at me. His eyes flitting between mine so fast it was hard to track them. My cheeks flooded with heat as his enormous hand held my elbow firmly, his grip tightening ever so slightly.

"Careful," his deep rasping voice surrounded me. Cocooning me. I shivered, prickles of electricity dancing all over my body. I'd heard it in a song, his deep croon underneath his brother's had filled my ears nearly the entire plane ride, but hearing it in person, up close and full surround sound, was a powerful experience. I couldn't seem to look away from the blue flecks of his piercing grey eyes. He made no move to urge me along.

"Shy." My uncle's voice broke me away from the trance and, in an instant, the noisy fans and flashing lights invaded. The hand on my arm tightened momentarily before disappearing altogether. My mouth dry, I spun around, jogging the rest of the way to the limo. Not at all *careful*. I was lucky I didn't land on my face.

I stopped before my uncle, my other hand covering the still warm area around my elbow, keeping the tingling from spreading outward. My uncle looked from me to Walker and back again, a guarded look in his eye. But he didn't comment on my very obvious flushed face. He ducked inside the limo, waving me to follow behind him.

I slid across the leather seat and looked up to take in the others already settled. My uncle was sitting beside Julie. They were on the left side of the limo while the band was on the opposite side. The rest of the people who were on the flight had departed in two other cars. Before I could even think of moving away from the back, someone moved to sit next to me.

My breath seemed to clog inside my throat, swelling as the warmth of Walker's body seeped into my right side. I did not dare look at him. I'd already made a fool of myself. I was not going to allow myself to get caught gawking at him twice in one day.

The limo drove off and I stared out the window as we left the airport. I zoned out, exhausted from the flight.

A few people chattered inaudibly near the front of the limo, Jameson and Lake's boisterous laughter filling my ears. They were teasing each other about the show tomorrow night and discussing plans for the afterparty.

I learned in that twenty-minute ride—the first twenty minutes of being in their collective close proximity—that they were the furthest thing from reserved. No topic was off limits, no matter their current company. Apparently, the old adage, *sex, drugs, and rock n' roll* was fully embraced.

My uncle, whom I knew as an old-fashioned gentleman, didn't flinch a single moment as the conversation grew more and more vulgar.

I, however, knew I could not hide my discomfort. I wouldn't consider myself a prude. I wasn't a virgin, despite my first and only experience being awkward and a bit painful. Far from earth shattering, but the topic of sex did not make me uncomfortable. But these men spoke of women like disposable tissues. Crudely. There was a severe lack of respect when they shared their most recent experience with groupies and hangers-on. Listening to them just hammered home how out of depth I was in this new environment.

I could feel the blood rush to my face, embarrassment as Jameson described his experience last night with the 'stacked blonde with pierced nipples' in great detail.

"So fuckin' hot for my dick, man," he purred with a lewd grin. "She did this thing with her tongue—"

"*James,*" a low voice rumbled beside me, cutting him off.

Jameson looked to Walker, then at me and his grin grew. "Am I makin' you uncomfortable, sweetheart?"

I shook my head.

"You sure?" He crooned, leaning over Brooks to try and catch my eyes.

"*James,*" Walker barked. The booming sound startled me and I glanced at him. Walker glared at his brother, his brows heavy over his stormy eyes.

Jameson chuckled, leaning away.

I stared at Walker, unable to take my eyes away from the anger in his or the tight press of his lips.

"Shy," my uncle called out. It was a struggle but I tore my eyes away from the enthralling man at my side. "Everything okay?"

"Yeah," I plastered on a smile, though the attention was draining.

He watched me closely but eventually went back to talking with Julie.

"He's harmless," Brooks told me. He appeared as tired as I felt. "Those girls know the score."

I bit my lip to stop the sharp retort that wanted to come out. Those women may have known what they were getting in Jameson and Lake's bed—a good time and nothing more—but I doubted any woman anticipated being spoken about in that way.

Brooks cracked a grin. "You're a little thing. How old are you?"

"Twenty-two," I muttered, surprising him.

"No shit?"

"No shit," I deadpanned.

He chuckled quietly. "V said you just got outta college. What are you doin' hangin' out with a bunch of bums?" At least my uncle hadn't shared I *dropped* out of college. That I couldn't hack it.

"Y'all are hardly bums," I retorted dryly. Millions of dollars, mega mansions and exotic cars. These guys may have come from broken homes and families that were barely scraping by, but they were living the dream now.

He raised his brows, waiting for another answer.

I shrugged, unwilling to dive into all my issues for this stranger. "Nothing else to do."

He slapped his chest, cradling his heart. "Nothing else to do? You mean to tell me you aren't having the time of your life?"

I cracked a smile unable to help it. Brooks so far was a gentle giant with a soft sense of humor. "Not yet."

"Not yet, she says." He shook his head. "We'll fix that, eh, Walk?"

Walker grunted, but I could feel his eyes on the side of my face.

"You grab a drink and loosen up, and you'll be singin' a different tune."

"I'm not much of a drinker."

"What's this, princess? You don't drink?" Lake jumped into the conversation.

Brooks shot him a scowl before smiling at me. "That's cool. You listen to our stuff?"

"Who doesn't?" I asked, grinning impishly.

"Good answer, honey," Jameson hooted. "Who the fuck doesn't?" He crowed and banged his fist against the roof of the limo.

"Alright," Brooks chuckled. "You ever see us live?"

I shook my head.

"Oh, baby, you're in for a treat," Lake purred, his eyes twinkling. "We'll get you a front row seat."

Just having the attention of one of these rock gods was a shock to my system, but all four of them focused on me? I was barely breathing.

"Nope," my uncle called absently. "Shy is off limits."

Lake rolled his eyes and leaned back in his seat. "V, what you got against us, huh? You think we're gonna sully your pretty little niece?"

"Yes," my uncle said dryly, tapping furiously away on his tablet. "Shy's too good for the likes of you."

I smiled at my lap, pleased.

A thick finger tapped on my hand, and my eyes shot there, my smile freezing in place.

"You shy?" Walker asked on a low rumble.

My brows scrunched in confusion. "Yeah." Everyone had been calling me Shy for as long as I could remember. Shortened from Shiloh, it wasn't exactly a weird nickname.

He frowned, his thick finger leaving my hand to lightly trace across my cheek and the blush I could still feel there. "You shy?" He asked again.

The small touch was fast but it elicited a visceral reaction in me. I barely managed to nod.

Shy. Socially awkward. Easily embarrassed.

My nickname suited me.

He grunted and leaned away from me. Sitting back against the seat and closing his eyes. I let out the breath I must have been holding.

Having their attention was a blow but having Walker's finger on my cheek was like entering a thunderstorm.

Lightening everywhere.

3

P ulling up to the hotel, everyone climbed out of the limo. Fatigue lined our faces. I could feel my own exhaustion all the way down to my toes and was looking forward to getting some rest.

Two doormen and the band's security escorted us into the hotel. The concierge along with the hotel manager met us inside the lobby, where the rest of the team was waiting for us to arrive. "Mr. Green," the hotel manager, Harold, greeted my uncle with a wide grin and a hearty handshake. "It's a pleasure to have you all here."

While my uncle spoke with the manager, I sorted his bags and mine from the others. I pulled my suitcase by the handle, the wheels squeaking across the marble floor and stopped beside him. The manager handed Julie several key cards to various rooms.

"Five hours of sleep, and then every one of you need to be in the lobby by zero six-hundred," my uncle told the group sternly.

Brooks grabbed a card from Julie, rubbed his eyes and marched to the elevator. Lake and Jameson were hot on his heels along with the concierge pushing their luggage on a cart.

My uncle gave Walker a key card. "Gym is on the first floor." He pointed in the direction.

Walker nodded and without a word headed down the hall.

"He's going to work out?" I asked in shock. He looked exhausted and tomorrow was going to be a long day.

"He doesn't sleep much," Julie said. "You're with your uncle. You need anything?"

I shook my head and she joined the rest of the crew, her heels clacking, to hand out key cards to their rooms.

In the hotel suite, I gave everything a fleeting glance. There were two separate bedrooms, a lounge, and dining area. Regardless of who my uncle was, I was a stranger to lavish environments of this magnitude. Any other day, the room would have simply blown my mind. However, I was too tired to appreciate it all.

Unlike Julie and my uncle who set up shop at the black sparkly dining table, I couldn't wait to close my eyes. I picked the closest bedroom and shut myself inside.

I washed my face in the attached bathroom, set my weekly medication organizer on the counter and left everything else in my suitcase, before flopping onto the bed, face first into the soft bedding.

The next thing I remembered was a sharp knock at my door. "Shy! Time to get up!"

I groaned, nearly falling out of the bed as I rolled over. Glancing at the blinking clock on the bedside table, I saw it was five forty-five in the morning. Where my uncle got his energy was a mystery. I could barely keep my eyes open as I jumped in the shower.

With no time to dry my hair, I braided it and wrapped the braid into a bun at the base of my neck. I applied moisturizer to my face, jumped into black leggings, and slipped on my black boots with the blue shoelaces, before putting on a tank top and a thick oversized knitted grey sweater. Mom and I had sewn little stars throughout the gaping holes of the knit after we found it at the local thrift shop. It was one of our favorite things to do, reinvent old clothes no one wanted anymore. The older, the better. I put on my old black button coat and then I was ready to go.

I grabbed my pill case and suitcase and rushed out of my room.

"Gotta hurry," my uncle told me jovially, sliding me a tall glass of water and a mug of coffee. Coffee could cause a flare-up for a lot of people suffering from Crohn's but, for me, I could get away with one mug in the morning so long as I didn't add creamer.

I swallowed my pills with the water and sipped my coffee as I pulled open my cooler. I had a personal blender that I carried with me everywhere. I kept it inside a cooler that was always packed with nutrient rich foods I could easily access.

I filled the blender halfway with water then cut up a banana, mango, and a bunch of kale, throwing it in to the mix, then topping it with a spoonful of coconut oil. It was my go-to break- fast smoothie. It would give me everything I needed to start my day without forcing my body to break down anything that it might struggle with.

I took the blender cup from the machine, dropped in some ice and popped on a sip lid, then packed everything back up. My uncle made a face as he bit into a muffin and I huffed a groggy laugh. He hated my smoothies. Back when I was younger and he would visit, my mom would experiment with different recipes using guests as her guinea pigs. She never gave me anything without having several victims taste test it first. I was a picky kid and with my limited food options I made things much more diffi- cult for her. Over time, I'd grown to love the foods I could toler- ate. I had no other choice.

"You're on Julie today. Shadow her and help with anything she needs," he told me as we went to the elevator. We split the bags between us. I felt a little guilty, but I was small, and my uncle had a lot of crap. I think he realized yesterday I would struggle as his mule.

Down in the front lobby most of the crew was already climbing into the waiting vehicles. The road crew was leaving straight for the venue to begin setting up for tonight's show while the band was heading to the label for an early meeting. Everything for the tour had already been arranged months in advance. This meeting was to discuss the upcoming album, and my uncle had implied it may have been to remind them how much time and money had gone into the album and how much work still needed to be done before setting them loose on the world.

The band was nowhere in sight.

My uncle kept checking his watch, growing impatient. Brooks and Lake came stumbling out of the elevator, ten minutes late.

"Walker's out jogging," Brooks rasped beside my uncle. He winked at me before he walked to the nearest chair and fell back into it, shutting his eyes.

"Jameson?"

Lake shrugged and walked outside, a pack of cigarettes in his hand.

My uncle sighed and pinched the bridge of his nose. "Go find him," he told the nearest person—Perry, Percy, or something— one of the band's handlers. It was going to take me a while to remember everyone's names. "Everyone else, outside."

We waited at the front of the hotel beside two idling black SUVs. Lake and Brooks were inside one, both of them asleep with their head pressed against the windows.

My uncle paced down the sidewalk, Julie's eyes following his every step.

"He knows better." She checked her silver watch again.

"I thought it was kind of a written rule that rock stars are notoriously late." I rubbed my hands together to warm them up. The wind was biting but the sun was still rising. Hopefully it would warm up in a few hours.

She huffed a dry laugh. "Not these rock stars. Varian won't allow the typical stereotypes with them. He knows they're too good for that. And when he can't get them in line, Walker steps in. That man defies every stereotype."

So far, it seemed that way. I was still kind of surprised he'd stayed up to work out. I half expected the entire band to get into all kinds of trouble my first night on tour with them. But I didn't think the others did anything other than sleep.

Jameson came tripping out of the hotel doors. His hair a mess and still wearing his clothes from last night.

"Finally," my uncle rapped out. His shoes smacked across the concrete as he marched to Jameson's side. "You're late!"

The singer trudged past him without a look. "I fucked up." But when he caught sight of me, his steps slowed, and a sneer came over his face. "What're you lookin' at?"

"Leave Shy alone, and no fuckin' shit you fucked up," Uncle V snapped. "They're looking for a reason to fuck you over. Breach of contract is an excellent way of opening that door for them."

Jameson sighed. "Chill man, it won't happen again."

"No, it won't." My uncle held open the door for Jameson, glaring at him as he slid into the back seat. "Let's go."

Julie and I jogged over to the car and climbed inside, then shut the door. I sat between Jameson and Julie while my uncle took the front passenger seat.

My nose wrinkled and I had to hold my breath to keep my eyes from watering. He smelled like sweat and smoke.

"You stink," Julie hissed at him, leaning around me.

Jameson rolled his eyes, leaning against the door and closing his eyes. "Put a cork in it, Viper."

My uncle shook his head, ordering the driver to go.

The day wasn't looking great so far. Thankfully when we got to the tall, gleaming building everyone's mood seemed to brighten a little. I still hadn't seen Walker, and though my uncle was so angry about Jameson, he didn't say a word about the missing drummer.

So it surprised me to see Walker waiting inside the record label's lobby, grey sweatpants and black hoodie up, obscuring his face. I would've missed him if not for the tattoos on his knuckles and his massive size. "You're late," he said to Jameson. His voice was gruff. Angry.

"V already gave me shit, bro." Jameson brushed past him.

Walker, sighing, followed behind my uncle at the same clipped pace.

We packed inside the elevator like sardines. Brooks' elbow was in my spine, and Jameson's leg bumped against mine as the elevator jolted up. I fell forward into Lake's backpack and had to hold onto it before I knocked him against the doors.

"Sorry," I squeaked, letting go as he glanced at me with tired eyes.

A heavy arm draped over my shoulder. It was Brooks. "You're so tiny." I smiled crookedly. I couldn't tell if that was an insult or not for the way he scowled at me. "What's that shit you're drinking?"

I looked down at my nearly finished smoothie. "Banana, Kale, Mango, and coconut oil."

He made a face and took it from me, sniffing the lid.

"Looks nasty," Jameson said from behind me.

I took it back from Brooks. "It's good." Once you get used to it.

The elevator stopped and we all piled out. I took a deep breath Rock stars stunk. Particularly one. For all the beauty Jameson was, he seriously could use a shower. It was funny but knowing that about him kind of took some of the shine away. I could feel my starstruck nerves fading away little by little.

Several men and women dressed in designer suits met us in a large conference room. Over twenty seats at a long white table in the center of the room, Julie guided me to the back where a table was set up with food and drinks. "Just make sure the guys have everything they need so they're not leaving for anything," she told me.

"Got it." I took cues from her and started pouring mugs of strong coffee.

The suits started to discuss marketing details of the tour but mostly the upcoming album as I rushed around the table, handing out coffees and plates of pastries.

"Water, doll," Brooks gruffly asked with a sweet smile. I nodded and poured him a glass from a crystal decanter.

My hand shook as I placed a mug of steaming coffee in front of Walker, his stare was intimidating and entirely too focused. The man was not shy about eye contact. His appreciation was a low grunt but softened by a small tug on my sleeve. His eyes smiled and I stumbled as I moved away.

Where the band offered thanks and nods as I served them, the suits ignored me completely, handing out orders without meeting my eyes. I was fine with that. So much Armani made me nervous.

Once everyone was served, I sat in a chair in the back of the room beside the buffet. The pastries smelled so good and I was glad I took the time to make my smoothie or I would have been drooling over them. Gluten was a sore spot for me though. Sometimes I could get away with it in a pinch so long as the rest of my diet that day was good, but I didn't want to risk a flare-up during the tour.

I zoned out for a while, having a hard time following what they were discussing since I didn't have a deeper understanding of the industry. There seemed to be so much that went into it. Money. Marketing and advertising—apparently the two weren't the same. Dates and times. So many different locations and trying to juggle recording with tour responsibilities. I'd always thought you wrote some songs, recorded them and went on tour. After the tour, you started again. But now I wasn't so sure. It sounded like they were touring for their first album all the while writing and recording their second.

Hearing the amounts of money that was funneled into it blew my mind. So much money.

Mind-boggled by the endless stream of numbers, I tuned it all out, daydreaming. A bad habit of mine. My attention wandered sometimes at the worst possible times.

After another round of refilling mugs and glasses and fulfilling every task the suits gave me—go ask for this folder or that sheet or go find this person or that person—my feet were sore and I was struggling to keep up with all the demands.

"Shy," my uncle barked.

I jumped in place, dropping a stack of folders I'd just dug through the table to find. I blushed, embarrassed I hadn't heard him the first time.

"We need a few copies."

I rushed to his side, grabbing the paper he held out to me.

It took me ten minutes to find someone who could direct me to the copy machine then another fifteen to figure out how to operate it. Didn't the label have people for this? People far more skilled than me? The fact that I couldn't figure out which buttons to press on the big machine was more than a little disheartening. I was going to suck at this job.

I was flustered by the time I came back to the meeting, but it seemed me and my task had already been forgotten. I quietly left the stack of papers beside my uncle's elbow and returned to my seat. No sooner than I sat was everyone standing.

I grabbed my coat and my uncle's, and followed them out the door, glancing over my shoulder at the mess on the table. Was I supposed to clean the plates and mugs up?

"You work for us, sweetheart," Lake whispered, startling me. With a teasing smile, his heavy arm draped over my shoulder as he guided me out the door. "Don't worry about serving the stuffy suits."

I looked to Julie for confirmation. She nodded. "Don't worry about anyone but the band. Not the label. Not the roadies. Not our assistants unless Varian or I direct you otherwise. No sense taking on more work than you need to."

"Got it." Was I just supposed to refuse? "My uncle didn't need those papers, did he?" I asked Julie, suspecting I'd been sent away to save myself from doing too much. It seemed like something my uncle would do—quietly manage an uncomfortable situation.

She smiled gently.

"You'll get the hang of things," Lake promised me.

I hoped so.

♪♪

LEAVING THE FIFTY-FLOOR BUILDING WE SLID BACK INTO the cars and drove to the venue, an arena in the center of the city. Twenty-thousand tickets had been sold, selling out the show.

The rest of my day was beyond busy. My uncle had his fingers in every piece of the event. Following him around everywhere was exhausting. The band retreated to the buses to sleep as the stage and lighting was being set up, only waking up three hours before the show for a sound check.

Then my uncle had me running around like a trained monkey. Having found the band a few years ago by sheer chance when they were performing in New York and immediately recognizing the talent in front of him, he was invested in their career as well as them as people. He had a difficult time giving up control to other people which meant he checked and double checked every little detail, often to the point of stepping past his usual job description. And so I was very busy.

Food was set up in the band's dressing room but I still ordered hot meals for me, Varian, Julie and the rest of the team. By the time I had a second to eat, my hands were shaking. I sat on the edge of the stage, my feet dangling down and gazed out at the empty stadium.

So many empty seats that would soon be filling at full capacity. They seemed to go on forever.

How must it feel to have that many people there to see only you? To have their every bit of attention on every single thing you did? I just couldn't imagine it.

So many people moved around me. All of them focused on their tasks. I didn't know any of them. Didn't even recognize any from the team. Some were roadies, but I knew most had to work for the venue.

It was kind of mind-boggling to witness all that went into one single show on tour. All the effort and time and *so many people* that worked tirelessly to make it all a success. And all that effort came down to four people. Four rock stars responsible for making sure not a single fan was disappointed in the show. All these people's labors could be completely wasted if the band failed to pull off their part at the end.

Thousands of people could walk away either loving or hating you. The pressure had to be crippling.

I nibbled on the grilled chicken breast, sipping my protein shake in between. I was going to have to stock up at a grocery store if takeout was the go-to on the road. Without knowing how things were made it was difficult to find something I could eat. I knew my uncle was aware of this and likely expected me to just order whatever I needed, but I was nervous to use his credit card. He'd told me it was for anything I needed, but I didn't feel like I earned anything yet let alone the use of his money.

I wanted to *earn* money before I started to spend it. But I would be no good to him if I broke my diet out of nerves.

After the band was back preparing in their dressing room, I broke down and searched out Julie. We found a local grocery store which was open and put in a large order. I gaped at the price but barely an eighth of what she ordered was my own.

She got a little excited over the prospect of fresh groceries on the buses and ordered for everyone.

Why she never did this before when she so clearly preferred it to fast food was mystifying. I guessed I gave her the excuse she needed.

From there we went to the dressing rooms.

It was like walking into another world.

One hour before the show started there was no one here. Now that the arena was filling up and the opening band had just taken the stage, the dressing room was *packed*.

I couldn't spot a single member of the band through all the people swarming around.

Assistants, hairdressers, make-up artists, and the fans...the scantily dressed female fans. I wasn't sure if it was normal to have fans in here but Julie didn't seem bothered by them.

She muscled her way through the large room like a professional linebacker. She was used to this, but I was overwhelmed. Music blared from the speakers throughout the room. Everyone shouting to be overheard.

We found Lake and Jameson first, both on a sunken couch with several women pawing all over them. Jameson's tongue was down one woman's throat like he was trying his level best to swallow her tonsils.

"Over here," Brooks called to Julie. He was standing with my uncle and a famous baseball player. My dad was a massive fan of baseball, dragging me to every game he could. I knew what this man's butt looked like on a big screen and now in person. I could not wait to tell my dad I shook his hand.

Brooks chuckled at me, then leaned in and whispered in my ear, "A fan?"

"Of like everyone in this room," I told him in awe. I was noticing several celebrities in the large dressing room now. I didn't think parties like this started until *after* the show.

He squeezed my shoulder. "You'll get used to it."

So everyone kept telling me.

"No woman for you? Or two?" I asked Brooks, unable to ignore the tongue show the two other band members were putting on not even three feet from us.

He observed them over his shoulder briefly before shrugging. "I got something special back home."

I smiled up at him. "A girlfriend?"

He nodded. "She's my everything."

I immediately liked him. Brooks became my favorite fast. To see all the beautiful women in the room drooling over him and his attention hadn't wandered their way once. Whoever this girl was, she was lucky.

He grabbed a bottle of water from the ice bucket and handed it to me. "You'd like her," he said.

"Does she come on tour with you?"

He sighed. "Soon. But she's got some stuff goin' on right now."

"I can't wait to meet her," I told him.

He smiled and pulled me into his side. It was a brotherly sort of affection, keeping others from knocking into me. My uncle saw the move but didn't comment.

"Where's Walker?" I asked, looking around.

"This ain't his scene." Brooks got pulled into a conversation with another famous person that left me starstruck.

I quietly snuck away, bumping into people, trying to make it through the crowded room. I found a chair in the back and claimed it, pulling out my earphones and stuffing them in my ears, drowning out the chatter with my playlist.

This wasn't my scene either. One thing Walker and I had in common.

4

Standing in the private area side stage, I watched them in total awe.

My fingers tingled, the hairs on my arms standing on end. Their music was of course *amazing*. But seeing them live was like watching a wild animal. A predator stalk through the night.

Jameson worked the crowd. His voice crooning and raspy all at once. Women screamed his name, desperately reaching for any piece of him they could get their hands on. He kept them on edge, teasing them. He loved it up there. You could feel his passion for the music and eager audience.

Lake also ate up the attention, working his guitar like it was an extension of him while he grinned and winked at the crowd.

Brooks was in his own mind. His gaze on his bass guitar and his flying fingers or up into the night sky above him. When he added to Jameson's vocals, he closed his eyes, a peaceful look coming over his face.

And then there was Walker.

He took my breath away. All that raw masculine power exploding out from his center as he used every shred of himself to hammer into the drums.

Sweat dripped down his bare torso, highlighting every last drop of colorful ink etched into his skin. He glimmered under the blue spotlight, his eyes closed as he pounded away. He didn't sing under Jameson's vocals as often as Brooks or Lake, but when he did, his thick, jagged tone sent static awareness over me. I found myself standing stage right, my every molecule aware of him and his every movement.

"He's hot as fuck," a voice to my left pulled me from the desire that had suddenly impaled me to the floor. I looked to the girl standing inches from me. We were the same height but that was where the similarities ended. Where my style was subtly quirky, hers was *loud*.

My coffee brown locks couldn't compete with her bright lavender hair. It was pulled up in a messy bun, several braids and a small neat dread lying against her right ear interwoven throughout. She wore a black and pink cropped top with no bra. I could never pull that off with my bigger chest. An obscenely short, pleated, black skirt paired with grey skull-design knee high socks and ass-kicking boots. Her boots were far more expensive than mine but artfully grunged up.

She looped her arm through mine, the layers of chain bracelets nearly snagging on my knit sweater. She sighed and leaned her head against my shoulder. "I'd bang him."

I didn't know this girl, but I'd put her to be around my age if not a year or two older. I'd never seen her around the band but then I'd only been here for less than two days and she had the bright green wristband on her right arm that let me know she was granted backstage access as part of the crew.

"You're kind of quiet," she remarked, her eyes locked on the stage.

"You're kind of forward."

She snorted. "That I am."

"I'm Shiloh," I told her, my eyes wandering back to Walker.

"Of course it is. Adorable name for an adorable chick."

My nose wrinkled. I didn't want to be adorable. I looked down at my clothes, plucking at my sweater.

She tugged my hand away and held it to her chest. "Don't worry. Adorable is hot as fuck too. I'm Mavis."

"That's a cool name."

She was hugging my arm like it was her favorite pillow. I should have been disturbed by this stranger's invasion of my space but somehow it just came off as friendly. Odd, but I liked odd things and people.

"Named after my evil grandma," she told me. "But it's cool, I guess. We have cool names in common." Her blue eyes latched onto mine. "Want to be besties?"

I stared at her. Lost for words.

"You're new here," she told me brightly. "But you're with the band, right?"

I nodded warily. "Why are you here?"

"I'm with the band, too. Just not that one." She nodded to the stage.

"One of the opening bands?" I didn't know much about them other than one was pretty good and the other one wasn't. Uncle V had been complaining about the latter on and off today.

"I'm with the shitty band."

I tried to hide my wince. They wouldn't be around much longer. They were shit musicians and even shittier performers. I had no idea how they even got on this tour, especially with their horrific attitude. There was potential there. Their lyrics were sultry and powerful but they didn't have the talent to back it up. The guitar line had the bones, but it's musician just couldn't hit the melody like I suspected it had been written. Unless they got their shit together, I didn't think I would see much of Mavis around.

She snorted a dry laugh. "Yeah I know. They totally suck. But the lead is my boyfriend."

My wide eyes dropped to my toes to hide the pity I felt for her. Van Driver, the lead singer, was the worst. He had several women hanging off him today and had tried to climb so far up my uncle's ass this morning I thought Van would have shit coating his nose by the time my uncle escaped.

"Besties?" She asked again.

I shrugged. I had no friends on tour. It wouldn't hurt to have someone to pass the time with while I was here. "Sure."

"Sweet," she said under her breath, shooting me a bright smile.

We watched the show together. My arm ached from how often and exuberantly she shook it when she got excited and started to sing and dance along with the band, but it was kind of nice to have someone to share the experience with, so I didn't complain.

♪♪

SHE DROPPED A DRY KISS ON MY CHEEK AND BOUNCED AWAY, her head bobbing to the music as they hit their last song before the encore. I watched her go, completely mystified and a little charmed by her character.

The band left the stage to thunderous screams and applause. I held several cold waters in my arms and dry towels over my shoulder. I handed them out, my mouth dropping as Walker stood before me, pools of sweat dripping off of him. It should've been gross. But it was *not*. The little droplets slithered down his bare torso, dipping in between the ridges of his abs. My mouth watered and I may have drooled as he poured an entire bottle of water over his head, washing most of it away.

He ran his hand through his hair, spritzing the water behind him. My breaths came fast and I couldn't tear my eyes away from him. Enthralled, I didn't feel the last bottle of water leave my hand as he gently pulled it from me, sucking most of it down in one breath. My eyes followed the line of his throat as his sharp Adam's apple bobbed up and down.

His eyes twinkled as he glanced at me. His finger coming up to my chin to gently tap close my gaping mouth. I licked my lips, swallowing hard.

He winked, then returned to the stage. I swayed in place, nearly falling flat on my face.

Face like an inferno, I made myself scarce for the encore.

♪

THE AFTER-PARTY STARTED BACK NEAR THE VIP LOUNGE. IT was a much larger room for a much larger group of people. I was to make sure the band had everything they needed after the show. Most of it had already been placed by the arena crew before they arrived: water, Gatorade, food, an abundance of alcohol, and strangely—per Walker's request—the muscle cream, Icy Hot.

I found out pretty quickly it was for his overworked muscles as Julie escorted a woman in that began to rub the Icy Hot cream all over his back and arms. He sat on a couch and she sat on the back of it, her bare thighs on either side of him as she massaged the cream into his skin like she'd been doing it for more than one show. Her hands were familiar on him as were the smiles she shot him.

My face flamed the entire time she worked. My gaze caught on the path of her hands as they worked over him. But Walker seemed completely unaware of the beautiful woman talking low in his ear.

His eyes were all for *me*.

He sat hunched over, his elbows on his thighs, hands hanging loosely between them. His head was down to give her access to his neck but his eyes were up and tracking me, his damp hair almost obscuring them.

"Big bro seems fixated," Jameson remarked to Lake as he approached me with a list of more demands.

Unsteady and a little breathless, I tried to focus on their food orders, but it was impossible as Lake and Jameson both looked from me to Walker pointedly.

"You know what that means?" Lake asked me.

"Means Uncle V's gonna be pissed," Jameson crowed loudly.

I scanned the crowd for my uncle. I needed this job. I could not fuck it up by drooling over my employers. "I don't know what you're talking about."

They laughed.

I took in the long list written in Jameson's messy scrawl.

"Not only can I barely read this but where the hell am I supposed to find all this?" It was food. So much food. Pizza, burgers, various fried foods, ice cream, something barely legible, and buffalo wings. Then there were the other things. Condoms written in all caps. And a few other listed items that made me uncomfortable to read while they watched me with burgeoning grins. Usually things like this were taken care of prior to the show, but everything Jameson had written now hadn't been on that original inventory list.

Jameson shrugged. "A store?"

I just gawked at him, flabbergasted. Was this the deal after every show? This would take me hours to get through. Wouldn't it be easier to give this list to my uncle or Royce, the tour manager, *before* the show?

Julie came barreling into our little huddle. "I'll take that." She swept away the long list. "Shy is here to help but she isn't your errand girl."

"No, just V's." Lake grinned at me.

"You're no fun, Jules," Jameson said with a sharp smile.

"Call me the Queen-of-no-fun," she crowed.

"Sorry," I told them, but I so wasn't. Getting only half of those things would have taken me all night in a city I was unfamiliar with.

"We're just fuckin' with you a bit," Jameson told me, tugging on my hair bun.

I winced, pushing him away.

"James," Walker called out, loud enough to catch the attention of several people around us.

My eyes shot to his, surprised as he shrugged the girl off and stood like he was going to physically remove Jameson from my person.

Jameson shrugged and snagged a girl who was dancing around her waist and tossed her over his shoulder. She shrieked until she realized who had her and then she melted against him, her hands roaming to low places. He slapped her ass and whooped loudly. "Let's move this party to the bus!"

The crowd cheered and I searched for my uncle again, absolutely avoiding the tall man I could still feel staring at me from a few feet away. So far out of my comfort zone, I was decidedly *uncomfortable*. What was I supposed to do now? Follow them to the bus?

I thought I had a pretty decent handle on my duties but that was before I was actually thrown into the job. Now that I was here, I was realizing just how much it entailed. I was worried I'd bitten off more than I could chew.

Lake grabbed my hand and shadowed Jameson. "We're just teasing you," he told me. "You're the new shiny toy."

"I'm not a toy." And I didn't appreciate getting jerked around.

Lake stopped suddenly and I rammed into his side, teetering. He caught me with a wince. "That came out wrong. You're Varian's girl and we owe a lot to that guy. You're safe with us, okay?"

I nodded, appeased by his sincerity.

Lake kept me by his side as we moved to the exit and walked through the double doors that led outside. I was thankful for his closeness when we were nearly mobbed getting out the door. He shielded me as excited fans screamed from behind the barricades, reaching out for him and Jameson. Phones and cameras blinded me with their flashing lights. Everyone wanted a piece of them. My ears were assaulted by the excitement.

They'd slowed their pace and Jameson set down the woman he was carrying to pose for photos and sign autographs. Strangers' hands were pawing and tugging him, but he barely flinched, and his smile never wavered. He was in his element.

I caught sight of Brooks at the end. He was also signing autographs, but where Jameson had several sets of tits as his canvas, Brooks ignored all those women and focused more on the younger fans and those that stood in a line guarded by several security guards. These people were far more respectful as the world-famous bassist shared his time and attention with them.

It was surreal. I didn't know how anyone could get used to this kind of adulation. They had to feel like *gods*. It had to take a toll. What did that kind of power do to a person?

From there the walk was tame. More security lined the way as we reached the gate that held the buses. There was still a crowd of people beyond the gate but apart from a few fan passes hanging around necks, all of them had the green wristbands that gave them access as crew.

The bus was a steel monstrosity with black glittering accents. In no way was it marked with the band's name. It could have been any old mega expensive streamline and gave them an air of anonymity as they traveled.

Inside, the bus was beautiful. Sleek black leather and chrome everywhere you looked. There was a small kitchenette up front behind the deep driver's seat and from there I walked back into a sitting area. A massive leather couch I wouldn't have expected to fit inside a bus and a small dining set with padded bench seating. Lake waved me to the couch, and I dropped into it, looking deeper to the bunk area. The bunks were curtained and not much to look at, but there was a door at the end. The door was open, and I bent forward on the couch to try and peer inside but other than blue recessed lighting it was hard to make out.

More people climbed into the bus, mostly women.

"What's your poison?" Lake asked me standing by the kitchen counter that held nothing but booze—bottles and bottles of it.

"I don't drink," I reminded him.

He nodded. "That's right." He opened the fridge. "Who went shopping?"

"Me and Julie."

"Sick," he rapped out. "You gonna cook for us?"

"I'm not the best cook." And what few recipes I did know I doubt would go over well with their tastes.

"Sweet Shy, I won't turn it down, but we don't need you to mother hen us. We already got Jules for that. How about some water?"

Jameson cranked the music on and feminine squeals of approval filled the bus.

"Thanks." I took it from him and relaxed into the couch, and then I was alone. Well not exactly *alone*. Lake sat beside me, but two women were immediately there to crawl into his lap and steal his attention. I scooted over to give them room and bumped into two more girls sucking face. Jameson leaned against the table opposite the couch. His lips fastened onto one woman as he watched the girls on the couch try their damndest to eat each other's faces off.

I wanted to leave as I wasn't keen to take part in the scene unfolding before me but I didn't know where to go. Brooks was nowhere in sight, and the longer I sat there unsure, the more the bus filled up with groupies and hangers-on. I stood up but was knocked down by a woman gyrating to a tune that didn't match the music playing.

In minutes, nearly everyone around me was intoxicated or on their way to public indecency. Or both.

I didn't think my uncle would be happy to find me here. However, the socially awkward and anxious freak I was didn't allow me to draw attention to myself by trying to escape the drunk and horny sardines surrounding me.

Nerves shot, I searched for an escape and met Walker's eyes. I hadn't seen him come in through all the bodies but he stood by the counter, a bottle of beer at his lips as he watched me. One woman was latched onto his neck like a vampire but she might as well have been invisible for all the attention he paid her.

I could feel the panic growing inside me. In seconds, he extricated himself from his leech and pushed his way through the crowd toward me. Then he was standing above me, that powerful hand that had twirled a drumstick like it'd been ingrained in his DNA held out to me like an offer.

I wasn't sure what came over me. Maybe it was how uncomfortable I was or just that those swirling eyes were hard to turn down when they were focused solely on me, but after only a brief hesitation, I took it.

His large hand curled around mine and tugged.

5

W alker didn't take me off the bus, instead he guided me to the back room. I could see now that it was a small recording studio. Padded walls, and several instruments. A few people lingered inside, more than one stripped down and showing more skin than I ever needed to see. All he had to do was look at them with a impassive expression and intent in his eyes and they scattered. He shut the door behind them, smothering the loud music, and dropped into a small two-seat leather couch.

His left arm was relaxed along the back, his right balancing his beer on his knee. He glanced to the empty seat beside him pointedly. An invitation.

I took an involuntary step toward him but common sense smacked me in the face and I spun around, observing the small recording studio as I fidgeted self-consciously. It wasn't close to being set up to record a full album but with a guitar, small drum set, mixer and other bits and pieces, I suspected they could record rough tunes they wrote while on the road. All the equipment didn't leave much room for moving around but I did my best to avoid the silent goliath observing me.

"This is cool," I squeaked out, so damn nervous and restless.

I didn't know what was happening to me. I was a withdrawn and often cautious person but not normally this jumpy. Walker Lawson did something to me that I couldn't explain and I barely knew him. Barely exchanged more than a few words with him.

He hummed a low sound.

There was only so long I could touch a cymbal before it became awkward so I faced him, holding my breath. "You all fit in here together?"

He shook his head, clearing his throat. "No."

Okay. His eyes were hooded, his thumb at his mouth as he observed me. He dragged that thumb across his bottom lip as he watched my face. I probably looked like a spaz, twitching in place and blushing so bright I could blind a mole.

"I don't think I'm supposed to be here," I told him to fill the edgy silence. "I need to find my uncle."

"Why are you here?" he asked me.

I looked to the door, avoiding eye contact. "Lake brought me here. I'm still adjusting and I was tagging along before I realized."

"Why are you *here?*" He waved his beer around and to himself meaningfully. Walker Lawson had a way with words. Or a lack thereof.

It was annoying how much I liked that about him.

I shrugged. "My uncle gave me the job. But you already know that."

His head tilted to the side.

I sighed, not wanting to spill all my baggage at this man's feet in the back of a million-dollar tour bus full of picture-perfect groupies. "I needed a job."

"That it?" He challenged me, narrowing his eyes.

I narrowed mine right back. "Yeah, that's it."

He shook his head slowly, a quirk to his bottom lip. "That ain't it."

I huffed, annoyed and turned on. It was a disconcerting mix. "I don't know what you expect me to say. Why I'm here isn't your business."

He grinned. It was a small thing, just the barest flash of teeth and a little wicked but it lit my entire body on fire. "Fair enough."

"Why are *you* here?" I shot back, angry at my body's response. It chooses *now,* this man, to turn to mush? I'd been basically asexual since I dropped out of college.

He chuckled, his eyes smiling. "I'm here to make money and get my dick wet."

My mouth dropped open with the crude response. That word. I *clenched* around air. Walker watched my thighs tighten and his grin kicked up another notch.

"That's not it," I said a bit breathless. This man was much, much more than the rock star stereotype I had so quickly boxed him into yesterday.

"No, that's not it," he affirmed, pleasure in his gaze.

"What is it then?" I asked, *needing* to know.

He looked at me and I could feel his response, though he was kind enough not to say it.

None of your business.

I nodded. "That's fair."

He looked at the seat beside him again, a dare in his eyes.

I swallowed hard.

This man was potent. I wanted to run from him and jump him all at once.

"I'm not like those girls," I told him.

He smiled softly and stood. Towering over me, he thumbed my bottom lip, dragging it down to bare my lower teeth. I lit up like a live wire, my hands limp at my side as I fell into his dark eyes.

I wasn't sure what I expected him to do. Maybe replace his thumb with his lips but that was so far and away from what I *should* want him to do. I held myself still, just savoring the feeling of his warm skin touching mine in a place and way that I would never have through to be so erotic before this moment.

"You're on V's bus," he told me, his eyes flitting between mine.

I nodded, "But I don't know which one is his." Startled by how disappointed I was when he dropped his thumb, I looked away.

"Come on." He grabbed my hand, gently leading me through the crowd and off the bus.

Silently, he walked me down the line of buses, several of them spilling with music and gyrating bodies. I caught sight of Mavis for a second, standing on top of a bus all alone, she twirled and twirled with her arms in the air, a bottle of liquor dangling from her fingertips. One man stood on the ground staring up at her with a scowl on his face. I wanted to go coax her down, it seemed dangerous, but though it was dark, I could see the man was Van and he was calling her name sharply and I figured he was there to do just that.

The drummer holding my hand didn't give me much time to ponder it as he pulled me past all of them to a dark bus at the end. The lights were off. He knocked sharply on the door and a tall man opened it, rubbing sleep from his eyes.

"What's up, Walk?" the man asked.

"This is Shiloh," Walker told him. I shivered as my name rolled off his tongue. "She's V's niece."

The man waved me on, disappearing back into the bus.

"Dale, V's driver," Walker told me gruffly. One second I was standing beside him and the next I was standing on the first step to the bus, his hands still on my waist from boosting me up. I was now at his height, my eyes level with his. "Go to sleep."

I narrowed my eyes at the order.

He was amused. His eyes filled again with that lit pleasure as my face scrunched in affront. One quick tug of fabric at my stomach and I fell into him. "Sleep," he ordered me again, his voice low, his hot breath dancing across my lips.

"Don't tell me what to do," I replied, that breathy tone once again inflicting my words and fighting off how serious I had meant them.

He nipped at my lip. It was so fast and surprising adrenaline flooded my body and I swayed into him, my hands latching onto his broad shoulders.

His eyes darkened and his hand curled tight around my hip. "What're you gonna do about it? Huh?"

Lust, hot and sweet pooled low. He licked at my lip, soothing the sting.

And then he was gone.

♪

SLEEP WAS ELUSIVE. STRANGELY I WANTED TO OBEY, GOING to bed like he'd ordered but I also couldn't stop the urge to defy him even if he would never know. I did not know one thing about Walker Lawson other than the man was sex personified. He was quiet but so communicative with his expressions. He was one of the best drummers I'd ever seen live and he threw his entire body and soul into the music. I also knew he wanted me.

Me.

Plain, shy, awkward—me.

It was alarming. Shocking. It completely baffled me when so many beautiful women had been available to him, he'd wanted me. I knew if I had given him the signal, I would have been under him in a second last night. I couldn't deny how crystal clear he'd made his desire for me.

It was intoxicating.

His attention.

His desire.

His touch.

His lips.

Teeth.

It was also very dangerous.

Walker was irrevocably dangerous to me, my libido, my emotions, and my job. I wouldn't betray my uncle's trust. Walker had taken me off guard last night but I couldn't allow that to happen again.

I knew it wasn't likely going to be a problem. He wanted me last night, but the sun brought a new day, and I knew it was highly likely he'd moved on to someone else after he dropped me to my bus.

That some other woman spent the night under him.

Jealousy threatened to overwhelm me, but I refused to succumb to that foolish and unfair emotion.

I'd turned him down and I was okay with that. I had to be okay with that because that man was unattainable. He wasn't built to be chained down by anyone or anything. And even if he were, I wasn't the girl that would get that chance. She would be something otherworldly. Beautiful, smart, funny, creative, and...not sick. She wouldn't need heaps of pills to get her through the day.

I looked down at the pharmacy I carried with me everywhere I went feeling sorry for myself which I absolutely loathed. I wasn't dying. I knew how to manage my disease. I could lead a healthy and normal life if I made my health a top priority.

I wanted a family. To get married and have babies and though that may look a little different to some people, for me it was still possible. Hospitals were a familiar home. Last minute cancelled plans were a common occurrence. My diet would always be abnormal and affect the man I married, but hopefully, that man would be supportive.

Then, there were always the effects of the disease that were hard to talk about. Or even think about.

I took spare clothes with me everywhere I went in case my body betrayed me. Thankfully, that had only happened to me twice in my life, but those two times were so mortifying they haunted me.

The first in a supermarket that had a bathroom for employees only. Standing at the front of the store on my own while I begged the manager to let me in wasn't something I was willing to do so I'd fled, leaving my full cart at the checkout line. The cashier had known something had happened and was kind enough not to call me on it, but I never went back to that store.

The other instance, and the most embarrassing, happened during a college party where it was so hard to hide that I'd changed clothes in the bathroom and had to bag the spoiled ones and carry them out with me because of a deep-seated fear that my peers would find them in the tiny trash can and call me out on it.

My future husband would need to know that there were times I would get sick. So sick I would need treatments that would make me useless for days and leave my immune system compromised. He would need to know that I didn't know what my future would look like. That there may come a time when surgery would be the only 'fix', and that single surgery would mortify me for the rest of my life. Leaving me to carry a bag around attached to my stomach that would take some creative fashion to hide under anything that wasn't a baggy sweatshirt.

Not a lot of awareness was out there about Crohn's disease. But it was a debilitating illness and caused even more problems throughout my life.

Therapy had brought me to a point in my life where I accepted this disease as something I couldn't change. I was in a good place mentally, apart from how difficult it was to manage sometimes and keep a steady job. Some days that place tilted under my feet and left me unbalanced. It was a disease that lived in my gut, but that didn't mean I wasn't suffering from it in other areas. I could get depressed, anxious, and paranoid about fevers and stomachaches.

I could feel amazing one day and a mess the next. My emotions could swing without warning, and sometimes I couldn't find the physical or mental fortitude to get out of bed.

But I was a person. I had dreams and desires, aspirations and expectations. I wouldn't let it beat me. So every minute of every day I was fighting back against something that was hell bent on dragging me down.

I would find that man that would accept me and every bit of scary baggage I carried. He would be good, kind, and supportive. He would be my superman.

But Superman was not a rock star.

♪♫

FOR MOST OF THE MORNING, WE WERE ON THE ROAD. I wasn't sure when we left the city, but I realized we had when I finished getting ready for the day and sat on a leather couch that was a replica of the one the band had in their bus, folded my arms along the back with my chin propped up on them, and watched the scenery fly by out the window.

We were heading to Boston. From there we would be in the US and Canada for nearly two months before we went overseas. Not having traveled too much I was pretty excited to see everything possible.

The travel accommodations weren't too shabby either. My Uncle's bus was just as large and ritzy as the band's, only we didn't have to share it with a bunch of stinky rock stars.

I made a smoothie for myself and whipped up eggs and toast for my uncle, knowing he would be up by nine as per the schedule Julie had emailed me.

He came out of the bedroom dressed in his suit and set his laptop up at the table. He took a bite of the toast I made him.

"You can have the bedroom, Shy," he told me absently as his fingers flew over the keyboard.

I shrugged, trying to take notes on the tablet he'd given me to use but still a little unfamiliar with the programs. "I don't mind the bunks."

He looked at me over his screen, one brow raised high.

I chuckled. "They're pretty comfortable."

He snorted. "You don't want the privacy?"

"No. You've changed my diapers," I told him around a snicker. "I don't care if you catch me drooling."

He chuckled, taking the tablet from me and showing me how to access the note icon in the app.

"Besides," I told him. "I feel kinda bad taking your bed when I filled your bathroom with all my *girly* products."

He groaned. "There are just some things a man shouldn't have to see in his own bathroom."

"Afraid of a few tampons?" I teased him.

He shuddered. "Terrified."

Thus, ladies and gentlemen, why my forty-three-year-old uncle was still single.

I shot him a sly grin. "Even Julie's tampons?"

He scowled at me but his eyes were laughing. "Hush."

I knew they had something going on. It was obvious when his gaze wandered to her ass so often. They weren't official and knowing my uncle that was either because he didn't want to be official or—and what I suspected—he didn't want to put Julie in a position that anyone questioned her hard work and dedication to her job.

I wondered how that would work now that I was staying with him on this bus. I didn't know where Julie stayed, but she wasn't on this bus and that could be my fault.

"I don't want to get in the way—" I started.

He cut me off. "You're not. She wouldn't stay with me even if you weren't here."

Yup. It was a secret.

I nodded, appeased I wasn't messing with their time together.

"Where is she?" I liked Julie. She was sweet and patient, and really good at her job.

"She often takes a flight to the venue to prepare," he said as he typed. "That's where she is now, but other days there's another bus for her and the other managers."

"And the roadies?" I asked. I knew there was the band's bus following behind us along with two haulers for equipment.

"They have their own accommodations."

"So shitty buses and shittier hotels?" I teased.

He snorted. "Something like that. They know the score and most of them live for this life."

Yeah, I could tell. The roadies were busy from sunup to sundown, but they partied last night just as hard as the band. They were friendly for the most part and really did seem happy to be doing the grunt work.

Uncle V put the kibosh on anymore chitchat and we got to work. Though he was here for this band and it was his top priority, he still had a lot of responsibilities for the label and other musicians. I fielded most of his calls through the day and organized his emails by priority.

One of his work phones rang for the thirtieth time in so many hours and I picked it up. "Varian Green's phone."

There was silence, then a weird crackling sound.

"Hello?"

I could hear the person breathing but they didn't speak.

Confused, I pulled the phone from my face, glancing at it before calling a greeting again.

Mouth Breather continued briefly exhaling and then hung up.

My uncle looked to me, his eyes raised as he listened to another call on his other phone.

I shrugged and handed him the phone, showing him the last call.

His eyes darkened and he placed it on the table, face down.

"Who was it?"

I saw him hesitate, something creeping over his face. "No one."

I didn't want to pry, though I could tell just by the dark mood that had descended over him that is wasn't *no one*, but I let it go.

By lunch time he had taken over his phones, returning several calls, and I was on my own time to do whatever I wanted for the last hour of travel. I decided to pull out my camera and fiddle with the settings, hoping to get a few shots of the city when we stopped.

Despite my confusion when I first joined the tour, after my meeting with Uncle V, I had a much better grasp on what was expected of me leading up to the show. I was to do any and everything Julie or Uncle V asked and make sure things were moving smoothly. I was basically a water girl but that was fine with me. I would be the best water girl my uncle ever had, if that was what it took to remain employed.

Last night I was nervous after a long and hard day, but a smooth day of travel had allowed me to relax and gain perspective. We traveled for five hours today, but other days would be longer so I was glad I had packed my e-reader. I was also going to take full advantage of the traveling and fill my photography page with cool new sights from the cities we were stopping in to help build my following on my social media accounts. I'd include photos of the shows and the new people I met. Cool people like Mavis. Maybe even make some new friends.

By the time we rolled into the arena, I was excited.

I was ready.

Too bad my anxiety's favorite meal was confidence.

6

Anxiety.

It was a finicky bitch on a good day. But when you were at your most vulnerable? It was a beast.

I had been doing good. I got to work right away, fulfilling Julie's checklist immediately.

Talking to the arena vendors was hard enough due to my lack of brain to mouth coordination but when the band finally rolled off the bus? I just about lost all my smooth marbles.

Brooks was starving and had no idea what "half the shit in the fridge" was. Jameson apparently flooded the shower—or rather one of his many female friends flooded the shower when she barfed her guts up and clogged the drain. Hangover plus a swaying bus did not equal a settled stomach. After finding someone to clean that up—because I *was not* doing it, Lake then needed help excavating his own admirers when they absolutely refused to leave the bus.

Frazzled and tired, I ran from place to place to put out all the fires that seemed to ignite when the band came on scene and smacked into Walker.

The man was a ninja. Sneaking up on unsuspecting women when they least suspected. I stood in the middle of the parking lot, gaping at him as his focused stare moved over my sweaty hair to the mascara I knew was likely rubbed all over my face.

"Hi," I squeaked, stepping out of his hold on my upper arms. I hugged them to me, looking for an escape all the while wondering if his lips were really as soft as they felt last night and how upset he would be if I climbed him like a tree to test them out.

Standing there so silent only heightened my spastic nerves and I found myself spinning on my heel and running from him before I really did try to climb him.

The rest of the day I beat myself up for running off like a lunatic. I couldn't meet his eyes any time he was near, and if I thought he was even thinking about confronting me I made myself look busy or—ran. Again. I couldn't seem to help myself.

Then I obsessed about running and the night before and what he must have thought of me and replayed my every interaction with him in my mind over and over no matter how small or insignificant.

Like I said, spastic.

By the time all three bands had gone through stage rehearsal and were getting ready in the back, I was a total mess. I had to make myself a smoothie to calm my upset stomach, all the while reassuring myself that my nausea was a product of my mind and not my Crohn's.

I had no idea when my 'off' hours were but after the long day I didn't think anyone would mind if I washed up. I made a pit stop at the bus and jumped in the shower to wash off the day and the worries. With my hair dried and thrown up, I went for leggings, and an old, pale pink T-shirt that came from a campground me and my parents visited a few years back, and my grey sneakers. Not exactly rock attire but I figured getting all dolled up for every show would get old fast so why worry about it at all?

A little calmer, I made my way backstage, flashing my pass to every security guard that tried to stop me. Just outside the dressing room doors my phone vibrated against my hip. I took it out from where it was tucked between my skin and waistband and saw several missed calls from my mom. I'd texted her last night but I knew she wanted to check in with me.

Seeing the seven missed calls made me feel guilty for not making more time for her yet. It was only bound to get worse, so I needed to make her a priority now before I got in the habit of ignoring her calls.

"Mama," I greeted her.

"Shy," she breathed into my ear. Audibly relieved. "I've been calling and calling."

"I know. I'm sorry. I've just been so busy."

"Busy is good," she perked up. "What kind of busy?"

I smiled as she prodded me. "The busy kind of busy."

She chuckled. "Okay, I promised I wouldn't pry too much. How are you liking it? Are you having fun? Are you taking your medicine? Is your uncle taking care of you?"

"Mom," I groaned. "I'm fine. Everything's fine. I'm having fun. Uncle V is watching me like a hawk." I left out that he sort of forgot about me last night. It wasn't his fault that I needed my hand held. He was used to the people around him being on the ball twenty-four seven. I was going to have to learn to keep up.

"That's good. You know I worry."

"I know," I leaned my shoulder against the wall. "How's dad?"

"Missing you. Like me."

I huffed a laugh. "I've only been gone a few days."

"He has no one to watch the games with and I need my scrabble partner back." I was quiet and she sighed. "I'm sorry, I don't mean to guilt you about leaving. We all know this is a good move for you."

Yes, it was and we all needed it. My parents couldn't put their entire lives on hold for their adult daughter. I would not be a burden my whole life. I refused to.

People all around the world led independent lives with this disease. It wasn't crippling in that way, I just hadn't found my own path yet. I was young and had time but my parents were helicopters and made everything that much harder. I was loved. I was so loved, but I was too dependent on them and only some of that was because of my disease.

We chatted some more. About what Mrs. Fenhill was doing to her garden next door and the sale prices on ground beef at the local market. All things that were absolutely titillating for my mother and then I caught sight of a person coming out of the dressing room. I stiffened as Walker spotted me.

My mother's voice went static as he swaggered my way, a curious smile in his eyes.

"I-I gotta go, Mama," I hastily whispered.

"Oh. Is everything okay?"

"Yup, just gotta get back to work."

"Oh." She sounded disappointed and guilt slithered through me for lying. "Well, I love and miss you oodles. Your daddy will want you to call back so he can talk to you."

"I'll try in a little bit," I promised.

"Okay, kisses," she smooched dramatically.

Wincing, I smooched back, my eyes on Walker's as he stopped in front of me.

Sex on a stick watching or not, my mom was the best woman in the whole world and I would never diss her.

Hanging up, I flushed as his lips twitched.

"That's my mama," I told him unnecessarily. "We have this thing," I kept babbling. "Never hang up without a kiss. She would've got her feelings hurt."

His eyes twinkled in that way that told me he was highly amused.

I fiddled with my fingers, having put away my phone. "Did you need something?"

"Can I get one of those?"

I blinked at him, looking at my empty hands. "What?"

He stepped closer, backing me into the wall. His finger gently tapped my lips purposefully and I shuddered, sagging against the wall. "We can't do that anymore."

"Why not?" he whispered playfully, his lips now at my ear. All I saw was his big shoulder, the dark shirt stretched tight over it.

"My uncle would be very upset," I reminded him, my voice squeaking out of me.

He backed off a little, just a little, ducking down to catch my eyes. A question in his that never left his lips.

"This is a very bad idea," I told him unsteadily. It was. It was a very bad idea. I just had to keep remining myself of that very fact. Not an easy feat when a guy who looked that good in a washed-out T-shirt was crowding you against the wall, his lips a hairs breath away from yours.

He tugged on my shirt at my stomach, briefly glancing at the little smiling bear with the ranger's hat. "Cute."

Cute. Adorable. That was me.

Walker kept waiting. Keeping me trapped though I didn't feel that in a scary way. It was a protective sort of trapped. We were in a dark corner and his big body kept me hidden, and I knew if I pushed from the wall he would back away. But I didn't, and that knowledge was written all over his determined face. My mouth could spew excuses, but Walker was a body language kind of guy and my body was telling him to keep doing exactly what he was doing.

"I can't sleep with you," I whispered against his lips. "I'm a good girl."

"Give me a kiss, good girl," he ordered.

My lips fell abruptly into his. Zero coordination, all excitement. Completely betraying the very real reasons I had told him we shouldn't be doing this very thing not even two seconds ago. He chuckled at my clumsy excitement, bracing my back with one big hand spread the length of my spine.

Lips against lips, I just breathed him in. Neither of us moved to make it more, we just stood there, savoring the press of them together. The soft feel of his against the softness of mine. His minty breath kissing mine. Shivers danced along my spine and a soft sound left my mouth as his hand drifted around my hips.

"Thank you," he said against my mouth.

"You're welcome," I breathed into his.

I sagged against the wall as he left me. Bereft and cold, I watched him march down the hall.

What exactly was happening? The man made it impossible to turn him away, but when I gave in, he barely took a thing from me. Other than my wits. Those were in his back pocket.

A delicate hum drifted into my ear to the tune of a teasing kissing playground melody and I looked over my shoulder.

"You have a beautiful voice," I told Mavis.

"You just kissed Johnnie Walker Lawson," she sang, making the damning words sound both raspy and melodious. "You naughty, dirty girl. Tell me *everything*."

♪

MAVIS WAS LIKE A DOG WITH A BONE AND I JUST DID NOT possess the mental fortitude to deny her bubbly personality. I kissed Walker. A tiny one. Just a peck really. Could that even really be defined as a kiss?

Apparently, Mavis thought it was the hottest kiss she ever saw. She was massively disappointed no tongue was involved. I had to agree with her.

But that thinking was bad. My uncle wouldn't let this go if he knew. He'd be so disappointed in me and yell at Walker. Or no, I couldn't imagine anyone yelling at Walker. He would do *something* to Walker. I would be fired and my parents would be kind and understanding but they would be disappointed too. A casualty of relying on them too much as an adult.

Mavis didn't see things my way or even pretend to understand my reservations. She wanted me to jump Walker's bones and then give her a play-by-play.

I let myself get carried away in her hyper personality during the show. Both of us avoided the stage this time and took over an empty dressing room. While Mavis binged on fried arena food, I ate from my pre-packed cooler. She was curious but didn't push me. It was kind of nice not to have to worry about her judgment. Mavis seemed like the type of person who didn't know how to judge; she was just too accepting. She didn't understand personal space or hold back any of her thoughts no matter how inappropriate or strange. But she was kind and sweet, and I was glad she'd asked to be friends. Just like the night before, once the show was over, she disappeared and I figured it was to find her boyfriend and his band.

I didn't personally know Van, the lead singer and her 'boo', but from what I'd seen of him I knew he didn't deserve someone as awesome as Mavis.

The after show went much like the previous night only this time, after I made sure food and drinks were where they were supposed to be, I kept to myself. But I couldn't help but notice Walker and Brooks were on the other side of the room, neither of them partaking in the many women on offer.

However, the woman who had rubbed Walker down returned. I refused to watch her do so this time. If anything, it was confirmation that what he'd been doing with me was just fun on his part. We weren't in a committed relationship. Hell, we barely knew each other and shared nothing more than a peck on the lips...and a bite.

But I knew myself. I got too hung up. Too clingy. Walker Lawson wasn't a man I could latch onto no matter how hard he was to resist. I needed to make that clear to him the next time he cornered me.

Instead of allowing Lake to escort me to the buses, I learned my lesson and left ahead of them. There were disappointed boos when the fans spotted me and no rock stars followed, but no one bothered me as I made my way to the buses.

I grabbed my camera and sent a text to my uncle that I was going for a walk. I was in a strange place and without a buddy, so I didn't leave the gated parking lot and instead walked around the partygoers between each bus, snapping candids of their fun.

Most people ignored me, but some posed and had fun with it, asking me for group pictures. I dutifully wrote down emails and promised to send them the photos and filled my entire night behind my camera.

That night I slept good, sure in my decision not to get involved with any rock stars. I was going to soak up every last experience this tour offered and then I would go home to my small town and find my place. My independent, content little place in the world.

7

So it happened by accident. And if we lingered a little longer than we should have or ducked behind a few equipment crates to not be seen, it meant nothing. Absolutely nothing.

We weren't eavesdropping—exactly. We just happened upon them and felt bad about interrupting, so we hid.

Not to mention, the argument we'd stumbled on was so loud and distracting, we were a little nervous to be announcing ourselves.

If held up under oath, I wasn't sure what I'd say, but for now, I was going with accidental snooping. That and peer pressure.

Mavis clamped her hand around my mouth, shushing me.

"He keeps calling V," Walker growled, his face a mask of rage. It was kind of shocking to witness to much emotion from him when he was normally so stoic.

Jameson stood, watching his brother with indifference. "So what?"

Mavis and I ducked down as he turned. We were only here to get my camera bag I'd left behind, they hadn't even heard us enter the massive room and now it felt like if we tried to leave, they might catch us.

"So what? So *what?* Are you still talkin' to that fucker?" Walker asked him.

Jameson chuckled a dark, humorless sound full of anger. "Worried I'm on somethin' again?"

"I went away for you," Walker rumbled quietly. "Did you forget that?"

"No," Jameson said quietly, pissed. "How the fuck could I forget that?"

I couldn't hear Walker's reply.

Jameson growled, "I haven't spoken to him in years."

"You're lyin' to me."

"He loved her too, ya know?" Jameson hissed. "You weren't there after she died. You didn't see him."

"I don't give the first fuck about him. He got her killed."

"No," Jameson returned deadly quiet. "I did."

Silence.

Then Jameson again, "Just fuckin' say it, Walk. I know you want to."

"If I find out he's dealin' to you again, it won't be him I fuck up, it'll be you."

Something slammed and then boots stomped out of the room.

Mavis bugged out her eyes, wrenching me to the side. We crawled out the side door.

"We shouldn't have heard that," I hissed to her, standing in the hall. "That was private."

She shushed me again, ducking into a nearby closet. "Jameson Walker on drugs again?"

"Again?" I slapped the wall, searching for a light and finding none. All I could see were her wide eyes.

She made a sound of shock and clamped her hand down on my arm. "How do you not know? It was all over the place a few months ago. The media got ahold of a friend from Jameson's hometown and the chick squealed all his dark secrets."

I shook my head. I liked the band before I knew them, but I didn't stalk them online.

She leaned closer to me, whispering. "He and his sister were all fucked up on drugs as kids. There's a theory that Walker went away after beating the shit out of their dealer."

I remembered his sister. The band spoke of her often. She was the baby in the family and all the guys knew and loved her. But I did remember that she'd died of an overdose.

"That has to be who they're talking about. Walker must think Jameson is talking to him again."

I sighed. "Mavis, this is all just sad and wrong. We shouldn't be whispering about them in dark closets."

She looked around, as if just noticing our hiding spot and winced. "Sorry, I'm a chronic gossiper. It makes me feel better to shit on everyone else's problems than obsess over mine."

"At least your honest about it," I told her.

She grinned wide, her white teeth flashing in the dark. She poked her head out of the door, dragged me out behind her, and we dipped out of the hall and quickly walked back to the bus.

"Movie night?"

I nodded. Probably best to keep clear of any lingering animosity floating around the band tonight.

I wasn't sure what to think about all we'd heard. Not all of it made any sense, but Walker seemed concerned about Jameson. And Jameson seemed a whole lot of *not concerned* about his brother's worries.

It wasn't any of my business anyway and I felt bad for over-hearing it. Mostly I spent the rest of the night making sure Mavis didn't have any plans to spread it around. But she assured me she had no intention of getting kicked off the tour, so I let it slip from my mind and focused on spending a carefree night with a new friend.

But one thing did keep coming back to me. The reminder that Walker had beaten a man. I wasn't sure what it was about that conversation that reminded me of it. I didn't know why Walker had said he went away for Jameson when he was the one who beat that guy. Walker was the one to put him in the hospital.

But all of it was a stark reminder that Walker was not always a calm, quiet man. He could be violent. Had been violent, and every time he latched those eyes of his onto mine, I seemed to completely forget that fact. Uncle V may vouch for him but that did not mean Walker was a man I could get myself involved with. I didn't know him. Not at all.

Now if only I could remember that the next time he touched me.

If there even was a next time.

♪

LATE THE NEXT NIGHT, I WAS SITTING ON MY OWN AFTER the show on a fold-out chair in front of my uncle's bus. He and Julie were inside, either having a meeting or discreetly trying to spend some time together. Either way I didn't want to interrupt. So I settled in with my laptop and camera, downloading some of the pictures I'd taken that night.

A few of the band on stage, but mostly the fans.

My favorites were of them waiting in line. Their excited faces were bright and luminous and I could feel the palpable air of anticipation through the photos.

"Those yours?" A voice startled me from behind. I jumped and would have knocked my laptop to the ground if it weren't for Walker's hand snapping out to catch it. "Didn't mean to startle you."

I gaped at him, my face flooding with embarrassment. I shouldn't feel embarrassed. There was not a thing to be embarrassed about, unless you counted the way he stared at my lips so intently it was like he was willing the words to come out of my mouth.

Unfortunately, all I could focus on was the conversation Mavis and I had snooped on the day before.

After thinking it over, and over, and over, I suspected the girl they had referenced was their sister. And it broke my heart remembering the way Jameson might blame himself for her death.

But with Walker just standing there, staring at me, I was forced to refocus on the present.

"Uhm," I glanced down at my laptop and then back. "They're mine."

He tore his eyes from me and looked back at the photos on the screen. "You're pretty good, huh?"

Swallowing thickly, I nodded. I wasn't the best at accepting compliments. I never knew how to respond to them. I got it from my mother. She was the worst at accepting them and she passed the trait on to me. A simple 'thank you' always seemed too arrogant but not saying anything at all was just rude. I had a hard time falling into a comfortable middle and wound up just fumbling the entire exchange.

Walker didn't seem to mind though, he just crouched down at my side and casually flicked through the photos.

Silence descended over us as he perused my photos from the night before.

I couldn't seem to tear my eyes away from the side profile of his rugged face, and he knew it by the tiny smirk playing along his lips.

If only he knew what I was truly thinking in that moment.

My head was clearer than it had been during our previous exchanges. I could see his fist wrapped around the edge of my laptop from the corner of my eye and I imagined that fist turning on someone in anger.

The man he'd put in the hospital had been a year older than him. Nineteen at the time. I wanted so badly to look it up. Now having known him at least a little, I knew I would look the story over and draw different conclusions. But years of listening to my uncle berate the media about how they withheld certain facts and went with their own assumptions, their articles littered with judgmental opinions, held me back.

I didn't want to be that person. It felt wrong to look more into it when I saw this man every day. I didn't want anything coloring my opinion of him—an opinion I wanted to draw from experience. Not from an article online.

Staring at his face, the smile still playing on his lips, it was nearly impossible to picture him doling out any kind of violence. He had the size and strength for it. He was easily at the very least eighty pounds heavier than me and over a foot taller. Even to most average men, he dwarfed them.

His physical appearance, I could see, could be scary. But my father and uncle were large, strong men, and so size didn't necessarily intimidate me.

If anything, his strong jawline, pillow-soft lips, and gorgeous eyes intimidated me. But only because it made me hyper aware of my own insecurities.

Staring at those lips now, Walker's small smirk pulled into a full smile. "Shy girl ain't so shy."

Heat flooded my face and my eyes flew to his. To my shock and surprise a matching blush colored his own cheekbones.

We just sat there, staring at each other, his blush slowly fading as my own grew hotter.

I knew my embarrassment was filling my eyes but his own seemed pleased, and if not mistaken, a little *hungry*.

I tore my eyes from his, clearing my throat. I tugged the laptop from him and he released it, standing again.

"You take any of those for us?"

I refocused on the photos, flicking through them all without much intent. Trying to distract myself from the sudden heavy atmosphere lingering between us. "Uhm, no, not yet."

"You want to?"

Yes, Yes, I did. Badly.

But they had a photographer. A team of them actually. Professionals, which I was not.

"Maybe."

He huffed a chuckle, his chest shaking as he crossed his arms. "You want to."

My blush faded and a scowl fell over my eyes. "Walker, are you teasing me?"

He licked his lips, eyeing mine. "Like how you say that."

My scowl falling away and an uncomfortable heat falling low in my stomach, I asked, "Walker?"

He hummed, backing away. "I want to hear more of that."

I shook my head. "Now I don't want to say it at all."

A sharp bark of laughter fell from him and I grinned, ducking my head. Pleased that I'd obtained that response from him.

"Come with me," he told me, tilting his head even as he backed away.

I looked away from him, biting my lip to smother my smile. "I'm busy."

"You busy tomorrow?"

"I'm always busy."

He shook his head grinning. "Full of excuses. I can read you like a book, shy girl. You want to come with me."

Oh boy did I. But that was bad.

As he walked away, I reminded myself how bad it was to follow him.

But just once, I wanted to break the rules. I wanted to experience something bad for me.

But I was a good girl, a shy girl. I was proud of myself for dueling with him a little rather than running the other way as I had in the past and I wanted more of that feeling.

I was always good. Always safe.

It was exhausting.

I wanted to put myself in the path of something dangerous for once.

8

I remained on edge for a week just waiting for Walker to corner me again. I practiced my speech in the mirror every morning. But he never came close. It was like he could tell. He knew I was on a hair trigger and instead, gave me space. But that didn't mean I lost his attention. His eyes followed me every time I walked into a room. Those dark turbulent orbs locked onto me and didn't let me go until I was out of sight.

I kept waiting and waiting for him to catch me unaware but he never did. Instead I settled into my job. It actually wasn't as hectic and draining as it had been the first few shows. Once I got accustomed to my duties and what was expected of me, I felt more comfortable throughout my days and managed to find quite a bit of downtime for myself. There weren't really days off in this lifestyle. There were show days and travel days.

During travel days I helped manage my uncle, but I didn't mind that work. I was learning all sorts of programs and found I kind of had a knack for assistant duties. Show days were my busiest. On my feet for long periods of time and running from place to place, but every night I had a front row seat of my choosing to one of the greatest shows by one of the greatest bands I'd ever seen or heard live.

When each show ended, Mavis would come to my uncle's bus to hang out with me if she wasn't with her boyfriend. We'd watch horror movies we rented and binge on my gluten free popcorn while painting our nails and going over the photos I'd taken that day. With her around, I never felt like I was missing anything as the parties went on and on throughout the night. She'd crash in one of the bunks on our bus when her asshole boyfriend was messing around with another girl.

She knew. Of course she did. Not much got past Mavis.

I tried to talk to her about him but she got so defensive and, for Mavis, that was a rare occurrence. Seeing the hurt in her eyes had me backing off the topic fast. Something about him kept her hanging on, and it wasn't my place to tell her that her choices were wrong or reckless. They were *her* choices. I knew the importance of making your own choices and mistakes all too well.

Mavis and I liked going for a walk early in the morning when the bands and crews were still asleep. We would search for healthy food restaurants for lunch. In some cities, they were hard to find while in the larger ones, there was always a plethora of choices. We'd made it a ritual in every city we stopped at. Today was no exception. We sat together at a wooden table in a courtyard, across the street from the venue with a spread of takeout. Mavis had purchased a stack of fashion magazines which we were flipping through as sunshine beamed down on us.

"I like that one," she said as she circled a bright yellow handbag with a glitter pen.

"It's too loud for me," I murmured, eyeing its burgundy twin. "And I don't really carry handbags."

She motioned to my neon orange soft cooler with her head.

"Not a handbag," I told her.

"It could be," she hit back. "That thing lacks personality. Why not transform a cool bag like this into a cooler." She tapped the magazine. "Or fix up that cooler. You're good at that." She tugged on my shorts, noting the little lace patch I'd sewn on the hem.

"I have before but this one cost too much money to mess up." My parents spent a whack on it, hoping it would keep my smoothies cold all day long. So far it worked like a charm.

"What are you looking at?" Brooks asked over my shoulder, having snuck up behind me.

"Girl stuff," Mavis chirped.

Brooks rolled his eyes and sat with us.

"My girl's birthday is coming up," he told us, stealing a handful of Mavis's fries. "Can I bribe you girls into helping me shop for her?"

Mavis clapped excitedly. "Shopping!"

"What does she like?" I asked him, pushing one of the magazines his way. Brooks had become sort of a tagalong buddy of ours. We kept him out of trouble when his female admirers were around and we benefited from his ability to keep the horny roadies away from us. He made things interesting yesterday when he came with us to lunch. The paparazzi getting wind of him at the restaurant cut our meal short, so I doubted he'd be tagging along much more in the future.

He sent me a blank look and I chuckled.

"Favorite color?" Mavis asked him.

"Uh, pink."

"Hobbies?"

He shrugged. "Girl shit?"

"What does she do?" Mavis asked him unimpressed with his ignorance.

"Hair." Brooks nodded. "And nails. And that eyebrow thing with the strings..."

"Threading," Mavis informed him. "So a girly girl."

"Woman," Brooks corrected her. "She's twenty-six."

Mavis just shrugged and flipped through her magazine. "Get her diamonds. Girls like her like diamonds."

"No. She hates diamonds," Brooks retorted vehemently. "She doesn't wear a lot of jewelry."

I pulled out my phone and handed it to him. "Show me her profile."

He typed in her name—Reese Donovan—and handed it back to me.

Mavis hung over my shoulder, her lavender hair tickling my nose. "Blonde Barbie." Brooks scowled at her and she waved him away. "It's not an insult, Blonde Beard. She just dresses like a Barbie. Cheerleader I bet."

Brooks nodded. "Captain in high school."

I flipped through her photos. They were mostly her with her girlfriends and little videos of her doing someone's hair or nails. Surprisingly, nothing about Brooks.

"You sure this is your girlfriend?" Mavis looked at him doubtfully. "It says she's single."

"We keep it private," Brooks said gruffly. "I don't like Reese gettin' hounded about me."

Mavis huffed a laugh. "That's gotta bite at her ass."

"What?" Brooks leaned against my shoulder, looking at her recent picture outside a rose garden with a small smile.

"Having caught you and the world not knowing?" Mavis looked at him like he was an idiot. "That girl is a saint for not calling you day in and out to make sure you're not touching anyone on the side."

Brooks shook his head. "I don't cheat. She's my world and she knows it. She doesn't need to check up on me."

Mavis and I exchanged a glance. Reese may be keeping it from him but no woman in her right mind wouldn't worry about Brooks cheating, no matter what he promised. I knew he wasn't but that was because I was around him nearly every minute of every day. He didn't check out another chick. This girl though, she had no idea what was going on during the tour.

"Don't we have a break coming up?" I asked him.

He nodded. "In two weeks. We'll get three days and I already got my plane ticket home."

"But her birthday is before that?" Mavis asked. "Virtual date," she declared confidently.

I smiled brightly. "That's actually a really good idea. If she can't come here, take her on a date while you're apart."

"Scavenger hunt!" Mavis crowed. "We'll send her a bunch of presents and her friends can hide them around her home or around her town and then you can FaceTime her and give her clues on where to find them. Then send her a romantic dinner and wine and dine her." She closed her eyes and clutched her hands to her chest. "Then you can have hot phone sex."

Brooks laughed while I shook my head. He looked to me. "What do you think?"

"I think it could be romantic. Does she have a friend that could help?"

"Yeah, her best friend, Josie, would help."

"Call Josie," I told him. "She'll know what to get her and you can get her measurements. Send her an outfit for your date. Make an appointment to get her all dolled up and cater the food from someplace she loves."

"I still want to buy her stuff," he told me. "Come out with me tomorrow to help me look?"

"I can take a long lunch," I said.

Mavis clapped excitedly. "I'm inviting myself."

Brooks stood up. "Thanks, ladies."

♪

ONCE LUNCH WAS OVER THE REHEARSAL BEGAN, AND I rushed to the stage to help Julie check everything over.

Walker was pounding away on the drums, moving fluidly and so fast it was hard to keep up. I didn't understand how someone could keep a beat like that. I was so bad at coordination.

I grabbed a few water bottles and moved passed Walker to place one behind him so he'd have something to drink during his set.

He abruptly stopped playing and I felt an arm wrap around my waist. Startling me, he pulled me onto his lap in one sleek move.

Jameson trailed off into the mic, glancing at us over his shoulder. "What's goin' on?"

"You know how to play?" Walker's deep voice rumbled into my ear, ignoring Jameson.

"No." Acutely aware of all eyes on us, I attempted to stand. He moved me so my legs hung over each of his and spread his thighs to put his feet on the pedals. I shivered as his hands grabbed mine and curled my fingers around the drumsticks.

"Well, Shy girl, you're about to learn." Still holding my hands, he hit the drums in a rhythm for a few seconds and finished by striking the cymbal. "Give it a shot."

Hesitating for a moment, I flicked a quick glance back to see if he was serious.

He raised his brow. "Come on, play for me."

I gripped the drumsticks and smacked them against the drums in no particular order from one side to the other.

I looked back at him in question and he huffed a quiet laugh, shaking his head. His arms came around me and he guided my hands again, hitting in a one two beat, his thigh jumping under mine as his foot hit the pedal.

Brooks and Lake chuckled, clapping dramatically.

"Let me know when you're ready to get back to work," Jameson jumped from the stage, settling into a seat and pulling out his phone.

I shot to my feet, somewhat embarrassed. Walker frowned, tilting his head to follow my retreat. "Ignore him. Come play with me some more."

The words did something to me. Tingled in places that made me jumpy.

He reached for me, but I danced away, frustrated and hot all over and then peeked over my shoulder to see Walker scowling at his brother.

Standing in the shadows off stage, I listened to Jameson tease him as he jumped back on stage.

"Need to up your game for that one, bro."

Walker smashed the sticks against the drums in a beat so fast and melodic, but it sounded like frustration. "Just sing the fuckin' song."

I ducked away as his eyes searched for me and ran back to the bus like my ass was on fire.

Every moment I spent around Walker imbedded itself inside me, and the euphoria I felt after each and every encounter was intoxicating. I wanted more of that feeling. The steadily growing attraction was starting to override all my common sense.

9

Leaving with Brooks was a production that had to be planned and, as my uncle's assistant, I helped with that planning. The experience taught me that him tagging along with us to lunch was a huge no-no the other day. I was lucky my uncle hadn't reprimanded me for it.

Now we had three vehicles. One for just Brooks, Mavis, and me. The other two were for Jules and the security team.

To my surprise, when Brooks met us at the cars, he wasn't alone. Walker was with him. It would be rude to back out now so I pasted on a smile and climbed into the car ahead of them.

"Shotgun!" Mavis crowed and jumped into the front passenger seat. Our driver, Joe, was a giant and had a suspicious bulge at his chest and side. "You carrying a gun?" Mavis asked him.

"Jesus, Mavis," I laughed. "Filter."

She winked at me and threw her boots up onto the dashboard.

Joe scowled at her and she slowly removed them with a rueful smile.

Both doors in the back opened and I found myself wedged between Brooks and Walker. I hunched closer to Brooks, keeping all my parts away from Walker's.

The heat of his body alone curled around me and enticed me to lean closer.

Fans who had gathered at the gates, were screaming as we pulled away from the arena. They couldn't possibly know who was in the cars, but that didn't stop them from throwing their bodies up against the windows.

Brooks shoved his face into his phone and Mavis fiddled with the radio effectively leaving me to sit awkwardly next to an equally silent man beside me.

His arm was spread across the seat behind me, the hairs on his arm tickling the back of my neck. I sat ramrod straight, my eyes glued to the windshield.

Traffic was slow and it felt like it took forever just to get on the highway. At this rate, it would take us forever to get there.

It started out as a tickle. I first thought I imagined it, but then the pressure firmed and I knew it was Walker's thumb. Back and forth his thumb dragged across the back of my neck. Side to side, up and down. His nail lightly scraping and raising goosebumps all down my spine.

I held my breath for a moment, but then the tremble started in my toes and moved up to my thighs, eventually flowing over my entire body.

He chuckled a low, amused sound that tickled the hair against my forehead as his thumb circled just under my ear. I sat forward more but then his hand circled the back of my neck wholly, gently guiding me until I relaxed against the seat.

I caught sight of Mavis's eyes as she watched me over her shoulder, a smirk playing on her lips.

"Bitch," I mouthed to her.

"Whore," she mouthed back.

Walker used his grip on my neck to turn my head to face him. He didn't say anything, just gazed into my eyes. He held me trapped like that the entire ride.

It was the most erotic twenty minutes of my entire life, and he was barely touching me.

When we pulled up to the strip mall, Joe parallel parked and got out, first opening Mavis's door and then Brooks'. The moment Brooks slid out, Walker leaned in and whispered against my lips, "You done hidin' from me?"

"Who said I was?" So damn taken with the interest aimed my way. When he was like this, it was hard to keep myself still. I wanted to hand over anything he asked of me. Problem was, Walker was *always* like this with me. How was I supposed to fight dogged determination when it came from a six foot two, powerhouse of a man that had sex appeal dripping from his every bone?

A flash of teeth for his grin and then he took my mouth with his.

There was no question with this kiss. I didn't have to wonder. It was positively a *kiss*. It caught me off guard enough that I gasped and he immediately took advantage, swooping his tongue inside with flawless precision. He licked along the length of my tongue and I sagged against the seat, opening wider for him. Slow and calculated, he licked at my mouth, exploring every dark corner. My hands found their way to his chest, twisting into the fabric of his grey shirt and pulling him closer.

He made a dark sound of masculine approval in the back of his throat that I inhaled into mine with a shiver and wrapped his free arm around my waist. His other hand smoothed up my neck and twisted into my hair, pulling my head back with a small bite of pain that had me whimpering and clutching him tighter.

His tongue was warm and slick, his taste minty and intoxicating. He groaned low and I squirmed against him, pressing my thighs tight together.

A sharp rap on the roof of the car startled us both and I tore my mouth away, looking at Brooks who was peering in through the window. "You done sucking face?"

"Fuck off," Walker barked without any heat and gently pried my hands away, sitting back and adjusting his pants. I kept my eyes firmly on his even though I badly wanted to look down. To peek at what I'd felt along the outside of my thigh. He licked his top lip, his eyes amused.

Scrambling out of the car, Brooks righted me as I stumbled onto the curb. Mavis was aiming a shit-eating grin my way as she took my arm and pulled me to the doors of the store.

"You ready for the consequences of that?" I heard Brooks ask Walker from behind.

Walker's response was unhurried. "I'll take care of V."

Brooks snorted. "You don't fuck with fire, man."

"Don't worry about it."

The shop door closed behind me then and I put Brooks' warning out of my mind to pull out and obsess over later. I already knew there would be consequences, and Brooks just confirmed it. I was off limits. That's what my uncle had told them. Walker didn't seem inclined to listen, and I wasn't sure how to feel about that. He was the money. The show. The rock star. I was just my uncle's assistant. If anyone was going to feel the consequences of their actions, it was going to be me. What did it say about Walker that he wasn't at all worried about that?

It implied what happened to me as a result wasn't on his mind. I would be lying if I said that didn't hurt just a little. Or a lot.

♪

BROOKS WAS EITHER THE PICKIEST MAN ON THE PLANET OR this girl was so special she had him all worked up about a pair of shoes. Studs or no studs? That was the question, and Brooks just about asked every single person he could rope into his decision. The salesclerk had been all too happy to help—for about twenty minutes. Mavis gave up after the third time Brooks changed his mind. I was pretty sure Walker was asleep while holding up the wall. That left me and Joe. Joe was for no studs. I was for them. At this point I just wanted Brooks to buy both and move on. We still had so much more to get.

"You like the studs, get the studs," I told him again.

"I don't think she'll like them."

"Too biker babe," Joe agreed.

I sighed. They were a pale pink with a peep toe and silver studs surrounding the heel. They were awesome and I wished I could pull them off. The plain pink ones looked boring in comparison. Plus, we were doing this backward, you should choose the dress than the shoes but Brooks said he loved her in heels and nothing else, so I let him be.

"Buy both," I urged. "You'll know when you find the dress."

He didn't seem convinced. "Walk?"

Walker lazily rolled his head against the wall, looking to me first and then down to the shoes. "Shy likes the studs."

Shy. God, hearing that from him did something to my lady bits that should be illegal. If me calling his name had done even a fraction to him what it did to me...

I couldn't stop the blush from flooding my face. "It's not about what I like. What will she like?"

Brooks groaned. "I don't fuckin' know."

"Call Josie," I suggested.

Brooks sighed and pulled out his phone, stepping away when he put it to his ear.

Mavis groaned dramatically, stomping around in a circle with an expensive fedora on her head. "Are we there yet?"

I snickered, pulling the hat from her and carefully putting it back with its expensive peers much to the relief of the clerk. It was clear *we* weren't here to spend money. Mavis in her torn T-shirt dress and striped stockings and me in my black biker shorts and cropped sweater. Neither screamed haute couture, rather second-hand dime bin.

The only reason we hadn't been thrown out of the high-end store on our asses was due to our company. All three clerks about fainted when the guys walked in the door. At first, there had been gushing and blushing but now even they looked tired of all of us.

Leave it to Brooks and his indecisiveness to put off the ladies.

Finally, a decision was made, and Brooks was going with the studs on the word of her bestie that Reese was trying to broaden her fashion horizons. Personally, I hoped none of it even mattered to the woman who'd stolen Brooks' heart. When you had a man that amazing, so devoted to you, who cared if they cost twelve-hundred dollars or two? They could've been dollar store flip-flops and I would've been a happy girl.

"Finally!" Mavis breathed dramatically as we left the store.

Brooks winced. "Sorry. This is harder than I thought it'd be."

"No biggie," she replied. "You're just the *only* man on the *entire* planet who can bore two girls to tears while shopping."

"I just want everything to be perfect," he said.

"And so it will be," I replied, tugging him into another store. "Maybe just keep Josie on speed dial to help narrow it down faster."

"Got it."

"Oh," Mavis breathed in delight. "Look at all the pretties."

Everything inside the dress shop sparkled and Mavis and I split up digging through the racks. This time we were more than happy to take our time, holding up several options and having fun with the upbeat tune drifting through the shop speakers.

"I need to find a sugar daddy," Mavis declared so seriously as she held a deep green strapless number up to her chest and twirled. I touched a silky black dress, the straps wide and delicate like ribbons. Mavis ooh'd and ahh'd and held it against me. The hem flared out like sharp knives of various lengths and stopped just below my knees, the gaps between them coming up high on my upper thighs. The bodice would be tight down to my hips but it was like liquid silk and I fell in love with it. "Sorry, chickee. We'd need a couple rounds on the corner to afford this one."

I gaped at the tag and immediately shoved it back on the rack. I'd need to sell an organ to afford it.

Thirty minutes later and Brooks chose a tight grey bandage dress that sparkled like diamonds. Mavis hated it. I thought it would look cute with the baby pink heels—*with studs*. She'd look like a rock princess. I was invested now and I hoped she posted pictures online so we could see how her date turned out.

After waiting for Walker to extract himself from the flirty cashier —and biting my tongue before I made a fool of myself—we moved to the jewelry store. Brooks had claimed she didn't wear jewelry, but Josie must have said otherwise because Brooks walked out with pearl studs and a delicate silver chain bracelet.

The man swaggered back to the cars. All his bags in hand and a pleased smile on his face.

"I'm hungry," Mavis whined dramatically, throwing herself into the back seat beside me. I squeezed her tight in thanks and she winked at me. She effectively sat between me and Walker and the man knew it was on purpose. He just shook his head at me, laughing at me silently. His arm went back against the seat and Mavis snuggled into his side, shooting me a wicked smile. Walker didn't push her away, instead it allowed him to reach further and fiddle with a lock of hair that escaped my bun.

"I could eat," Brooks told us as he sat in the front seat.

I pulled Walker's hand away, but he caught my fingers and pulled me sharply against Mavis, his arm trapping me around my shoulder, and resumed his fiddling with my hair.

Mavis elbowed me in my gut and wiggled forward, climbing over my lap and into my seat while I shuffled over. Walker put his arm around my shoulder so I was now cuddled into his side.

"Tacos," Mavis declared.

I scrunched my nose but didn't say anything.

She read me though and winced, an apology on her lips.

I waved her away. It wasn't her place to constantly remember my approved foods.

"I could eat tacos," Brooks announced. "Bring some back to the guys too."

"No tacos," Walker rumbled, his arm sliding down my side.

I looked up at him and he winked.

"I've got my food at the bus," I told them. "Get what you want."

"It's a long drive back," Joe added as he passed a slow-moving Honda. "There's a sandwich shop up here."

Mavis looked at me in question and I shrugged. I was sure I could find something there to eat. I didn't want to draw any more attention to myself than I had already.

A phone rang and I shifted away as Walker reached into his front pocket to pull it out.

Something ominous and dark moved over his face before he silenced it and shoved it back in his pocket.

It was only a glance, but I could have sworn it was the same number that had called my uncle. The mouth breather. I'd answered only two more calls from that number after that first time and none since but only because my uncle had strangely stopped having me field them. But those three calls were memorable. The caller never spoke. Not once. Only breathed. And then the third and last time, my uncle had snatched the phone from me, disappearing into his room on the bus and talking quietly, for a *long* time.

Brooks exchanged a weighted glance with Walker and my eyes narrowed, my mind turning the possibilities over in my head.

We pulled over and went inside and I was forced to let it go. I ordered a veggie gluten free flat bread for myself–leave it to the ritzy part of town to have rarer options.

We sat at a table, eating as fans inside surrounded the guys. I felt bad that they'd barely been able to eat, but neither of them seemed to mind. It only got worse the longer we were there. Word must have gotten out because before long security was ushering us to the cars through a mob of scarily excited fans.

A foot from the car, one fan was so excited she nearly tackled Joe to get to them and I would have went down flat on my face if Walker hadn't been behind me. He scooped me up in his arms and security surrounded him, barreling through people until we slid into the car.

Arms clutching his shoulders, I panted as we squeezed together in the back seat. Brooks and Mavis were squished in the back with us, a security guard in the front passenger seat.

"That was nuts," Mavis shouted over the screaming and banging on the windows. "We can't take you guys anywhere!"

I shifted on Walker's lap, extracting my feet from under Mavis. "Maybe you should consider online shopping," I told Brooks.

He just chuckled and banged against the window, waving and smiling as the car pulled slowly away.

Brooks started texting again and Mavis being nosey watched his every move over his shoulder. I shifted again, trying to find somewhere for my feet. Walker put his arm under my knees lifting them so my heels rested on one of his thighs and my bottom on the other.

I looked up at him as his arm dropped over my knees, his fingers cupping my calf and his other hand pulled me by my waist so I was resting my side against his chest. He cupped my hip then, his head dipping down to my shoulder.

I heard him inhale and his chest lifted me up a few inches before falling back down.

"You smell good," he whispered in my ear.

I licked my lips and folded my arms around my stomach. "Uh, thanks?"

He hummed, inhaling again behind my ear and tiny little sparks danced down my neck and butterflies took flight in my stomach.

Something long and thick twitched at my hip and I stiffened, my eyes shooting to his in question even as a ragged breath drifted from me.

His eyes glinted devilishly and he snuck a thumb under my cropped sweater, playing with the waistband of my shorts around my upper waist.

Pulling at the waistband lightly, he slipped that thumb underneath, stretching the fabric and dipping so low he found my hip bone.

I trapped his hand there with my arm, my breath catching.

He cocked one dark eyebrow, his eyes dancing, and circled his thumb to the front, finding the band to my panties.

"Walker," I warned quietly. I couldn't help it. The rough, calloused skin of his thumb against the sensitive bare skin above my panties, I was seconds away from combusting.

His entire body tightened, that thick rod under me jumping. I bit my lip as his thumbnail gently dug into my skin, falling into his hungry stare.

"You're making me horny," Mavis mulishly declared, verbally dousing me in ice.

Brooks broke away from his phone and followed her narrow-eyed stare to Walker's hand under my sweater. "Man." His voice was exasperated as was the warning stare he shot Walker.

Walker's hand moved—not away—but flattening against my lower belly under my shorts. I shivered at both the warmth and the glare he gave Brooks. Brooks just sighed and looked back down to his phone.

The rest of the ride was tense. Mavis hummed under her breath but I was a living, breathing ball of static electricity. Every bump in the road or sharp turn tightened Walker's hand at my belly and it wasn't long before his fingers were playing with the front of my panties. For his part he was just as tense, his body stiff as a board—*everywhere*.

Moisture pulled in my mouth and it took every bit of concentration not to squirm against him.

When we pulled into the gates of the arena, Brooks got out for Mavis but then sat back into the car, his eyes latching onto Walker's with a warning in them. I didn't dare move as they had their silent standoff. Then I exhaled roughly as Walker pushed open the door and helped me off his lap.

My legs were wobbly underneath me and I gazed up at him, blinking away a dizziness that was solely his and his masculine potency's fault.

I counted each one of his dark lashes as his swirling grey eyes swam with a thousand words he held back from me.

One hand under my chin, he tilted my head, curled his muscular body over mine, his eyes flitting between my own. Waiting for his lips, I sagged in relief—not at all in disappointment— as they only touched my cheek.

Then he walked away and I was left with only my stumbling wits.

Brooks sighed heavily as he stopped at my side. "Careful with Walker, Shiloh. He can be intense."

No kidding. "I'm trying."

"Try harder," he said, walking me to my bus. "Walker's got a lot of shit in his head and I don't want to see you messed up with it."

"He's dangerous?"

He stopped suddenly. "No. Walker isn't dangerous. He would never lay a hand on you or anything like," he paused. "He's got some shit that fucks with his head and you deserve better than someone that can only give you half of themselves."

With that warning filed away to the forefront of my mind, I hugged Brooks and hopped onto the bus. Shaking my limbs and anxious nerves, I tried desperately not to obsess over every single question Brooks' words demanded I find answers to.

I was not successful.

10

I obsess. It's a flaw of mine I will admit to anyone who accuses me. Funny thing about obsession though, no matter how many times someone tells you to cut it out, take a breather, let it go...it is *never* that easy. That's why it's called an *obsession*.

Walker Lawson was fast becoming the worst obsession I'd ever had.

I obsessed over his touches. His looks. Every twitch of his lips and twinkle in his eyes. I obsessed when he was in front of me. When he was far away from me. I obsessed even about the obsession I had of him.

I was a disaster.

My therapist would tell me to walk through what drew me to my thoughts.

Identify the obsessive thought.

In this case, person. Easily done. Rock star. Sexiest man to ever look my way. Walker Lawson.

Next, *How is this obsession affecting you – both positively and negatively?*

Negative: Well, I can't stop thinking about him.

My mind is my own and I hate lacking control in that area.

A positive: Thinking about Walker was enjoyable. The thoughts he provoked were very enjoyable.

Negative: I was a horny ball of nerves. No one could go around lusting all day long. How was I supposed to get anything done?

Third, *allow yourself to obsess. Even if for an hour a day, give your mind that time and permission to go for it.*

Again, easy peasy. I was chomping at the bit to allow my sexy thoughts of him to go haywire as well as my nervous thoughts.

Walker Lawson defied every attraction I thought I had for the opposite sex. He was unlike any man I'd ever dated in the past. Quiet and pensive. Thoughtful. Impossibly sexy. I had a specific thing for his arms. He had fantastic arms.

When he looked my way every last thought evaporated from my mind. He only left room for thoughts of the two of us together. Naked, alone, his skin brushing against mine...

But with the sexy thoughts came the concerns.

What exactly was Brooks subtly telling me? What fucked up shit haunted Walker so much that Brooks was genuinely worried about me?

What was with that argument with Jameson? Why were he and my uncle getting phone calls from the mouth breather? Who *was* the mouth breather?

I came up with no answers.

Then, after you've given yourself that time to fly free, snap the obsessive thoughts away.

In my case I had a rubber band around my wrist. When I couldn't seem to stop myself from obsessing, I would quite literally snap myself out of it... or at least try to. This also helped when my mind would wander or I had trouble focusing because I was too busy daydreaming.

Then, if the pain of a piece of rubber doesn't do the trick, ask yourself if you can change it. Can you stop thinking about Walker?

Hah, not likely.

So finally, Forgive yourself.

The man took no prisoners when he came at you with his sexy eyes and sexier smirks and hot as hell subtle touches. He was seducing me one touch at a time. How the hell could I resist all that? I couldn't, so I forgave myself.

Going through all of this of course did nothing to slow my mind down when it came to the world famous drummer.

Not to mention if my therapist knew I was obsessing over a man she'd likely throw a party. She'd been trying to get me to open up more for the last two years and meet new people. Relationships were good for the soul. Secretly, I suspected her and my mother were in cahoots to get me knocked up so she could have a grandbaby.

I couldn't talk to anyone about Walker. No one around me could know unless I wanted to be fired. There wasn't a written rule that I couldn't fool around with a band member, but my uncle's warning to them kept ringing in my ears and I just *felt* that it would be a very bad idea to test that.

Plus, I wasn't the fooling around type. I needed a connection with someone to go there. I needed to feel safe, at the very least, and though I felt physically safe around Walker—despite his past—my emotions were walking on a tight rope fifty stories up. My balance was growing shakier by the day.

Leaving my bus in the morning was a test of my nerves like never before.

Would I see him?

Would he be waiting for me?

What would I say?

What would *he* say?

Would any words be exchanged at all or just tense lusty looks that soaked my panties in seconds?

Would he kiss me again? Did I want him to?

I could go on and on but you get the picture.

Mess was long gone and my mental state was now a *disaster* of massive proportions.

A tsunami of questions terrorized my anxieties. Emotional tornadoes and hurricanes were obliterating any logic in its path.

How was I going to function like this?

Of course, no answer came. I could ask Mavis to distract me but she'd likely just toss me in Walker's destructive path and call it a day.

I was on my own.

I walked through my day on autopilot, my normal habitual worries taking a back seat to all things Walker Lawson.

Direct a crew of twenty roadies to unpack the stage? No problem.

Handle transfers for over thousands of dollars' worth of merch? Easy.

Maintain calm when the suits came a knockin' because we were hours off schedule? I *had* this.

Things that normally would have had me stumbling in tension and worries—socially awkward queen over here—were nothing in the wake of Walker's lusty looks from afar and sexual promises lurking in his eyes.

By the end of the day, when we were getting ready to load up and hit the road, I had to change my panties before going over the checklist with Julie. I could not stand it another minute. The lust, the *want* for him.

Walker was unknowingly cruel in his pursuit for the sole reason he was a tease. A massive, sexy, confusing *tease*. He hadn't spoken a word to me or laid a single finger on me all day, but I felt his hunger for me like it was a physical thing.

If he did corner me, there was a strong possibility that all my concerns would jump clear out the window and I would throw myself at him.

I stood beside my uncle as he reviewed our progress for the day and I *knew* he suspected something. How could he not when Walker stood not three feet from me, his back against the wall while his brother smoked? Every ounce of his attention was locked on me. I could feel his eyes caressing my body as if his fingers were dancing up and down to a slow, sultry beat.

Dread coursing through me, I watched my uncle narrow his eyes on Walker. Breath clogged in my chest, I gaped at Walker as he met my uncle's eyes with a challenge. My uncle sighed heavily and looked to me.

"What?" Playing dumb was all I had here.

"You and me," he said. "We're going to have a chat."

I swallowed tightly. This was it. I was going to be fired and I hadn't even been here three weeks.

Mortified, I glanced at Walker. He frowned as he took in the anxiety soaking me from head to toe. His jaw ticked and he took a step toward me but panic overwhelmed me, and I hastily followed my uncle onto the bus.

We sat on the couch side by side, staring at the window across from us. The crew carried on outside, waiting for the word to get going. Here I was holding everyone up. I could not have felt more ashamed in that moment.

"Shy," he paused, cursing beneath his breath.

"I'm sorry," I squeaked.

He shook his head. "I promised your parents I would look after you and I haven't been doing a very good job of it."

He was a busy man. My parents had to know he wouldn't have his eye on me all the time. He made sure I made it on the bus each night after that first one. He checked in with me throughout the day, but he expected me to use my brain and sadly, Walker had turned it to mush.

And besides, it bit at me that every member of my family thought I needed my hand held. I was *grown*. I was twenty-two goddamned years old. I could look after myself.

"It hasn't gone anywhere—"

He held up his hand, stopping me.

I didn't sleep with him! I wanted to scream it.

"You're an adult," he said firmly. "You don't have to explain anything of that nature to me."

"But I work for you," I said, confused.

He huffed a laugh. "I don't interfere with my employees' personal relationships. That said, you're my niece and I love you and so I am worried."

I nodded accepting that no matter my age, he would have an opinion on how I conducted my personal life.

He pinched the bridge of his nose. "If he were anyone else, I would stay out of it. Hell, if it were anyone else, I wouldn't worry. It could be fucking Jameson and I wouldn't worry because I know you're a smart girl and you won't fall for any shit."

I bit my lip, surprised as he cursed. My uncle normally held back around me. Habit from knowing me as a baby.

"You warned them all away from me," I reminded him.

He shrugged. "That was for your sake. You're a beautiful young woman and I didn't invite you here to put you in the path of careless musicians. I brought you here to see the world. To get out of that small town. It can be stifling."

"And I am so grateful for it," I gushed.

He pulled me into his side. "I love you, Shy. I love having you here. But Walker isn't the man for you. For one, he is several years older than you. But more importantly, he has some things he needs to work through and I won't let him use you as a distraction."

And there it was. From the mouth of someone I trusted. I was a distraction for Walker. Nothing more.

"I can see you're going to take that all wrong and I'm tempted to let you if it will keep you away from him."

I just looked down at the floor. My scuffed sneakers next to his shiny loafers.

He sighed again. "Walker is a good man. Deep down he has the makings of an excellent man, but he gets fixated and—" He stood up, pacing in front of me. "Look. Just be careful. That's all I ask. I know I can't talk him away from you. I could threaten him and believe me I am going to do my best. But I know him and, if he has his sights on you, nothing I do or say will make him back down."

I flushed bright red, a mixture of dread and excitement.

"But you have the power here. If you tell him to back off, he might push a little but ultimately if you mean it, he will respect you. I don't doubt that. It wouldn't be fair to either of you if I exposed all the reasons this is a bad idea." He stopped and ducked down to catch my eyes. "And trust me, Shy, this is a bad idea. He isn't a good bet. He's been through a lot. Too much."

So many questions. So. Many.

He resumed pacing. "You've been through your own fair share and I just want you to consider it." He huffed a laugh. "I know I likely sound like a paranoid lunatic right now. Dating is healthy. Go on a thousand dates. Go on none. It's none of my business. I just want to warn you. It wouldn't be dating with Walker. It would mean much more to him than that. He has never once pursued a woman on the road. Not seriously."

Shock. I was struck by shock. Gaping at my uncle, my mind emptied completely.

"I should've seen this sooner. I haven't been paying attention but I saw him out there. He's completely enamored with you." He chuckled to himself. "How could he not be? Look at you!"

I looked down at my sneakers, purple leggings, and then my white tank top with a happy kitty on the front. My fingers touched my bare face. Not a drop of makeup. My hair could use a cut—it was in a tangle around my bare shoulders.

"Your father is going to kill me." My uncle shook his head for the millionth time. "Is anything I'm saying making sense?"

I blinked at him, at a total loss for words. Not a bit of it made sense. Walker was using me as a distraction but then he directly contradicted himself by saying Walker pursuing me was serious. I was so confused.

"If he hurts you, I'm going to kill him," he declared. And with that parting statement he stomped off the bus in a huff.

Frozen in shock, I startled as he hurried back up the steps. "Julie said she's seen you taking photos of the crew and scenery. I want to review them with you tonight and we can see about you taking a few for the band's social media."

Then, he was gone.

11

I left the bus in a daze.

There was *so much* to unpack there. What was Walker dealing with? What was so worrying that not only Brooks had warned me but now my uncle as well? Did it have anything to with his past? The mouth breather? I was an anxious mess hounded with the need for answers.

And then...no women on tour? Not even one? I found that so unlikely it was ludicrous. He had to mean emotionally. There was no way a man that famous and tempting was wearing a self-imposed chastity belt. He had a girl rub him down after every set. The same girl every set. She had a knowing smile on her face every time. She'd definitely done the dirty with him. No question.

Then, there were the women. The women that were around every single night. Throwing their panties at him during the set to then reclaim them after the show. Since that first night, I never hung around to find out who he spent his nights with, but Jameson and Lake were always asking me to get rid of their female friends.

Just because Walker was more discreet, didn't mean they weren't in his bed the next morning too. I had no reason to believe he was celibate.

But I would be lying if said the very possibility that he hadn't been with anyone else since meeting me didn't *thrill* me. Because it did. A lot.

But I didn't truly believe it.

I didn't even expect him to be. We weren't in a relationship. There was no commitment to be made after a few kisses and lusty touches.

There had to be a conversation for that and Walker didn't do verbal communication well.

I'd thought for sure my uncle was going to send me home, but he ended up telling me it was none of his business.

Thinking this entire time Walker was off limits for the sake of my job and now finding out that my employment was secure no matter who my sexual partners were kind of threw me off track. Like tossed me right off a high-speed train.

But just because my job safety wasn't a fear anymore didn't mean I wasn't afraid for other reasons. I would still disappoint my parents if they knew I was being careless in that area. I still worried about my habit to overthink and put too much emotion into surface relationships.

But now that this giant obstacle had been removed. I sort of wished that conversation with uncle had never happened.

I was so lost in panic and lusty want for Walker that I was defenseless when Mavis cornered me. "The next tour stop is only two hours away," she said excitedly, pulling on my arm. "Van wants to go to a club tonight."

Van was the boyfriend. The asshole that couldn't carry a tune to save his life.

"You're coming with us," she told me stubbornly.

I didn't put up much of a fight and before I knew it, I'd agreed to go out and into a situation I would've normally avoided.

♪

AT THE BEGINNING OF THE TWO-HOUR RIDE TO OUR NEXT stop, Julie was on board to go over the itinerary for the band. We were going to be there for four days as the band was doing two shows back-to-back, a radio show, and then a talk show performance the night before we took off again.

My uncle delved into his work, his nervous eyes watching me in concern. I had officially made him uncomfortable and I kind of hated myself for that. Things had been fun and light and now they were stilted and awkward.

However, it wasn't going to stop me from taking photos he wanted for the band. He seemed to love what I'd been doing in my free time and promised to lighten up on my assistant duties to make time for me to shoot the band during their shows and during their rehearsals.

I was both thrilled and horrified. I could tell he felt the same, impressed by my photos too much to deny Julie's insistence to get me behind my camera.

But I wasn't sure he realized he had just thrown me directly into Walker's path.

♪♫

MAVIS SCROUNGED THROUGH MY MEAGER WARDROBE AND decided nothing I had was good enough. After we parked the buses, she was off to her boyfriend's and back with several outfits and a giant bag of makeup.

It was fun to play dress up with her, but then everything with Mavis was fun. We settled on black booty shorts, ripped stockings with a gold sparkly cropped tank and leather boots. It was a racier outfit than I would normally wear, but I felt better when Mavis slipped into a dress that was so short, I could see her panties when she bent over.

My hair was braided up and circling the back of my head. I popped in a pair of my own gold stud earrings while she directed me to 'do something with my face.' I wasn't a makeup girl but I did swipe on some mascara and gloss.

After the buses were parked, my uncle waved us off with a promise to call if we needed a ride. I was somehow dragged into a van with her boyfriend and his band mates, the Blue Dudes—dumbest band name ever. Seriously, but I was not surprised.

Van and Mavis made out in the back seat while I sat beside Billy—a guy so high he barely noticed me. Maybe that was a good thing.

For the hundredth time, I wondered how these guys got a slot on the tour.

The club we pulled up to was large—grander than anyplace I'd been in the past. Muted yellow lights gave the outside a sultry atmosphere. They had a valet that gave Van more than a little entitlement, even as his rusty van was driven away, the engine backfiring the entire time.

The Blue Dudes were well enough known—due to their connection to Chains and Dames—to get us into the club without having to wait in line. Loud music pulsed through the club and the colorful strobe lights throbbed in time with the music. We were shoved through the crowd, looking for an empty table.

"We'll get in the VIP section when Jameson gets here," Van shouted to Mavis and me.

My friend barely heard him, already rocking to the music, but I immediately scanned the club for Jameson and the rest of the band. If he was coming, that meant the others were too.

That meant likely Walker was coming.

How I got myself into these situations was a mystery. The tour life had really changed things for me. Some of them good, some of them bad. Namely my recklessness.

I wasn't sure if I would have refused to come tonight if I'd known there was a chance of Walker showing or if I would have jumped at the opportunity.

Alcohol was passed out quickly. I didn't partake and where Mavis didn't mind, her friends weren't so understanding. They pushed and pressured until I was fiddling with my phone for a distraction, seconds away from calling for an Uber.

"Let's Boogie!" Mavis shouted in my ear. Her boyfriend and his bandmates hooted and hollered but she just rolled her eyes, tugging me out into the packed floor of dancing bodies. "Loosen up!"

I sighed and tried to do just that. At home, Mom and I danced in the kitchen while we cooked or twirled around the house as we cleaned. I loved to dance but I never really put myself in a position to do it publicly. Typically, when you were the friend that was always the designated driver, you didn't have the opportunity to find that freedom to let loose through imbibing. I could never find that fearlessness so many girls my age seemed to have in spades.

Mavis grabbed my hips and smiled, rocking me dramatically. I huffed a laugh, giving in. I was wound so tight I would do just about anything to let off some steam. I threw my hands up in the air, emboldened by Mavis's courage as she got lost in the music.

The warm bodies around me heated up my own and soon a fine layer of sweat coated me. I was bumped and jostled but no one was paying me any attention. I closed my eyes, feeling the stress melt off me with every beat and thump of the bass.

I felt him before I saw him.

It started as a tingle in the back of my neck, slowly moving down my spine.

Startled by the sensation, my eyes flew open and collided with a raging storm.

Walker stood above me, watching me from the mezzanine. He had both forearms resting on the railing with a bottle of beer dangling from his fingertips.

An inferno started in my core and I kept moving, unable to tear my eyes from his as I rocked and rolled my hips to the beat.

At first it was just surprise to find him there watching me that kept me on the dance floor, but soon it was this newfound courage I seemed to be acquiring on tour that kept me there.

The corner of his mouth lifted as he watched me and I fed off his attention, unable to stop the show I was putting on for him.

Hands in my hair, my breath caught as he tipped his beer back, draining it without taking his eyes off mine.

With this strange new desire to shove aside my fears and doubts, I ran my hands down my neck, on either side of my chest and to the bare skin of my stomach. He swung his empty bottle to the

side. Jameson caught it, looking for what held his brother's attention. When he spotted me, he threw his head back with a laugh I
couldn't hear and he gave Walker a shove.

The music pulsed up and down as Walker made his way around
the mezzanine to the stairs. I spun in a slow circle to follow his
progress, vaguely catching Mavis call my name with a wicked
edge.

Down the stairs he came and I felt every one of his steps the
closer he was to me. A throb in the deepest parts of me. He
moved through the crowd that were so caught up in the music,
they had no idea that a rock god walked among them.

Two feet from me, his eyes smiled.

A foot and his lips followed.

In seconds he was in front of me. He placed his hand on the
small of my back, hauling me against his large body.

He leaned down, his breath dancing across my ear. "That all
for me?"

"Maybe," I shouted over the music. It wasn't. And then it so was.

Eyes glinting, he ducked down again, inhaling the sweat from
my neck. I shivered in his hold, pressing closer to him.

I hadn't had a drop of alcohol but I was wholly intoxicated
on him.

"Dance for me?" he whispered in my ear. I swallowed hard.
Vitalized now on his want for me, I did dance. He stood still,

watching my every move, his hands wandering over every inch of me. I turned, unable to take another moment of his possessive stare. He pulled my hips back into his and I rested against him, rocking against his solid build. His fingers drifted over my bare stomach, leaving tingles in their wake.

On a gasp my head dropped back against his shoulder, tilting to the side as his lips trailed down the side of my neck.

"You want me," he teased.

I nodded, unable to deny it anymore. It was *so* obvious.

"What did V say to you, Shy girl?" he asked into my ear, his hands now moving down my hips more forcefully.

I turned my head to his ear and he ducked around me deeper, pressing it against my lips. "He said you were a bad bet."

He pulled back and frowned.

I was standing still now. His fingers started to tap a rhythm that matched the beat low on my hips and I pressed into them.

When neither of us said anything more, he turned me around so my chest was pressed to his and bent to my shoulder, nosing my top's strap aside to nip at my shoulder. "And what do you think?"

I swallowed tightly, cupping the back of his warm neck in my hand. "I'm a bad bet, too."

Nobody knew that more than me. The doctors. The pills. The disease that hounded me day in and out. Walker had no idea just how bad of a bet I was.

He hummed into my neck and I dropped my forehead to his shoulder, tired of avoiding this thing that was brewing between us.

"I think you want me because I keep pushing you away," I told him loud enough to be heard over the music.

He chuckled a little in disbelief and tugged up my chin. "I want you because I *want* you."

I felt those words deep in my core and he knew it, sliding his thigh between my legs and pressing me firmly onto it. He was hard against my stomach and I gasped against his mouth.

"You're mine," he rumbled against my lips.

"You don't even know me."

He made a rough sound and licked into my mouth, shutting me up. We stood still on the dance floor, his thigh putting pressure against my core as it throbbed. My tongue battled his but he was stronger and more determined and I gave up, letting him have control as he wrecked my mouth for any other man.

Bodies bumped into us from all sides and his arms curled around me tight, blocking out everything around us with the width of his back.

Mavis had approached us and shouted over the music, "You've been spotted."

Walker tore his mouth away with a curse. We both looked around. People were noticing—stopping to point and gawk at Walker. Phones came out and flashes brighter than the club lights went off. Walker lifted me quickly, cradling me as he marched to the stairs.

"Mavis!"

"Go!" she shouted, waving me away. "I'm fine! Have fun!"

"Shiloh's not so shy," Jameson called from above. It wasn't a gentle play with my name. He said it with a sneer. I didn't know what Jameson had against me, or if he had anything at all and I was just in the way of his anger toward Walker that seemed to follow the pair of them.

"Fuck off," Walker barked as we crested the stairs and strode to a curved vinyl couch.

Tucked in his lap I could've been swallowed by his attention if I allowed it but I made myself glance around. As per usual, Jameson and Lake were both entertaining several women each while Brooks sat on his own, looking as bored as humanly possible. He spotted me and sent a half smile but his eyes were wary as he watched Walker rest his chin on my shoulder.

For all the worry he and my uncle were expressing, neither of them seemed compelled enough to step against Walker. I didn't know how to feel about that. It didn't necessarily seem that their concern was about Walker *the man*, but about something I couldn't see.

The song switched to something slower and Jameson carefully extracted his limbs from the bevy of beautiful women, sagging into the bench beside us. "Shy."

I smiled tightly, warily watching as several women clambered onto the couch beside him...on top of him. I got an elbow to the side and a woman latched onto Walker's arm, whispering something in his ear.

"Off," he ordered coldly without lifting his chin from my shoulder. She pouted and moved away, shooting me a catty glare.

"Come here, sweet thing," Jameson told her, guiding her to his knee. "Walker's chained up for the time being."

I looked over my shoulder, meeting Walker's eyes. "For the time being?"

He just chuckled, nipping at my upper arm with his teeth. "You want a claim on me?" His eyes sparkled with mischief.

I rolled my eyes and moved forward but his arm banded around my waist, keeping me firmly in place.

"Calm down," he crooned with a pleased smile.

"Don't tease me," I begged him. "I'm not like them. I don't want to share you."

"You won't have to," he whispered in my ear.

As his hands began to pet me from thighs to belly, he nodded to several men at the bar. "Look at them wanting you."

Surprised, I noticed he was right. More than one man was watching his hands move on me with desire and want.

"They can't have you," he purred. "You're mine."

I was. It happened too fast for me to put up a decent fight. I was defenseless against him from that first day.

And now I was trapped.

I hoped I didn't regret giving up the fight.

1 2

Wanting to leave the club with Walker and the band, I scanned the dance floor below for Mavis. She was dancing with her boyfriend, unaware that his eyes wandered everywhere but to her. I wanted to drag her away from him but it wasn't my place. So I sent her a quick text to make sure she was okay and to let her know I was leaving.

I climbed into the car, slipping in beside Walker.

Jameson and Lake took the other car with a several women. Brooks rode with us. He was chatting quietly on his phone since we left the club.

"Stay with me tonight," Walker insisted. It was barely a whisper. He took my hand in his and startlingly sweet, kissed every one of my knuckles.

"Uncle V will know." I shook my head. Just because he said he would stay out of my business, didn't mean I was going to knowingly add to his concern.

Walker just smiled in that infuriating way. Like he found me highly amusing.

When we returned to the buses, he took my hand and led me to my bus, rapping his knuckles against the door.

My uncle opened the door, his headphones in his ears and his thinking face on. Whatever work he was deep in cleared from his mind the second he saw me standing beside Walker.

"Shy will be staying with me," Walker told him low and steely.

My uncle sighed, rubbing his hair. "Walk."

Walker shook his head. "Make up your mind, V. You either step up now or back off."

"Walker." I was horrified. I didn't want this confrontation. I didn't want to draw a line with my uncle and make things more awkward than they were already.

"It's not my decision," my uncle said. "It's Shy's."

Stuck between a rock and a hard place, I felt the panic creeping up on me. I took a step toward my uncle, my loyalty to him forcing me to extract my hand from the man beside me.

He didn't let me go.

"Anyway, I'm leaving in the morning for California," my uncle paused. "Are you going to be okay on your own?"

I knew this was coming. I knew he had other clients, but I hadn't realized that time had come already. "For how long?"

"A few weeks."

"Julie's staying?"

"Yeah, she'll get you started on the band's social media sites."

The three of us exchanged awkward glances. Well, it was awkward for me. Walked looked determined, my uncle wary.

"Nothing I say will change your mind," my uncle finally told him. "Shy is special, but I think you know that."

I blinked away a burning behind my eyes.

Uncle V relaxed against the door with a sudden roguish grin. "Anyway, it won't be me you have to sway. You haven't met her father yet."

I huffed a surprised laugh. My father was the sweetest man on the planet—*to me*. He was right, Walker would have a hell of a time with my dad if this went anywhere. But I still wasn't entirely convinced it would last more than a night so that confrontation might never happen.

Without another word, Walker tugged me away from my uncle. I looked over my shoulder and met my uncle's eyes. He smiled softly, winking at me and suddenly I wanted nothing more than to go with Walker. For all his freaking out earlier, my uncle wasn't really trying to stop me. Either for all his warnings, he really did trust Walker, or he trusted me to make my own decisions.

Either way, it only shored in my mind that it had nothing to do with Walker as a person.

On the band's bus, the party kept going. Low tunes filtered through the space.

On the couch were Lake and two women, their mouths and hands exploring each other. I averted my eyes as clothes came off. Walker watched me with that twinkle in his eyes, guiding me farther back on the bus.

Low moans came from one of the bunks and my face heated. Hiding it in Walker's chest, he chuckled as he slid open one black curtain on an upper bunk.

"Up," he whispered and patted my bottom.

I braced my hands on the bunk as he gave me a boost. Once there, he playfully tickled behind my knees and pulled off my boots.

I scooted farther on the bunk, laying on my side with my back to the wall. One heave and he was up, his heated eyes crawling over me.

I wasn't sure what I expected. Maybe for him to pull me under him and strip off my clothes but that's not what he did. He laid on his back with a groan and hauled me against him, my head on his chest and then guided my thigh over his.

He had a small television screen like I had in my own bunk and several notebooks tucked in the pockets on the wall. Clicking off the overhead light he began tapping a rhythm out down my spine. I relaxed against him and tried not to squirm as Jameson made the woman moan his name in the bunk across from us.

Walker moved my hair aside with his warm fingers, then gently placed earplugs into my ears, muffling everything.

I smiled gratefully and he curled his chest up, pecking me playfully on the lips.

Walker was sex on a stick. The most intoxicating man I'd ever encountered, but that night he didn't act on any of the sexual desires brewing between us. Instead he soothed me, drawing me into a deep sleep at his side.

Somehow this was so much more intimate than baring my body to him. So much more dangerous. But I just didn't have the resilience to stop myself from falling into him. For him. It felt too right. Inevitable in a way. I should've seen it coming the first time he caught my eye.

Walker Lawson had me before he even knew my name and he knew it. Reveled in it.

♪

HE WAS A RESTLESS SLEEPER. HE SHIFTED EVERY HOUR, AND I shifted with him like we were choreographing our own dance. He would put me on my side and curl around me from behind. Then I would be on my belly and he would settle into me, keeping me trapped under him.

I woke up lying on him like a blanket. My head was on his chest, tucked under his chin, my legs spread on either side of his torso, and my hands were imprisoned under his arms. I was so warm I didn't want to move.

I heard snoring, feminine and masculine, and realized my earplugs must have fallen out sometime in the night.

Walker was awake, his warm hands smoothed up my spine, under my shirt and down my sides. I shivered, squirming closer and he chuckled a raspy sound, wrapping his arms around me.

"I don't want to get up," I groaned, rubbing my face against his shirt to clear my fuzzy eyes.

He rolled me onto my side and kissed the corner of my mouth. "Go back to sleep."

He didn't have to tell me twice. I closed my eyes as he left, covering me with a soft blanket.

I dozed on and off, finally waking up when the bus rocked with a loud noise.

"Wakey, wakey, Shiloh!" Brooks called. "Jules is looking for you."

I jumped up, smacking my head on the padded ceiling.

I grunted and rolled off the bunk.

Brooks stood at the end of the hall, a shit-eating grin on his face. "Walk slept the entire night."

"And that's weird?"

He huffed a dry laugh. "You have no idea."

I passed him, my mind reeling with that little nugget of information, and got off the bus.

"I've never seen him so bright-eyed and bushy tailed." He trailed after me.

I didn't feel as bright and could've easily gone back to sleep.

"Where is he?" I asked as I stepped onto my bus.

He came in after me and sat on the couch.

"I left him at the gym. Man's been at it for hours," he said as I dug through my suitcase.

Walker spent a lot of time in the gym. When most of the guys were sleeping or lazing around, he was lifting weights or jogging around the arena.

The imagined visual caused little sparks of excitement to explode in unmentionable places.

The sight of him bare chested and perspiring in loose sweats was lust inducing and something I normally would have avoided watching at all costs for my own sanity. Mavis had no such reservations and often gave me a descriptive review of his performance.

But now, after last night, I suddenly wanted to go and find him and have him see me watching him like the women on the crew often did.

But I had a job I was late for.

I jumped into the shower and rinsed off, swallowing my pills and dressing in jeans and a sweater. There was a chill in the air this morning and the farther north we traveled I figured I would need to start dressing more warmly. I was due to go back home in two weeks, and I had plans to pack nearly my entire winter wardrobe.

I grabbed a coffee with Brooks, listening to his final plans for Reese's birthday.

"She has no idea still?"

He grinned. "Not a clue. Thinks I have a show that night."

I laughed at his deviousness. "She's going to love everything."

He sighed. "I miss the hell out of that girl."

"Is that who you're always on the phone with?" I asked, prying just a little.

"Her and my mama," he said proudly.

The mention reminded me I needed to call my own mama. I called her almost every night and having missed her call last night, I knew it was only a matter of time before she blew up my phone.

We parted, and on the way to the stage I spotted Mavis by the exit in a corner. Headphones in her ears, she didn't hear me approach her. She was scribbling furiously in a notebook she always had with her, her feet tapping a beat only she could hear.

My eyes scanned over the page. They looked like lyrics—good ones too.

The second she noticed me hovering over her, she slammed the book closed... blushing. Mavis never blushed. The girl wasn't shy or modest. Ever. She looked cagey as hell right now though.

"Heyyy. Have fun last night?" Her question lacked her normal mischief.

"I didn't know you were a writer," I said, impressed but holding back since she looked so uncomfortable.

She shrugged. "It's nothing."

An understatement. I only saw a few lines but they were haunting and seductive.

We chatted a few minutes and it was uncomfortable and stilted and I was sorry for interrupting her. I felt as if I stepped over a line somewhere and was unsure how to fix it.

Dwelling on it, I took the time to call my mom.

Our conversation was short. I gave her snippets of my activities but left everything about Walker out of it.

I wasn't sure why. Maybe because it was so new.

Maybe because I wasn't sure if it would last.

But either way, it felt like I had this secret. This secret I wanted to keep tucked close just in case voicing it out loud jinxed it.

I didn't want to jeopardize it. I wanted to keep it forever.

13

Walker sat on the couch. He cracked his neck to the side and smiled at me. Wide and wicked, hunger and lust building in his eyes.

I shuddered in place, my feet glued to the floor.

Mesmerized by him, my feet carried me in his direction. I came to a halt upon spotting a woman zeroing in on him—the one there for his rub down. I felt my brows drop down heavily and my hands fisted at my side.

When I moved my scowl to him as she came up behind him, he frowned searching my eyes, his head tilting in question. Her hands slowly moved across his bare glistening shoulders and I felt something uncomfortable coil in my gut like a snake.

He glanced over his shoulder, becoming aware of her presence. Humor lighting in his eyes, he smiled at me. So damn pleased. "Come here," he mouthed.

I didn't find a thing funny and shook my head, anger igniting a blush on my face.

He frowned back, patting his thigh sharply.

"Go stake your claim," Jameson whispered in my ear, his tone a dare.

I could've run. I could've turned my back on Walker and walked right out the door, but that's not what I did. That was the old Shy.

The girl I was so desperate to leave behind.

I marched over to him and stood so close to him I could feel his heavy breaths against my skin. I scowled at him and her hand moving over his shoulder pointedly.

Tenderness moved over his face. He shrugged the woman off, pulling me down onto his lap with force. "You gonna rub me down?"

"Are you sore?" I asked, my feelings a little bruised.

He nodded, shrugging his shoulders. I looked at the woman seething behind him, courage finding me. That and determination to make my own intentions clear even if Walker's were still a little fuzzy. "I've got it from now on," I told her.

Hate beamed from her eyes and she called Walker's name with a whine.

"You heard her," he said to her with his eyes locked on mine. "Shy's got it."

She stomped off in a huff, and Walker maneuvered me so I was straddling his lap. He tugged my hands up to his shoulders and grabbed the jar of cream.

"Who is she?" I asked, dipping my hands into the jar. The white cream tingled my fingers as I rubbed it across his shoulders, my chest pressing against his face as I reached to his back.

"No one," he mumbled, nosing his face into my chest. My breasts tightened and nipples tingled from the friction.

"She didn't seem to think she was no one," I pushed for an answer. Did she warm his bed each night before I was there? Or was she not the only one? Just how many women was I going to have to compete with?

"You like the show?" he asked, his fingers dipping into my shirt at my chest and peeking down.

"It was great. It always is." I sat forward and trapped his nose in my shirt and he chuckled, licking the skin there.

I shivered and squirmed on his lap and he sat back, dislodging my massaging hands. His dropped to my bottom, supporting me. I peeked over my shoulder, making sure we weren't being watched but I should have known better; envious eyes were everywhere. I wondered how many women here coveted the attention of the man who was solely focused on me. It was both an intoxicating and disconcerting feeling.

"Hey," he called my attention with a gentle scolding. "Don't worry about them."

"I can't help it. There are so many people here."

"You want to go?" he asked, searching my eyes.

"Do you?"

"You want me all to yourself?" he teased, biting at my chin with a playful growl.

Oh boy, did I.

"You have to talk to the suits," I reprimanded him with a hitch in my voice. They had an interview tomorrow and without my uncle here, I had to make sure they all were up bright and early.

Walker and I stood up. He grabbed my hand and found Silvia, one of his managers.

I stood at his side as he listened to her talk about who was here to see and talk to him. Lake and Brooks joined us and I dropped my head against his shoulder as they went over the schedule for tomorrow.

The radio station they were going to for the interview was over an hour away. From there, they were going to a television studio to perform on an evening talk show. It would be a really long day and there was so much involved. Wardrobe, set build. Each guy had a long list of things they would need to perform, and Silvia went over the list Julie handed her before the show.

"I think that's it," she said. "Julie has a few fans with VIP Passes she'd like you to meet with, take some photos and sign some merchandise, and then you can go."

Walker kept me at his side as we stood in the next room for as long as he could, but eventually he moved away to mingle.

Several fans had paid for the private meeting while others had won their spot through radio show competitions and online promotions. Many of them were women. A few were young kids —the fans that all four guys gave most of their attention to.

Jameson and Lake were players through and through but regardless of their fame and fortune, they had all the time in the world for their true fans. They had their fun. Partied hard. But regardless of the fame and fortune, they had a wealth of gratitude for the people that looked up to them, and their younger audience was always a priority. It was that attitude that had my uncle handing over his loyalty, shoving aside his other clients to put most of his efforts and attention into making the band a household name.

One young boy, no older than thirteen, gushed as Jameson talked rifts and melodies with him. It was a sight to see, the normally vulgar singer on his best behavior.

From there the party moved back to the bus. Adult themed in every way, but I didn't find myself as uncomfortable this time as I had previously. Walker tugged me onto the couch beside him and leaned back, pulling my thighs over his, then wrapped his arm around my back to keep me close.

He closed his eyes, tapping a rhythm out on my inner thigh.

Brooks sat down on the other side of me with a beer in one hand and his phone in the other. "This is Shy," he told the bright-eyed blonde on the screen.

I waved tiredly at her with a smile and she waved back excitedly. "Brooks has told me so much about you," she gushed. "I can't wait to meet you in person!"

I looked at him in surprise and he winked.

"I've looked you up online. Your photos are beautiful."

"Thank you." I was thrilled for the praise.

We chatted a little, getting to know each other enough that I was genuinely excited to meet her which was likely Brooks' intention when he sat beside me. We weren't a pair if you looked at us side by side, but we had similar interests and she was engaging and seemed really sweet.

Brooks stole her attention back, their conversation blurring into a more intimate one before he jumped up and disappeared into his bunk.

I looked back to Walker. His head was still back against the couch, his fingers still gently tapping on my inner thigh, but his eyes were now open and hooded as he watched my lips.

"Tired?" I asked him. My own eyelids felt heavy.

He nodded but didn't stand so I figured he was happy sitting here.

Unlike him, Lake was with several other men and women in the small kitchen area, playing some drinking game while Jameson—surprise, surprise—was making out with a woman against the wall.

God, he was going to terrify my parents. They wanted a sweet accountant or a veterinarian for me. Something nonthreatening. Walker was the opposite of everything they envisioned for their only daughter.

And now I was thinking about him meeting my parents and I *knew* I was obsessing and overthinking and I couldn't help myself. Any sane man would sprint away from me if they could read the thoughts running rampant through my mind.

None of this may even matter once Walker got to know me. If he knew I wanted to cling to him like a koala, I doubted he would hang around. Then there were my fears that once he knew how hard a relationship with me and my illness could be he wouldn't be able to run fast enough.

I was going to scare him away. I knew it.

He moved against me, his arm wrapping me tightly. I held my breath as he stirred awake.

Stiffening at first, he then sighed and clutched me close, humming in the back of his throat as he nuzzled my hair aside so he could get his lips on my neck.

"Did I wake you with all my moving?" he sleepily rasped.

I shook my head, the rough stubble of his jaw scraping against me and leaving tingles behind.

He rolled me onto my back, coming down on top of me with my legs on either side of his hips.

"I move a lot," he told me gruffly, his lips trailing down my neck to the collar of my shirt.

"You have trouble sleeping."

He nodded as his hands found the hem of my shirt and lifted it, exposing my belly. I shivered, smoothing my hands over his broad shoulders.

"I like this," he told me with a tired smile, his fingers tapping against my belly. I laughed, squirming as it tickled. "Cute."

"My belly?"

He kissed my nose. "You. You're cute."

I frowned.

His eyes twinkled as he nipped at my pouting lip. "And fucking sexy," he murmured, smoothing the sting with a warm lick. "So damn hot I want to eat you up."

I shuddered from head to toe, my fingers curling deeper into the hard muscles of his back. Those thick muscles flexed as he bent low to trail a circle around my belly button with his tongue. My hips jumped and he chuckled, pressing them down with a hand on my hip. "Still."

My breath came in fast pants as he drew shapes on my lower belly with his tongue.

"Shy girl," he purred into my stomach. "You want something from me?"

I wanted so, so many things.

All I could do was nod. My eyes glued to the messy dark locks obscuring his face. His hooded eyes watched me from under his hair as his fingers sunk low between my thighs, trailing the band of my panties in the crease of my thigh.

My legs fell open wider at his silent command and I whimpered as he lifted the fabric of my underwear to the side, his callused fingers roughly teasing me.

My heart thumped erratically and I couldn't stay still, my hips chasing his fingers as they moved away and came back, again and again.

Watching me with those stormy eyes, engrossed as I writhed beneath him, his breath escalated in ragged inhales. Settling above me, he lowered his head to mine, staring into my eyes with stark need. His fingers zeroed in with intent, and I bit my lip to stifle the whine that came clawing out of my throat.

A rough protest came from him and he pushed his tongue into my mouth with force, eating my desperate noises.

He circled his fingers and my toes curled up to dig deep into his calf muscles. Masculine approval rumbled in his chest as I flew apart under him.

The slick sounds of our dueling tongues mixed with my ragged inhales. I clung to him desperately, coming down with a euphoric blend of wonder and need for *more*.

His hips flexed against me and I pulled them to my center tight, urging him on. He ripped his mouth from mine and snatched my hand from his hip, his other hand impatiently ripping open the button of his jeans. Seconds later he moved my hand inside and together we wrapped his hard arousal in our entwined fists. My eyes widened as I felt the length and girth of him, and he flexed once and then twice, his brows lowered over his dark eyes and then he growled down my throat, his thick release coating both of our hands.

For long minutes his tongue played with mine, his pleased rumbles teasing my throat.

"That was so fuckin' hot," Lake sighed from somewhere behind our curtain. I flushed from the roots of my hair to the tips of my toes.

Walker cursed furiously, tugging the blanket over me before slapping the curtain back. Lake was in his bunk on the opposite side, his sleepy eyes on us. Walker just pointed his finger at him, his nostrils flaring in anger.

Lake held up his hands. "Don't blame me, man. Her sexy little sounds woke me up." He smiled at me with bleary eyes. "It was a fuckin' great way to wake up, doll."

I slapped my hands over my face, mortified. That was by far the best sexual experience of my entire life and took place feet away from several bystanders. Something I never thought I would be down for.

"Don't give Shy any shit," Walker ordered him gruffly.

Lake crossed his heart and kissed his thumb. "I swear it."

♪♫

Lake may have promised but Jameson didn't have any such restraints. He heard it as well and so did the woman in his bunk. She gave me a flirty smile when we all piled out into the kitchen and I hid my face in Walker's shoulder.

"Hungry?" he asked me as he poured a glass of water for me.

"I'd say," Jameson chuckled, not so subtly extracting his arm from his friend.

"I need to go take my medication," I whispered to Walker, ignoring his brother.

Walker frowned at me and I realized what I said. My brain still wasn't firing on all cylinders after our morning activities. I flushed—more than I already was— and avoided eye contact.

"Come on." He pulled me from the kitchen and Jameson whistled knowingly.

"Gotta hit the road, bro. No time to hit that again."

"James," Walker barked. "Enough."

Jameson rolled his eyes and walked to the back of the bus, leaving Lake to deal with the singer's overnight entertainment.

14

Walker was silent as he accompanied me to my bus. Not normally an odd state for him but I could tell he had questions. Questions I wasn't at all in a place to answer right now.

The sun was just creeping over the horizon and we had about half an hour to get going or we'd be late. I let him onto the bus, oddly put off that my uncle was no longer here. This bus would still travel with the band for two weeks until he came back, but it would only be me on it. It felt wrong to keep all this space to myself when so many others were crammed together on other buses. Maybe Mavis would want to hang with me. Or even Julie.

But then the man behind me tugged on my shirt to gain my attention and I wasn't sure if I would even be on this bus. Maybe it would roll down the road with only Dale inside the entire time my uncle was in New York.

Or maybe Walker would want to stay on it with me. However, Dale slept here during the day and, though I was embarrassed the band heard me and Walker this morning, it would be infinitely more embarrassing if Dale heard anything coming from my bunk. Plus, it felt disrespectful to fool around on my uncle's bus. I wouldn't do it in his house and this was his house on wheels.

I stared up at Walker. The brief thought entering my mind that my worrying was for nothing and there would be no more fooling around, but he watched me just as hungry for me in this moment as he'd been since I'd known him and I realized it would be impossible to keep my hands off him. I was in too deep.

"I'm just going to..." I waved to the bathroom and his lip quirked, his eyes dancing at my discomfort.

I jumped inside, taking my medicine and turned on the shower. There wasn't time to dry my hair so I tied it up as I washed off. My skin was hypersensitive and knowing only a flimsy door stood between him and my naked body made the entire chore that much more exciting. I wrapped myself in my cotton robe and stepped out, searching for him. He was in the kitchen, an adorable frown on his face as he read the labels on my protein powders.

I ducked into my bunk while he was preoccupied, taking a little more care with my outfit knowing there was a good chance I'd be photographed multiple times with the band. That and I wanted to look more professional since I would be taking photographs of my own for the first time as a new addition to their social media team. But I also kept in my mind that I was employed by the music industry and didn't want to come off as stuffy.

Black jeans with rips that weren't bought that way but made by me and my mother, and a silky green tank with a slouchy knit black cardigan. I paired it with my only heels. Faux-leather wedges that peeped at the toe to reveal my shiny black toenails painted by Mavis. I twisted my hair up into a neat bun at the crown and grabbed my backpack and cooler.

He watched me intently as I unpacked yesterday's containers and repacked with fresh produce and my other go-to snacks. An abundance of frozen water bottles to keep everything cool and that I could drink as they thawed.

"You take that with you everywhere?"

I knew he would ask eventually. "I'm careful about what I eat."

He nodded, slowly, watching everything I put into the cooler like he was cataloging it and filing it away.

"You take your medicine?"

I winced. "Yes."

He bent down, catching my eyes. "You gonna tell me about that?"

I shook my head. I knew my avoiding it was only going to make him think it was more serious than allergy pills or birth control, or anything 'normal' compared to what I had to take.

It was right then Walker and I had our first ever fight.

It went a little something like this:

He pushed for more information, using more words in five minutes than he ever had before... only they were the same words repeated over me. *What medicine? What for?* And like an order, *Tell me.*

It was as if we'd traded places. It was my turn to be frustratingly silent. Doing my best to avoid his probing, I tried leaving the bus.

He blocked my path.

I huffed and puffed.

He chuckled and tried to grab for me.

I dodged him with a glare.

He frowned, folding his arms across his chest.

And then finally, I set him off. "Why do I have to share when you don't?"

The fight lasted maybe a few minutes and ended with his typical silence. Leaving me on the bus to stew in misery and regret for not letting him just have the long list of medications I took daily no matter how embarrassing it would've been. At least it would've been out in the open and I wouldn't have to keep wondering about how he'd react.

Instead, I hadn't had to tell him a thing to send him running. I'd just had to act like a brat.

Fretting in the backseat of the car beside Julie, I watched the car in front of us. The one Walker was inside.

I felt guilty for throwing something in his face that he hadn't even known I was obsessing over. We hadn't gotten to the part of a relationship where you talk about the hard things. Neither of us had even prompted it until that morning and instead of embracing his inquiry, I shut him down so fast I ended up hurting us both.

He knew my uncle warned me away from him, but he didn't know what he told me. That Walker was dealing with *things*. I could've just asked him and maybe he would've told me, but instead I silently turned it over in my mind and ran with it. That wasn't fair to him. He hadn't done that to me, he'd just come out and asked me.

He also walked away and that felt like a scary premonition. That I would see his back again one day, one day maybe soon, and maybe that would be the end of it. If it wasn't already.

I wanted to apologize but I also didn't want to spill all my sad baggage at his feet yet either.

My phone rang in my pocket and I answered it quietly as not to disturb Julie's call.

"Shy," my mother greeted me with a confused tone. "I just received a call from a man."

Julie looked at me in question, silently asking who'd called. I shrugged.

"A uhm, Walker? Do you know this man?"

My jaw *dropped*.

Julie's eyes widened in question again.

I shook my head, completely stunned. "I'm sorry, *what?*"

"He was asking all these questions about your medication. Said he was with the band? Has something happened? Do you need a refill?"

Leave it to my mother to not know who Walker Lawson was when her own brother-in-law worked directly with him, and his face was all over the internet and tabloids.

She kept babbling, worried.

"Mom," I called her sharply. "I'm fine. I have all my medicine. Everything's fine."

Julie hung up her phone and turned to me.

"What was he calling for? Who was he? Why did he want to know what your pills are for?" My mother rapped out.

I sighed, shaking my head, completely bewildered. And outraged. Appalled that he called my mother. How did he even get her number?

I calmed my mom down and hung up, gaping at Julie. "Walker just called my mother."

Her brows rose high. "He what?"

I ran a hand down my face. "He wanted to know why I take my pills. How did he get her number?"

Julie sat back, stunned herself. "I doubt V gave it to him, but you're an employee, all he would have to do is call the label and they'd hand it over."

"That's messed up."

"What's going on between you two?" she scooted closer to me. "V said you two have something going on."

I shrugged. "I don't even know." Flushing, I looked away. "He's hard to turn away."

"No kidding," she said with a laugh. "That man is potent."

"I'm so angry," I bit out. "It's none of his business. He can't just call my mother behind my back."

"I take it you haven't talked much with him. Walker is very private."

I nodded miserably.

She patted my arm, frowning. "I'm worried because Walker doesn't get involved with anyone. If he's pursuing you then it's serious on his part. He wouldn't risk his relationship with V if he wasn't. He's intense. You need to be careful with that one."

"What is there that everyone keeps warning me away from him?" I begged her.

She sighed, looking at the driver and ducked closer to me. "It's not my place to say but woman to woman? He has some personal issues he's dealing with right now. He's not concerned and V thinks he should be. Walker isn't taking it as seriously as he should."

"And this is something that makes you and everyone else think he shouldn't be in a relationship right now?"

"You're amazing, Shy. He's a lucky guy to catch your attention. *He* is the lucky one and he would treat you very well. I believe that, but if things go bad..." she hesitated. "We're just concerned if it could blow back on you."

I thought of when he went to prison when he was younger. "Did he hurt someone?"

She sighed. "It's not my place and I really should have you sign an NDA for what I *have* told you."

That Walker had a violent past was public knowledge. But there was something there. Of everything I'd heard, all the bits and pieces, made me believe it was about that. Or about Jameson and the possibility he was doing drugs again. Maybe my uncle knew and Jameson being Walker's brother, they were worried things could go bad with that.

I didn't know and it was frustrating.

We pulled up to our first stop of the day and I had no choice but to drop it. I had something else pressing anyway. There was a crowd of people gathered at the doors of the radio station, the band's arrival for the morning show having been broadcasted for weeks.

I ignored them all and marched up to Walker as he exited the car. "You called my mom?"

My voice was low but full of outrage.

Walker frowned down at me and took my arm, guiding me past security and screaming fans. It was far too early for that level of excitement. Just inside the door, he turned on me, scowling. "You wouldn't tell me."

"She didn't either." I knew my mother. She wouldn't have said a word. "You only freaked her out."

"Kiddies," Jameson called. "Now's not the time or place for your little spat."

Walker scowled at him and I turned my back. Causing an issue was the opposite of my job description but I just couldn't let this go. Not even for a second.

"You can't do that. I'll tell you what I want to when I want to," I said heatedly.

He cursed under his breath and tugged me into a semi-private corner of the lobby, angrily waving Jameson away. Low and controlled he whispered to me, "I wouldn't have thought twice about it if you weren't being cagey. You don't drink. You eat all that healthy shit and weird powders. You get real tired at night. Bags under your eyes if you work hard that day." He moved closer to me. "I'm worried, alright. Just tell me so I'll stop thinkin' it's somethin' serious."

Walker apparently paid close attention to me. Like *very* close.

I blinked up at him, stunned he'd noticed all those things. "It's not serious."

It wasn't right now anyway. But it still felt like a lie. It could be serious. Depending on the time of year or what my life looked like, it could affect many aspects and anyone in my life. My partner deserved to know, but I had to have their trust first, and Walker and I were still so new.

"You'll tell me if you need anything?"

God, who was this man? He knew nothing apart from I took a pill in the morning. He had no idea just how many I took or what they were for or the side effects or anything, but it didn't matter. *If you need anything.* He was creeping into my heart and setting up camp.

"I'm sorry," he told me gruffly, nuzzling the side of my face. "I don't like you keeping secrets."

"We all have secrets," I told him, softening. I was damn easy when it came to this man. I stared into his eyes as his hand cupped my chin, tipping it back. "*You* have secrets."

He kissed my forehead, the space between my eyes. "Nothing you need to worry about. Open for me."

I sagged against him, shivering with the raspy tone of his voice. I opened and he licked inside, no crevice unexplored by him. Gruff, "You'll get all my secrets when I know I have you."

I nodded, completely gone for this quiet powerhouse of a man. He passed out words like they were diamonds. Each one precious and beautiful.

Jameson and Lake stood beside a man with headphones and a mic, animatedly catching Walker's attention until we rejoined them.

I crouched down, pulling out my camera from the bag Walker had carried for me despite our earlier fight. It was ready to go, and I hung the strap around my neck. Walker grabbed my bag again and I followed at his side as the man with headset escorted us to the elevator with Julie.

"You're on for an hour," he started, going into detail about what would be asked of them and to just act *natural*, even as he gave them cues.

Walker tucked me into his side as we rode the elevator up seven floors. The show wasn't on for another hour but they had to be walked through the process. As they took their seats around the table, I took a few shots on both my camera and my phone, getting approval from Julie to upload the phone shots directly to their social account.

Jameson was the charismatic member, his quips on point. He had a magnetism that elevated the show exponentially. Lake was a close second but more philosophical with his answers. The host was enthralled by him as he dug deep into the meaning behind some of the band's lyrics. Brooks was both comedic relief and took on the harder questions, redirecting the host smoothly when he crossed a line.

Walker...my guy...he was himself. Steadily silent and completely bored.

Apart from one-word answers and a few grunts, getting anything out of him was like pulling teeth. It didn't help that he'd rather watch me behind the glass barrier than pay any attention. But Walker was the leader of the band and that was obvious. If

Jameson got out of hand all he had to do was give him a look and Jameson was backing off. His steady presence brought the band together and it wasn't lost on me how respected he was by both the hosts and those that called in. He was an amazing drummer and he had adoring fans all his own that wanted a piece of him.

Close to the end of the show, I was engrossed in editing some shots on my laptop for their website and even the radio show manager had asked to pass them along for their own site. I was just getting started though. I wanted to do so much more.

A question from the host startled me to the point I almost dropped my laptop.

"So Walker, I hear you have a new woman in your life. Is that who you brought with you?"

Walker's return to the question was awkward. He glared at the host, his eyes filling with anger, his lips sealed tight.

It was actually, surprisingly, Jameson that waded in, expertly deflecting both hosts' attention.

"Big bro's a private guy. Sorry ladies," he purred into the mic, "but you'll have to grab your gossip elsewhere."

Both hosts laughed it off, taking the conversation to Jameson's lack of a love life and Julie leaned into me. "They knew better," she hissed. "Walker and V both explicitly told them no questions about you."

"How did they even know?" It's not like we're in public all the time together.

176

Julie shot me a gentle smile. "Shy, you both are kind of hard to miss. He's always staring at you. You're together all the time even if you're not touching. And there has been a few photos."

The club. I knew that one was out there. Walker and I dancing together. Mavis had squealed in excitement, eating it up that everyone was talking about it. But I hadn't taken it seriously. My parents hadn't brought it up so I didn't think it was big news or anything. Not that my parents paid any of that stuff any attention. But still, it had been embarrassing at first, but I didn't bother to read anyone's reactions online, knowing I wouldn't like most of what I read.

I hadn't anticipated Walker getting asked about me and maybe that was my own fault. Of course he would. Of course people would be curious.

I could have dwelled on why he didn't want to talk about me, but I knew my uncle and Walker never had a bad intention toward me, and if I was to be kept private it was for my own piece of mind.

Just before the end of the show, the line was opened up for call-in questions.

Most of them were women, wanting to know this or that about the guys. Nearly half were for Jameson alone and he took them gladly, playing it up for the stuttering, excited callers.

It was the last question that kind of set the mood for the rest of the day though.

It was a man.

I didn't know what it was about him, but the moment I heard those short, harsh breaths coat the line, I immediately recognized him as the mouth breather.

"My question is for Johnnie," the man asked, his voice deep and coated with menace.

Julie's fingers twisted into her pencil skirt tight before she jumped up, slicing her hand across her neck for the producers to cut the call.

They didn't.

Walker stiffened, leaning closer to the blinking red light indicating the caller on the line. I'd never seen him so angry. Like he had every intention of jumping through the line and ripping the man from God knows where and beating the shit out of him.

"What's your question?" the host asked, his eyes on Walker's reaction, alight with interest.

"How you been buddy?" A wicked laugh preceded an abrupt cut from the call.

There was a breath of stunned atmosphere. Confusion on the radio crew's part. Caution from everyone who was not Walker.

Jameson placed his hand on Walker's shoulder, leaning in to say something quietly.

Walker shrugged him off and glared at the wall.

With nothing else to do, the hosts closed out the show.

Walker was out of that room in seconds, stalking off without a single look to me.

"What just happened?" I asked Julie.

Her eyes flitting nervously, she rushed to pick up her bags, dragging me from the couch. "Like I said, Walker's got shit going on."

♪

NERVOUS AND UNSURE ABOUT THE STATE OF WALKER AND what the hell was going on, I took shots when we stopped at an outdoor restaurant, catching the guys in their ease and then their softer disposition when they held a meet and greet at a local music and arts school.

Everyone but Walker anyway. Jameson seemed to shrug the radio show off but Walker appeared to carry it with a dark cloud.

I wanted to go to him. I wanted to demand answers, but it didn't feel like my place.

I hadn't been willing to open up about my own secrets and just before the show he'd told me he would tell me about his when he knew he *had me*. Whatever that meant.

He had me. He had me completely rock solid obsessed with him. I didn't know what else I had to do to prove that to him.

When we got to the talk show that evening, I was dead on my feet and happy to relieve the duty to the show's snobby photographer. The band's normal photographer was Jerry and he was a total sweetheart. Not this guy. He'd looked my secondhand camera over with disdain and relegated me to the back. Walker looked down on the guy like he was a piece of crud on his shoe, his temper clearly frayed from the day already. Jameson found this so amusing he immediately relieved any tensions the photographer had caused.

But where all day the guys indulged me, posing or not posing when I asked, they turned their backs on this guy. Walker straight up refused to move from his seat on a stool, me resting against him between his spread thighs. Any pictures he captured were with me spoiling the shot and Walker's glower. I kind of wanted to beg the show for copies.

And though Walker wasn't taking any of his turbulent thoughts out on me, he was still somehow distant. He was touching me, but he felt like a million miles away. Lost in his thoughts.

They performed for the audience and film crew halfway through the show and then played a trivia game before we were free to call it a night.

There were no probing questions about me this time.

I dozed against Walker on the drive back to the bus. Brooks shifted anxiously beside us as he prepared for his long night. It was date night and he'd begged everyone to give him a few hours of private time on the bus. Lake and Jameson wanted to go to a high-profile bar but Walker turned them down and dragged me to my uncle's bus.

I told him I was uncomfortable inviting him to my bunk without my uncle's approval. He just smiled and laid back on the couch, spreading me out across his chest and flipped on the television.

Enamored with that smile after so long with his stoic demeanor, I thawed easily.

I snuggled into him as he chose a scary movie about a masked serial killer. "You just want me afraid so you have an excuse to comfort me," I teased him.

Eyes glowing, he clenched my butt cheek in one fist. "I already got you. I don't need a movie to pull you closer."

I sat up, my legs spread wide across his torso, and wiggled out of my sweater. He was a big heater and I didn't want to sweat all over him. His eyes glinted in approval.

I shook my finger at him. "I'm just hot."

"Yeah, you are," he crooned, pulling me back down and shifting us to our sides so we were facing the screen. He lifted one of my thighs and rested my leg over top both of his.

"Watch the movie," he ordered with gentle scolding. "You keep squirming and I'll be fuckin' you before we get to the best bit."

Chastised and pleased for it, I refocused on the movie. Laughing when he pointed out the best bit—the girl got chased out of the shower by the serial killer, her glistening tits swaying as she ran away, screaming in terror.

He hummed against my neck, his hands cupping my breasts and squeezing playfully. The rest of the movie was torture. His thigh between my own and pressing just right, his thumbs teasing my pointed nipples.

But when it went on and on and he never made a move—I know, I told him not to—I eventually dozed off. He put me to bed in my bunk and kissed my eyelids. "Hittin' the gym."

"You're not tired?" I asked groggily.

He shook his head, his thumbs pressing my lids back down. "Sleep."

"I can come with you," I offered.

"Sleep," he ordered again. "Come kiss me when you wake up."

I nodded, rolling to my belly as he covered me with my sheet.

♪

WITH THE SUN SLIDING THROUGH THE WINDOWS, I ROLLED over and rubbed my eyes. A single white rose was on my pillow next to me. I smiled, inhaling it's sweet smell. Walker did apologies really well.

But I was past needing that apology for calling my mom. I just wanted to know what was going on, so at the very least I could help unburden him of the things that plagued him.

I didn't want it between us.

But I knew I didn't have the right to demand that of him. I was keeping secrets of my own.

15

One week later and nothing much had changed but yet *so much changed.*

No more sexy times took place but that wasn't for lack of trying. Every moment we tried to steal alone was interrupted, and when we fell into his bunk at night it was either his brother or another member of the band who chilled all our desire. I was having a hard time getting over the fact that they'd heard me that first time and Walker wasn't at all happy about it.

He never made me feel anything but safe and comfortable but his band mates felt his anger every time they tried to tease me. We were both walking shades of blue. We needed alone time, stat. Walker was spending more time in the gym, and although he told me he often did when he couldn't sleep, it was the first place he disappeared to when we were interrupted.

I suspected his increased workout regimen was more about his secrets than a sleeping problem or unmet sexual desires. But then again, the sleeping problem could be exasperated by the secrets.

I went around and around about all of it. About the secrets. Both his and mine. I wasn't sure what to do moving forward other than put it out of my mind. It felt wrong to ignore it but it felt worse to pry where I wasn't wanted.

We were all taking off for two weeks tomorrow, and I felt our inevitable parting like a desperate seething dragon.

I wanted so many things from him. Reassurance. Time. Communication. And all my physical lust for him sated before we spent time apart. It wasn't looking like any of that would happen.

After the last song of the show, I met him side stage with an ice-cold water and a kiss. A ritual of ours now. When my uncle came back, he was in for a shock. Not only had I not taken any of his warnings to heart, I'd jumped into this thing with Walker headfirst and without a safety net.

I was officially committed to seeing it through. My obsession for him had only grown, but I stopped seeing it as such a bad thing and embraced it. I felt his obsession for me and it was intoxicating. I only hoped mine could make him feel the same way.

Back in the dressing room, the VIP passes were let inside and autographs and photos were given as I got Walker's massage ready. My hands on him turned him on like nothing else, and I suspected the only reason we kept it public was so he wasn't tempted to bail on the after-party before his obligations were met.

When he plopped down in front of me, his hips wedged between my legs, he tugged my thighs tight to his sides. Sitting on the back of the couch, I wiped the sweat off his body with a warm towel, dipping my fingers in the cream and working out his knots. Pounding on the drums for several hours really tensed him up, but I loved my new duty as his masseuse. That girl may have taken care of him before but she hadn't gotten his hands on her in return whereas I did. He rubbed my calves, his fingers digging in to relieve the pressure and nibbled at my arms as they came close enough to reach.

He was as hands-on in these moments as I was.

"You two are adorable," Mavis said with a pout and dropped onto the couch beside us. She had bags under eyes again, a sign she and Van had gotten into it again the previous night. "I'd kill to have Van rub my aches away."

"Drop the loser," Walker told her, his head dropping so I could dig my knuckles into his neck. He groaned low and my lady bits vibrated against his upper back.

"Just like that, huh?" she asked, genuinely curious, and I held my breath, hoping she was really considering it.

"Want me to fuck him up?" Walker asked, peaking at her from over my knee.

Mavis guffawed, slapping her thigh while I smacked his muscular side. "Walker—"

"No," she interrupted me through her giggles. "Oh gosh, the visual is just too good. Big man like you'd make him go *splat*." She smacked her hands together. "Yes, please."

Walker nodded and went to stand. I jumped him, wrapping my thighs around him from behind and covering his face with my arms. "Mavis!"

She giggled harder.

Walker bumped me up higher, his hands cupping my bottom. "No?"

"No!" I cried. "V will be pissed if you get in a fight!"

Walker scoffed and dropped me onto the couch. "That little pissant can't fight me."

I shook my head at him like he was naughty and he chuckled, "Sorry, girl. My Shy says no."

"Big bad Walker Lawson, cowed by a tiny woman," Mavis called theatrically, her hands spreading wide as if it were a headline. "Panties are dropping all around the land."

"The land?" I giggled.

She shrugged. "Can I come home with you for break?"

My smile slid right off my face and I observed her more closely. I could see why she wanted a break from Van, but what about her family? "You don't want to go home?"

"To the wicked witch?" She shuddered. "Pass." Wicked witch being her grandmother.

Mavis and I seemed to have that in common. No home to call our own, we both lived with family when we weren't on tour. Only she hated her family and I loved mine.

"Yeah, my mom would love to have you."

She looked at me hopefully. "Really?"

I nodded and she squeezed between Walker's arms to hug me. "Thank you."

After she bounced away with a new pep in her step, I backed away to dislodge Walker's lips from my neck. "What about you?"

He raised his brow and he continued to kiss my neck.

"Where are you going for your break?" I pushed. It was the first time the subject had come up without me calling it out like a desperate loser.

"Don't know. Don't care," he growled, pulling me up by my waistband. "Come here."

He was so much taller than me, I had to stand on my toes to wrap my arms around his shoulders. He hunched down, pressing his lips into mine. Hands on my butt, he boosted me to wrap my legs around his waist and started to march from the room.

"Not so fast!" Julie cried, and Walker ripped his mouth from mine with a curse. "I need you Walker!"

"Shy needs me," he returned, his hands dipping down low enough that I began to squirm.

"Shy can wait," she called with a laugh. "Your adoring fans cannot."

Dropping my legs from his hips, he sighed deeply. "Don't move."

He left after another kiss and I waited for a while, but thought it made me look like every other girl in the room vying for the attention of a rock star so I made my way back to the bus to pack.

Walker didn't make me wait often if he could help it, so I tried not to let it get to me that I was left on my own for so long on our last night together. So many people competed for his attention after every show, I couldn't expect him to drop everything for me. After I packed up and had finished an entire episode of the Bachelorette, I made my way to my bunk, sulking and hating myself for it.

When I was woken in the middle of the night, it wasn't by Walker. It was Brooks and he was shaking me awake, handing me another rose. This one red. "He had to dip, Shy. He didn't want to, but his dad called him and James."

I rubbed at my eyes. "Is everything okay?"

He shrugged. "When it comes to Daddy Lawson? Not usually."

I held the rose to my nose, looking down on it with a frown as Brooks left.

It wasn't until the next morning that I realized Walker and I hadn't done anything in our relationship in the typical way. We hadn't ever had a real date and so we hadn't done the one thing you normally would—we hadn't even exchanged phone numbers.

Cursing myself and feeling so depressed it was pathetic, I boarded a plane with Mavis. I was leaving Walker for two weeks and had no idea if we were even anything to each other outside of the tour.

Did I mention I had anxiety?

Number one rule...avoid the things that make you anxious.

But I couldn't avoid thoughts of Walker.

Being in the dark about the man I was quickly falling in love with was all sorts of anxiety inducing. It was up there with standing naked in a crowded room.

16

I could have sulked the entire trip home. In fact I would've reveled in it, holing up in my room with a gallon of mint chocolate chip ice cream and an entire sleeve of Oreos, watching reruns of *Friends*. That sounded like the very best way to blow two slow-as-snail moving weeks.

Two reasons that didn't happen. One, Ice cream was on my no-no food list. Two, Mavis.

We both would've been sulking and so one of us had to pull up our big girl panties. That girl was me—after a firm talking to from my ball-busting mother.

Three days in and we dragged ass outside to show Mavis around our small town and blow money neither of us had at the mall.

Six days in and Mavis seemed to shake off her melancholy whereas I was just becoming best friends with mine.

On the eighth day I was officially driving my friend and myself insane. Why hadn't he called? He'd gotten my mother's number no problem. He could get mine...easily. Had he moved on? Found another shy girl to keep him company? Was he relieved to be rid of the weight of me?

My mother was clueless as to the reason behind my mood, worried the tour was the cause. She and my father decided to gang up on me to come home.

I was *this* close to calling my uncle and begging for Walker's number. However, I did have *some* pride—and an eccentric best friend that was prepared to tackle me to the ground before I made a fool of myself.

She snatched my phone from me. "The man isn't helpless. If he wants to call he will."

Heart dropping, I looked away from her and she sighed.

"He is *crazy about you*, stupid girl."

"But you just said yourself he'll call is he wants to," I told her moodily.

She frowned, kicking her feet off the ground as we swung on the kiddie swings in the park a few blocks from my house. "I don't understand men," she declared.

"I don't either," I agreed.

"What does he think you're doing anyway? Pining away for him?" She huffed. "When we get back to the tour you should tell him all about your sexy escapades."

"What sexy escapades?" I asked her with a reluctant laugh. I glanced pointedly at the rusty playground and she snorted.

"You've got to learn to play the game, honey-bear."

I sighed. "I don't want to play the game. I just want him."

"Well, I bet he's hold up in his daddy's mansion, staring at his phone, trying to find the words to express his undying love for you."

I couldn't help but laugh at that. "One, you *just said* he'd call if he wanted to. Two, I'll be waiting a *long* time for that. Walker hates words."

She wiggled her brows. "I bet he makes up for it in bed though, am I right?"

I flushed looking away.

"Oh my god. You haven't rode that bull yet?"

"Shh," I begged her, eyeing the couple walking their dog a few feet away. "Walker's not a bull."

"You haven't," she blinked, stunned. "How is that possible?"

"It's not me that's holding back," I grumbled.

Something soft moved over her face and she suddenly blinked away glassy eyes. "Wow."

"What?"

She shook her head. "You have nothing to worry about, Shy. If that man has been holding off getting you naked then—" she sighed wistfully. "Just you wait."

I could wait. I'd been waiting. But even if I could, I didn't *want to*. But Mavis had a point. Walker was waiting for some reason and I wasn't so naïve not to see that it meant something. That I was more than a fling if we hadn't actually *flung*.

But he hadn't called.

⋅♪⋅

COOKING ON THE GRILL IN MY PARENT'S BACK YARD A FEW hours later, I reluctantly chuckled as Mavis made faces to the smell of the grilling black bean burgers.

"They're good," I promised.

She looked dubious, backing away from me in her tiny bikini. We had an above ground pool. Nothing special, but we could float and tan. Mom pranced around in a racy one piece for my dad, thus why we were avoiding that side of the yard all together and had volunteered to grill the burgers.

"You still hearing from Van?" I asked her while flipping patties.

"Yeah. He calls about every hour still."

I shook my head. "For how often he calls it sounds like he misses you, but why drive you away in the first place?"

She looked away from me, squinting into the sun. "Yeah."

It was sighed, knowingly, as if it didn't confuse her at all.

"Mavis," I started, hesitant.

"I know, Shiloh," she said warily.

I flinched, so unused to hearing my full name in so long. "If you know what I'm going to say then you know why you should leave him."

She shrugged, not angry or sad, just indifferent, and that worried me more than anything. There should be emotion in a relationship no matter how messed up it was. Lack of emotion wasn't a relationship at all. I was a ball of emotions twenty-four seven and I wasn't even sure if I was *in a relationship.*

My father's phone dinged with an alert for the front door. He groaned as he got up from the lounger, his Hawaiian shirt plastered to his barrel chest.

My father's Hawaiian shirt, my mother's tanning, our bikini's, it was all hilarious in a satirical kind of way. We were in Montana. The temperature just barely warm enough and only because the sun was out, but it wouldn't last, the moment the sun peeked behind the clouds, the cold breeze would flow in, but that was my parent's way. Enjoying the sunshine even if it would only last a moment.

"I got it. You girls about done burning the burgers?"

I jumped, looking at the crispy patties. "Sorry, Daddy."

He just kissed the top of my head as he passed me to get to the back door. "Just how I like 'em. As black as your mother's soul."

"Hey!" she shouted, affronted as she sunbathed on another lounger.

My father thought himself hilarious as he disappeared into the house.

"My soul is rainbows and unicorns, thank you very much," she shouted.

"He's gone," I called to her.

She lifted her sunglasses from underneath her massive sun hat. "That man..." she sighed and lay back down. "I love him with all my heart and soul, I do. Girls, you find a man just as sexy and ornery as him. You won't regret it."

I silently gagged and Mavis giggled. "You're 'rents are the best."

I knew it.

The backdoor slid open and my father's voice carried a whole lot of heavy censure. "Shy, there's a few young men here to see you."

"Me?" I couldn't help but ask in shock. I never got any visitors. I'd lost touch with high school associations years ago and left what little college friends I had back when I dropped out.

"Yes. You," he replied, exasperated. He nodded, and through the back kitchen window I watched several big bodies move through.

My jaw dropped in shock as Walker, Jameson, and Lake stepped out into my parent's backyard.

Mavis huffed out a dazed giggle, her hand curling around my wrist and shaking it. "Your mom's gettin' a load of three sexy ornery men as we speak."

I couldn't tear my eyes from Walker as he cautiously quirked a grin my way.

"Well isn't this cozy," Jameson drawled, his eyes roaming across the yard and zeroing in on Mavis with intent.

She gave me a shove and that was all I needed to snap out of my stupor. Walker Lawson was in my backyard and I wasn't as oblivious to not know he was here for *me*. I did not attempt to play a single game with him.

I took off for him with a running leap, my arms wrapping around his neck and squeezing the life out of him. He chuckled and squeezed me back, his arms coming around my bare waist unimpeded by my own teeny tiny bikini.

"Unhand my daughter!" my father shouted and I winced.

"Really, Rodger?" my mother snapped. "Unhand?"

I let out a hysterical giggle but I didn't let him go, instead squeezed him tighter.

"What are you doing here?" I asked, breathless with excitement.

"You're here," was all he said.

MY FATHER WAS NOT AT ALL HAPPY WITH THE interruption. Not only because these were members of the band my uncle worked with, but they were rock stars. In his mind, they'd stolen me away for weeks, and they were untrustworthy, pretentious, and spoiled. He didn't know them to make that type of judgement, so I took his attitude as protectiveness and his love for me rather than be offended on their behalf.

Of course, it hadn't helped that I'd thrown myself at one of them.

Walker, after introducing himself to my father and mother—and it should be noted, he introduced himself as *Walker, Shy's man*— now stood with my dad by the pool, talking quietly.

Dad didn't look too pissed anymore, just a thoughtful frown on his face as he nodded along to whatever Walker was saying. Mom, completely flabbergasted by their arrival and my show of affection, ran around to serve Lake and Jameson food and drinks, while trying to catch my father's attention with wide-eyed curiosity.

"I didn't think he knew that many words," Mavis teased me as we sat the table.

I laughed in disbelief, dying to know what Walker was saying just as badly, if not more so, than my mother. "I didn't either." My father looked as if he'd barely gotten a word in as Walker made his speech. What could he possibly be saying to him?

Jameson leaned closer to me furtively with a horrorstruck look in his eyes. "What is in this?"

Mavis cracked up, spotting the disgusted twist to his lips. "Food."

"No shit?" Jameson looked at his burger, taking another bite. "Tastes like ass."

"Don't let Mom hear you, you'll hurt her feelings."

Jameson winked at me but he still looked dubious.

"Quit eating it, if it's so bad," Mavis mumbled around her burger. I was glad she'd ended up liking it because I thought they were the bomb.

"This your sister?" Jameson asked me, nodding to Mavis with a riveted gleam in his eye.

She and I shared a surprised glance. "Really?"

Jameson looked at her, his eyes heating as he explored every inch of her bare skin on display.

"She's not my sister," I told him slowly, astonished that he didn't recognize her. She'd been on the road with us since the start of the tour. Sure, different bands and different buses, but she was gorgeous with shocking purple hair and startling blue eyes— kind of hard to miss.

"Good. Won't have to butter up the old man like my bro," Jameson said to himself.

Mavis rolled her eyes. "You're a toad."

Her ass shook as she pranced away. I stifled my chuckle as he gaped after her. I doubted Jameson had ever been turned down. At least not so fast and so firmly.

Lake polished off his third burger and leaned around Jameson's stunned body. "So what's there to get up to around here?"

My mom came up behind us and took the opportunity to jump in. "Movie theatre is showing oldies this weekend. Then there's the laser tag and indoor golf course. Bowling alley..." she ticked them all off her fingers and Lake's eyes glassed over with disinterest.

"Not quite what they had in mind, Mom."

She looked adorably confused for a moment and then seemed to take in their long shaggy hair, tattoos, excess of leather and chains and made an ahh sound. "Karaoke bar?"

Lake snapped his fingers with a smile. "That'll do it."

"Is that a good idea?" I asked them both. This was a small town but they were recognized everywhere... "Do you even have any security with you?"

Jameson waved the question away, valiantly taking another tiny bite as my mother watched him with expectancy. "They're out front."

"Oh," my mom said in dismay. "You should've said so, I can bring them something to eat."

"They're good," Lake dropped fast. "They already ate."

"Well maybe they're thirsty..." she trailed off and went into the house.

"Joe would shit a brick if he had to eat this," Lake told me.

I laughed. "You seem to like it."

"Hungry. I'll eat anything."

Jameson snickered. "Ass is his main course."

I gagged and stood, walking away from them as they fell over in hilarity.

Walker spotted me making my way over and fell silent, nodding to my father.

"What are you guys talking about?"

"You," Walker said as he pulled me to his side.

I peeked at my father, other than a little concern he seemed completely fine. "Daddy?"

"Like the man said, baby. We're just talking about you." He patted my arm. "Walker here says you've been taking pictures for the band. Why didn't you say so?"

I shrugged. "It never came up."

"You're so talented, Shiloh. Your uncle's a smart man to utilize your skills. I hope he's compensating you for the extra work."

It didn't feel like work...

"So you're leaving us early?" my father asked.

I frowned and he gestured to Walker.

"Took another show early," Walker told me, watching my eyes.

"Uncle V didn't say anything."

"Just found out," he said dismissively. "You're coming back with us tomorrow."

I was disappointed for the break to be cut short and also immensely excited to get back on the road—and mostly Walker. It wasn't like my parents would've been down with him staying here with us, not that he would've wanted to...

He pulled me so my front was to his and pressed a heartbreakingly sweet kiss on the corner of my mouth. "You miss me?"

My father slowly backed away...the look on his face. Kind of like he wanted to give us privacy—but also deck Walker in the face. For a man that was normally a pacifist that was all kinds of surprising.

"You know I did," I said with a playful sigh. "I couldn't stop thinking about you."

He smiled smugly, his eyes dancing with male satisfaction. The sad part was every bit of it was true and he could read me like a book. I wasn't fooling anyone.

"You miss me?" The question was weighted with self-consciousness and a feminine need to be wanted by the man with whom I was madly infatuated.

"You know I did," he said. And he had come all the way here, just what more proof did I need?

All the proof...I was insecure like that. Anxiety was *fun*.

"You didn't call..."

Walker frowned heavily. "I didn't have your number."

I scoffed. "You got my mother's just fine."

His shoulders lifted and he squinted into the sun. "You didn't like it."

My heart filled so full. I hadn't thought he wouldn't try and get it because of how badly I reacted before. "I wanted to hear your voice."

He looked at me with amused suspicion. *Really?* He seemed to doubt me and I huffed a laugh. "It's rare that you ever use it but when you do it gives me shivers."

"Shivers, huh," he growled and yeah, my entire body shivered against his. "Can I get your number, Shy girl?"

I caught my mom's awed smile, the pitcher of tea suspended above Lake's head as it slowly trickled into the guitarist's lap.

17

"He is something," my mother gushed as I quickly packed my suitcase. We were going out to a karaoke bar tonight but would be on the first flight home in the morning. Not home—to some random city on the tour junket. But it felt like home. A bus that traveled night and day from place to place which felt like my home, and that was an unsettling realization.

"Yeah," I grinned like an idiot as I folded a sweater.

"Oh, Shy," she breathed fervently, "You really like him."

I did. So much. Maybe too much.

My worries must have been written on my face because my mom stepped away from the window where she watched the band sit around the fire pit with my dad and Mavis. "What is it?"

I slouched down on my bed with her and leaned against her shoulder. We were the same height, same build, but my mama felt like a steel wall. Always there to hold me up. "I think about him all the time. I miss him when we're apart, even if it's only for ten minutes. This break has felt like a year. My heart aches when he talks to me, in a good way." I rubbed at it now, thinking about him. "When he looks at me..." I shook my head, not able to put it into words.

Her eyes glassed over and her smile was wobbly. "You love him."

I nodded miserably and her laugh came out warbled. "Don't look so upset. I'm so thrilled for you."

"I barely know him. It scares me."

"Love can be scary. You're opening yourself up to another person in a way that gives them power over you. Your emotions can sometimes be chained to theirs."

Yeah, I felt directly linked to Walker. "I don't know if that's okay for me. I don't know how to handle not having control over my own happiness."

"When you find that person that you're willing to risk your heart for, you *cannot* rely on them to make you happy. Only *you* are responsible for your emotions. That's not to say they won't affect it, but whether they make you happy, sad, angry, you have to control how you deal with those emotions. You have to decide on your own if you want to keep them around based on how they make you feel." My mom had a way of putting things into perspective.

"Are you thrilled, really?"

"I am *so* happy that this trip has opened you up to meeting new people. Forming relationships. Mavis, Walker, your uncle...those funny boys... I'm just happy to see you forming bonds. You've been so closed off the last few years."

I felt a 'but' coming. "But?".

"*But* I worry," she quirked her lips slyly. "What can I say? I gave birth to you. Twenty-two years ago, I changed. I became a living breathing pillar of terrified *all the time*. And it's all your fault."

"Nice."

"He seems so taken with you," she said tenderly. "How could he not be? You're something special. That *is* my fault."

"At least you take the blame somewhere."

She wiggled her brows. "Your father can have your teenage rebel years. I claim all the best bits."

"You okay with them staying here?" I asked again, unsure after Jameson had all but volunteered her and my father to put them up when the local hotel was out of vacancies.

"Yes, I mind," she said with a dramatic glower. "It will be *so* diffi-cult to have three handsome, famous musicians in my home, telling me how amazing my cooking is...when we both know they hated every bite."

"Lake liked my burgers," I bragged shamelessly.

She shoved me away. "My recipe."

She helped me finish packing, a thoughtful look creeping over her face. "He's very observant of your habits and diet."

I flushed. "Is it wrong to keep it from him?"

She shrugged. "There's no right answer, honey. He'll have to know eventually. You've been lucky the last two months. It's only a matter of time before you have a flare-up. Wouldn't it be better if he knows how to care for you before then?"

She was a mother hen, so of course she saw it that way. A flare-up could mean chronic fatigue, or nausea, pain, or a long list of other things. Any one of them could be easily handled privately but if it were bad, I might need a few days to myself. I would never expect anyone to hover over me, but... "I don't know."

She huffed. "And when you're so sick and the discomfort is so great you can't leave your bed? You won't eat?" She narrowed her eyes at me. "I don't know him well, but that man doesn't strike me as the type to leave you alone if you're not feeling well. So unless you have that conversation, you could put him in the awful position of feeling completely helpless to alleviate your pain."

"It's too soon," I mumbled.

"Perhaps." She got rough with my clothes, punching them into the suitcase. "But I would feel better if there were someone other than your busy uncle to watch out for you. I know it would go a long way with your father as well." Meaning Dad might be more inclined to be nice.

I fidgeted nervously. "And if it sends him running?"

She stood up, blinking at me. "Shiloh. You have a condition. A draining, sometimes frightening, condition. You need those you love to have a care in some areas of your life. You're not dying. You're otherwise a healthy, happy, young woman. If he can't see past it to the amazing woman you are, then he doesn't deserve you anyway."

I was getting upset. She was pushing it a lot harder than I would've expected her to. Words spewed out of my mouth in a rush, coated in self-loathing and anger. "And if I start to feel so sick so fast, I have to cancel a vacation we'd been planning for months? What about when I blow chunks in a crowded airport? Or if he has to spend days in the hospital with me?" I blinked away tears. "And when we're out to dinner and I have an accident? I wouldn't blame anyone for being mortified to be with me when I grossed out an entire restaurant." It was a lot for anyone to commit to. He would be chaining himself to a woman that could be sick so often it could feel like a burden to him just as much as it was to myself.

My mother sat down heavily, gaping at me with tears coating her face. "I had no idea you worried so much."

I smacked my tears away, frustrated. "I'm not stupid, Mom. This isn't like I get a sore stomach or a fever every once in a while. It can be gross and draining. When I'm flaring, I have to always make sure there's a bathroom nearby *just in case*. It's humiliating and demeaning and sometimes I don't even want to leave the house."

"But you went on tour..."

"I was depressed and it was scary, and I could see myself living in your house for the rest of my life." I walked to the window looking to the bonfire. "I didn't want to be a party to my entire life flying by and not having *seen* anything."

Walker was glancing at the backdoor, likely looking for me. He had no idea I was upstairs, my heart breaking because I could picture a life with him and it wasn't all butterflies and roses. It was frightening, complicated and *exhausting*. I couldn't imagine it lasting with anyone, let alone *him*. Someone so perfectly gentle and understanding.

Quiet, my voice so small. "I don't want to be a burden for anyone, especially not for him."

"I'm sorry, sweetie. I shouldn't have pushed." She wrapped her arms around me from behind. *"You are not a burden.* We love you. You're in remission right now. That could end tomorrow but you'll get through it and reach the other side like you have every other time. And I understand that it's scary, that it could keep you off the tour but what is life if not a risk? This will always be your home. You're stronger than you give yourself credit for, and I *know* your father and I haven't been helpful in letting you believe it, but we're so damn proud of you."

I let her words wash over me. "I like being on tour. It's more than Walker. I liked traveling and managing the band. It's fun and now I get to take pictures and I get paid for it. But how am I supposed to stay if I go out of remission? How will I go to the doctors?" So many damn doctors.

"Shiloh, light of my life. I love you but you can be so very dramatic sometimes. The tour isn't forever. Take it day by day and if you start to feel like you'll need treatments, we'll deal with it when it happens."

I sniffled some more, rubbing my snotty nose into her soft shirt. "I'm not dramatic."

"No. Worrying about something that hasn't happened and so early in a relationship is not at all dramatic." She pushed me away with an exasperated sigh. "I will say this. That you're so worried about a flare-up when you're on the road says a lot about how much you've enjoyed working for your uncle, and that makes me very happy. Your uncle understands your ordeal well. He would be more than happy to accommodate, should you need time off."

She was right. Treatments could take weeks or months to get back into remission. And one day there might come a time where it would take longer... but my uncle would be understanding. I had to hope I made myself valuable enough that he didn't replace me if that happened.

She gripped my arm as I stepped around her. "Shy, I just want to say—" she sighed, "I want you to keep working for your uncle, I just want to make sure you're staying for the right reasons."

"I can't say Walker doesn't influence me. That would be a lie, and if things didn't work out, I can't say I would want to stay and see him move on from me, even though I really do love working. Maybe I'll feel differently when the tour is over as I have no idea what my job will look like then. Right now, I love it and those reasons have little to do with Walker Lawson." And that was true. Walker or no Walker, I felt like I was needed by my uncle. Every day I was challenged. Every day was new and exciting. I felt independent and more my age. I wasn't cooped up in my room, wanting to experience the world but not having any idea how to accomplish it.

I was *living* and I wasn't ready to let that go.

18

Walking out to the bonfire, I let my talk with my mother fall off my shoulders, trying to alleviate the tension. I wasn't sure whether I felt better talking to her about my fears or more afraid to tell Walker. I just knew I wasn't going to tell him yet. I wasn't ready.

He stood as I stopped by the logs my father and grandfather had chopped down to use as benches when I was little. My father tilted his head in question, reading me like a book, and I smiled at him in reassurance.

Walker missed nothing and ducked closer to me, his thumbs lightly running under my dry eyes. Mom had pressed a cold rag on them but I knew they were likely still puffy. A question in his eyes, he frowned.

"Mom and daughter stuff," I told him.

"Me?" His voice was low, intimate.

"No, she's already half in love with you."

He smiled smugly and winked.

"Ready to go?" Mavis asked me, looking at my jeans and sweater dubiously.

Take me or leave me but I was feeling kind of rough after the cry fest and didn't feel like putting much effort in for small town karaoke.

♪

THE BAR WAS A LITTLE TOO DARK, A LITTLE TOO GRUNGY, and a little too quiet. It was dead for a Friday night. When the best thing on offer for a TGIF is karaoke, what really could you expect?

We drew attention.

When three tatted oversized men—dressed head to toe in expensive grunge, one too many skull and cross bone rings between them, Jameson sporting black fingernails, Lake about four bajillion facial piercings, and their bodyguards trailing behind that were arguably smaller in size and threatening demeanor than the band members they were safeguarding—walk into a bar this side of Montana...Well, there was a punch line in there somewhere.

However, most of the patrons were older and a few beers into forgetting their shitty jobs and nagging wives, so that worked to our advantage. No one seemed to recognize them. They didn't even appear inclined to put much brain power into recognizing them.

Mavis whistled sharply, "Feels like home."

"Frequent many backwoods bars?" Jameson asked her.

"You have no idea." She flitted off to the bar, leaving him no opening whatsoever.

"We're not backwoods," I scolded him.

"Whatever you say, darlin'," Jameson drawled with a terrible northern accent. We weren't in the south.

I rolled my eyes and allowed Walker to tug me to an empty table. My heart swelling impossibly large, I watched him wipe his forearm across the tabletop and chair, clearing it of crumbs—so yeah, okay, it wasn't the cleanest place—before he let me sit down.

"Water?" he asked, and my heart jumped. He paid so close attention to what I drank and ate that not once had he ever offered me anything I couldn't have.

A few minutes later, he returned with a glass of ice water and a beer for himself. Mavis was trailing behind with a giant spiraled binder.

"We're singing together," she demanded, her eyes daring me.

I immediately shook my head. "No, no way."

"Let go of the *shy*, Shy," she ordered. "Live a little."

"It's not about being shy,"—except hell yes that was a big part. Socially awkward worry-wart present— "You don't want to hear me sing. *Trust me.*" It was like cat-on-a-tin-roof bad. I was under no disillusions about my voice. Too high, too croaky, too *awful*. I shattered mirrors.

"It's karaoke, not Broadway."

I chuckled nervously, sensing her heels digging in. "Present company, three extremely talented world-renowned rock stars. Hell no," I said.

"Aww, Shy, we won't laugh," Lake insisted *almost* sincerely.

"Much," Jameson added and the two of them chuckled like little boys.

"This is it!" Mavis cried, pointing to her choice in the massive song book.

I peeked down and blanched. "Absolutely not."

"It's ABBA," she said dryly. "Karaoke gold. No one can screw this up."

"Me," I hissed. "I can screw up ABBA."

She wasn't taking me seriously. "I'm calling it in."

I gaped after her as she flounced to the snoring DJ in the corner.

"This ought to be good," Jameson drawled, somewhat amused.

Walker put his finger on my chin and tilted my head. "It's that bad?"

I nodded, one-hundred and forty billion percent serious. "*Bad.*"

He smirked, his eyes lighting up. "I want to hear you."

"Shy." Mavis tapped on the microphone and feedback hit us like a brick. Everyone in the bar winced as she chuckled mercilessly. "Earth to Shiloh. Get your ass up here. We're the only two women in this bar. We need to shake it."

I made a frightened mousy sound.

"Go on, dancing queen." Walker rumbled against my mouth, giving my bottom a boost.

All the blood drained from my face and the pit of my stomach dropped as I dawdled to the tiny stage as if it were the gallows. Glancing over my shoulder, I mouthed to Walker, "Please don't make me do this."

"What's that I hear?" Lake called, putting his hand by his ear and making a clucking sound.

Jameson guffawed. "Is that supposed to be a chicken?"

Lake clucked again.

Walker just shook his head, nodding for me to get going.

Forget every last worry that had been on my mind since meeting him, this right here, this would send him running for sure.

"I hate you," I hissed to Mavis as I joined her on stage.

"You love me," she purred into the microphone in a sex operator voice. An old man not three feet from us whipped around so fast he about fell out of his chair.

The music started—the cheesiest music. I covered my face with my hands.

Mavis nudged me hard, nearly knocking me right off the two-inch high platform... at least we weren't feet above the patrons.

I might not be able to sing. I might not have the courage to dance in public, but my mother was nothing if not thorough in my seventy's music education. I hit the first *ooh* right on cue and Jameson and Lake both shouted in triumph.

Face now flooding with color so fast I could've melted plastic. I spotted Walker's pleased smile. It was so wide and happy, so unlike anything he'd ever given to me before, I decided right then to throw myself into the song for nothing else but to get another one of those smiles.

I *had* just told my mother I wanted to experience life. What was that If not making a fool out of yourself just to earn a smile from the man who held your heart?

♪♫♪

MAVIS WINCED, THE LACK OF APPLAUSE DEAFENING.

I just scowled at her and stomped off stage, slumping into my seat, *mortified*.

Jameson stared at me, his mouth hanging open.

Lake—loud, lively, Lake—blinked. "Well, you weren't kidding..."

No. No, I was *not*.

I'd really gotten into in the moment, but as the last note trailed off quietly, I'd opened my eyes to see gaping mouths and horrified stares. It was only then that I'd seen Mavis' microphone hanging down by her side as she too had gawked at me. I wasn't even sure when I'd lost her as my singing partner.

"Well," Mavis cleared her throat into the microphone behind me.

I slunk down into my seat, hoping everyone at the bar was drunk enough not to remember me or my singing.

"*Baby,*" Walker called so, so tenderly.

Too wary to really appreciate the new nickname from him, I asked, "I made your ears bleed, didn't I?"

"There ain't one damn thing about you that ain't beautiful," he whispered and I felt his smile against my ear. "We might have to limit your venues, though."

"Like only singing in soundproof rooms thousands of miles away from witnesses?"

"How about you just save all your songs for me from now on?" he suggested.

My frown melted right off along with my heart as it puddled at his feet.

"I sing in the shower." I meant it innocently. A warning if he was ever around, but I realized how provocative it sounded when I saw his eyes heat.

"New bus rule," Lake chimed. "No singing in the shower."

"I have my own bus with my own rules," I teased him. "I can sing all I want."

Lake grunted a loud buzzing sound. "Wrong. V has officially kicked you off his bus at Walker's request."

My eyes jumped to the man watching me closely. "You what?"

He draped an arm around my shoulders. "Are you my girl?"

I nodded, so in love with this man it turned my insides to mush.

"My girl stays with me."

Music started up again and I tore my eyes away, focusing on Mavis as she swayed her hips side to side, her eyes on the ceiling and her thoughts far away.

Then for the next three minutes and some odd seconds, she completely stole all my attention and enraptured every ear in the bar.

Listen.

Queen B's song, but Mavis's emotion, completely captivated us all.

For that short moment in time, I caught a glimpse of the hurt, pain and frustration she fought so hard to hide under a vibrant effervescent persona.

When she trailed off, her voice so powerful I felt it in my bones, I snapped back into my own skin and my eyes ached as I watched her wipe her wet face with the end of her sleeve.

Jameson drew closer to the stage, his eyes locked on her. She was completely oblivious of him, tripping off the stage and heading to the bar.

"Shy," Lake said low, his voice awed. "Why is that girl following her shit singer boyfriend around on tour and not on tour herself?"

I had nothing. I suspected she had an amazing voice but that...

That was something else. She should be in front of stadiums. It was a crime that she wasn't sharing that with the world.

He shook his head. "Damn shame." He looked to Walker. "Might want to get James before he starts humping her leg."

Walker slipped off toward Jameson, jolting him from his trance as he pulled him back to the table.

"You gotta talk to her," Lake whispered, watching her down a shot at the bar. "We can get her in front of the right people."

I was so down for that.

But something told me it wasn't going to be that easy.

19

Empty shot glasses littered the table, a few of them Walker's but mostly Lake's.

"It's like watching a wild animal being born," Lake whispered, his voice slurred. He was referring to Jameson and I had to agree, it was fascinating to watch. Jameson sat at the end of the bar. A full beer that had to be warm by now. He'd barely touched it all night. He'd barely *moved* all night. He just sat there and watched Mavis with this enraptured look overtaking his face.

I was going to have to tell him she had a boyfriend. A shitty boyfriend but I'd seen Jameson in action. The women he took to his bed every night after a show. He wasn't a better option for her. Not one bit, no matter how much he was growing on me.

For her part, she seemed oblivious. In her own little world at the opposite end of the bar, dancing and twirling to every song she punched into the jukebox.

I checked my phone, noting the time and looked to Walker. He seemed content to sit still, playing with the hole in my jeans. His blunt finger sliding in and out to dance along the bare skin of my knee.

"What time do we leave in the morning?"

He blinked, focusing on me with slightly glassed eyes. "Early."

"So informative," I teased.

He pulled me into his lap. "You tired?"

"Kinda."

He immediately stood, cradling me in his arms.

"Time to go," he told Lake before calling out to Jameson and Mavis.

Jameson didn't budge until Mavis started weaving over and then he was up and glued to her side. She flinched, surprised to find him in her space and looked to me with raised brows.

I snickered, burying my face into Walker's shoulder.

The bartender saw us leaving and dropped the glass he was drying on the counter. "You guys mind if I get an autograph?"

I looked up. "You know who they are?"

The bartender just regarded me like I was nuts.

"Small towns," Lake teased me. "They even know us all the way out here." And gladly took the paper and passed it around. Walker setting me on the bar top and using my forehead as a hard surface.

I pouted and he kissed it away with a chuckle.

We returned home and piled into the house as quiet as possible. The guys had the two couches and recliners in the family room while Mavis and I went to my room.

Walker stopped me at the stairs, his fingers tugging my waistband. "Go somewhere with me tomorrow night?"

"Anywhere." I leaned into him, accepting his kiss. "Wait. Where?"

"It's a surprise," he teased and patted my bottom.

"Like a date?" I teased back.

He nodded, his lip quirking.

"Our first date," I sighed happily.

We kept eye contact as I walked up stairs right up until I turned the corner.

Mavis was already in the bed when I came out of the bathroom in my night clothes. I climbed in beside her and she rolled over, burrowing into my side.

I thought of her singing, and what Lake had said and opened my mouth before I talked myself out of it. "Why haven't you pursued a music career? You should be at least singing with Van's band by now. He has to know how good you are."

She stared at the glowing stars pasted to the ceiling. "I don't know. You know, I used to want to be a doctor."

My head shot to the side and I gaped at her. She caught the look and chuckled. "I don't know where the idea came from, but for the longest time, I was going to go to a fancy college and be the best damn doctor on the planet. I used to have this Halloween doctor costume, little stethoscope and doctor's bag." She smiled to herself. "I used to wear it for so long my dad would have to pry it off me so he could wash it."

"What happened?" Obviously, she wasn't in school to be a doctor. She hadn't even gone to college. She left home with Van the moment she turned eighteen. Six years later and she was still with him.

"The wicked witch, my grandma, didn't like the idea and was always telling my dad to put me in etiquette classes and debu-tante balls. To train me to be a *proper lady*. Not to feed my *fanciful dreams*." She rolled her eyes. "But he never got along with his mom. He just doubled down in his own rebellion and it became more his dream than mine. At some point, it stopped feeling like an aspiration and more like an obligation. I never knew my mom, but I found these old tapes in the attic. She was so pretty." Her tone turned wistful. "She died when I was a baby so I never knew her. I hid those tapes in my room and watched them over and over. They were tapes of her singing to my dad on his birthday, singing to me when I was born. Standing in a room all by herself and just singing her heart out. She was singing in every one of them. I tried to ask my dad about her but he couldn't talk about her without getting clammy and upset. I got resentful that no one was willing to tell me anything about her and I don't know... I was young. I would imagine her as this amazing mom. Kissing my boo boo's and reading me stories. But I couldn't really connect with those images. I only had the tapes. Shy, she was such a good singer. Her voice so pretty. I started singing with her in the tapes and before I knew it, I was obsessed. It was the only connection I could have with her. I was singing all the time. I discovered boys around fifteen and met Van and his band and fell in love with music and that was it. I didn't want to be a doctor anymore."

Van was five years older than her, *at least*. It gave me all kinds of squickie vibes to know she met him when she was only fifteen. "What did your dad say?"

She chuckled again, this time a little thick. A little sad. "I stopped being his little girl and he pushed me away."

"He sounds like an asshole," I mumbled. So did her grand-mother, but I already knew about her. Mavis was never quiet about her loathing of that woman.

"He doesn't mean it. He's so smart you know? He's a scientist. His mind is always working, always developing and solving prob-lems. He didn't understand what fascinated me about music or Van. Without having anything to bond over, he became frus-trated and shut me out," she paused. "Or maybe it was the singing. Maybe I reminded him of Mom or something."

"You still don't talk to him?" I asked.

She shrugged against my shoulder. "I call him sometimes. Sometimes he answers. Sometimes he doesn't."

"When's the last time you were home?"

She fiddled with a loose thread in my blanket. "He lives at his lab, so home is with my grandma. She makes it hard to want to go home."

"You're really good," I told her. "Singing, I mean. You should be doing it for thousands of people."

She smiled at me. "I know... but I just can't do it."

"Why not?"

She turned on her side, playing with a lock of my hair. "You ever want something so bad you're afraid to reach for it? Like you could reach out but you're terrified it will shatter the moment you touch it?"

"Yeah." Walker was that thing for me. Before him, it was leaving home. I wanted it so bad but was afraid I'd fail. I was still afraid.

"I can't reach out. I don't want it to shatter," she mumbled sleepily, her eyes closing. "The dream is always better than the reality."

♪

THE NEXT MORNING WE WERE ON A FIRST-CLASS FLIGHT. I didn't know where to until we boarded the plane. "You have a show in Hawaii?" I asked Walker.

He grinned, his eyes gleaming with mischief. He shook his head slowly.

"We're not returning to the tour?" My voice was high and excited.

He shook his head again, watching me closely.

"Beaches and bikinis," Lake shouted, punching his fist in the air.

"Bitches and bikini's," Jameson shouted back with a sneer. Mavis sneered back and Jameson's face wiped clean—something akin to a blush coating his face.

"You lied to my parents," I accused, but I did it smiling.

"No," he rumbled. "They knew."

They knew? I tripped over my own feet, falling into a seat and Walker straightened me. "They lied to me?"

They *had* to like him. Mom might have gone along but *dad?* No way he would've agreed to lie to me or even let me leave early unless Walker had somehow won him over.

Excitement coursing through me, I hurried into my seat next to Walker's. He gave me the window and I bounced in my seat, grinning like a loon at Mavis across the aisle. "We're going to Hawaii!"

She whooped and stood to do a little dance, unaware of Jameson watching her bottom jiggle in her black leggings.

"Excited?" Walker asked me.

I'd never been to Hawaii. He had no idea how excited I was. "Best first date, ever."

♪♫

I'D NEVER FLOWN FIRST CLASS. THE CLOSEST THING WAS the trip to New York, and that was a whole other ball game, but first class was really nice too. The seats were wide and comfortable, and you got served full meals instead of the bags of peanuts and water-downed soda in coach. When Mavis started munching on snacks, Walker surprised me by handing me my cooler, fully packed. I knew my mom had put some things together, but I was shocked to see half of everything labeled with Walker's name. She'd packed for him too.

The flight was long but I shared a movie with Walker and dozed on and off. The entire time he touched me. A kiss here and there, or just holding my hand or knee or pulling mine to his.

Mavis sat with Jameson across the aisle. Her nose was in her notebook as he openly watched her, barely taking his eyes from her the entire flight. I'd never seen him sit so still or quietly. Once again, she was either completely oblivious to him or had a very good poker face. She neither encouraged nor deterred him.

We left the airport in blacked out SUVs to the sun shining and the smell of the salty ocean invading our senses.

Pulling up to a massive gated house, Lake took off for the front door as I walked more slowly tucked into Walker's side. Joe and the two other security guys grabbed most of our bags to bring inside.

Mavis skipped the house altogether and took off on bare feet down the side path to the empty beach beyond the house. Walker tugged Jameson out of his stunned Mavis-induced state by the arm until he fell into step beside us.

"Where did she come from?" Jameson suddenly asked me.

I watched her spread her arms out wide and throw her head back, letting the sunshine touch her face.

"Somewhere that didn't deserve her," was all I said.

The house was as massive inside as it was outside. Over six grand bedrooms, several bathrooms, a kitchen, dining room, cocktail room, theatre, and indoor pool. Then there was the wraparound porch that held loungers the size of beds overlooking the ocean.

Lake, in black board shorts, hopped on his feet as we stood on the porch. "We goin' out tonight?"

"No," Walker tugged me back into his chest as we watched the waves crest over the sand. "I'm takin' Shy out."

I looked up at him, my head leaning back against his chest. "You are?"

He looked down on me. "First date?"

Lake rolled his eyes and took off for the water as I smiled to myself. "Where are we going?"

"Secret." He guided me into the house and upstairs to a room at the end of a hall. Inside, he unbuckled a garment bag and spread it out on the bed. He unzipped it. "For you."

I peeked inside. It was the black dress from the day we took Brooks shopping. My voice breathy, I asked, "When did you get this?"

"That day." He ducked down to catch my eyes. "You like it?"

I loved it. It was even more beautiful than I remembered. "It's too much." I pulled it out and set it on the bed.

"Shoes in there too," he indicated with his head.

I dug into the bottom of the bag and, sure enough, there were the heels with studs on it—the same Brooks had bought for Reese, but black instead of pink.

I checked the sizes and looked over to him. "How did you know my sizes?"

His hands wrapped around my hips from behind. "You think I missed any of this?"

Back then, we hadn't touched. Not really. I flushed. I'd been doing a lot of that lately.

"Go on." He nudged me toward the bathroom. "I want to see you all dolled up."

I stood on my toes and pressed my lips just under his chin. "Thank you." He rumbled in satisfaction and made a move to grab me but I dodged him, shutting the door behind me with a thrilled laugh.

Showered, shaved, and lotioned all over, I blew out my hair. I was no expert with a makeup brush but I did all right. I didn't wear much, just a little something on my eyes and lips.

I let my hair hang down with its natural wave and pulled my dress on over the sexiest underwear I owned. A plain black thong. I didn't normally wear them much but the dress called for me to go outside my comfort zone and I couldn't wear a bra with it. The lacey silk was too thin and revealing around the chest, and the straps crisscrossed in the back and held me up. One cool breeze and the thin fabric would reveal my stiff nipples yet it made me feel sexy. I left the bedroom and walked down the spiral staircase, my heart fluttering.

Walker was leaning against the wall, his arms crossed and his eyes on the floor. My breath caught as my eyes roamed over him. He wore black slacks and shiny shoes, with a black button-down shirt tucked in around a leather belt. A perfectly fitting suit jacket hung open and the first few buttons of his shirt were undone, revealing a hint of his tatted colorful chest and neck. It was so outside his normal jeans, shirt, and boots that I nearly tripped over my own feet and fell down the stairs. He'd even slicked back his hair, the piercing in his left ear gleaming with a diamond.

"You look edible," Lake called from the kitchen, a spoon suspended by his mouth, a gallon of ice cream cradled to his chest.

Walker's head shot up and I watched his eyes flare, moving from my painted toes, up my bare legs, my belly and briefly stopping on my chest, then shooting to my face. He stood straight, his hands fisting at his sides before he shoved them deep into the pockets of his slacks. Holding me hostage with his predatory stare, he licked his bottom lip slowly as I stepped down from the last stair.

"Fuck off," he muttered to Lake before directing his attention to me. "Come here."

I walked to him, never feeling more beautiful in my entire life than I did in that moment as he visibly locked his body down until I stood a foot from him.

"Look at you," he purred.

"Look at you." My eyes taking all that was him in again.

His cheeks flushed just a little and my eyes locked on them, stunned. "You like it?"

I nodded fast, my chest heaving with how much I liked it. How much my body wanted to press against every inch of his.

He read me so easily, his eyes darkening. "Ready?"

Yes. I was so very ready.

20

The restaurant was outside on the beach but we didn't enter the pavilion dining area. A host stood outside by a private entrance and led us to a wooden walkway that led to an isolated quiet area on the beach. My fingers tingled as we approached a soft pad covered in silk under a canopy of gossamer curtains blowing in the breeze. Pillared candles sat in glass vases all around the silk pad and a small silver tray was at one end, holding two crystal glasses and a dark bottle in a fancy bucket of ice. It was intimate, held off in a secluded bend of the beach. Beautiful vegetation guarded us from the rest of the dining area.

Walker's smile was devilish as he took in the excited wonder overtaking my face. Holding his hand for balance, I gently toed off my heels and sat down on the silk bed, my legs curled to the side. Walker left his shoes on as he leaned against a pillowed back that offered even more privacy from any onlookers.

Stretching his legs out and crossing them at the ankles, he pulled me closer to him with a wicked glint in his eye.

"Your menu has already been approved," the host said. "I will leave you to your waiter," and with that he left.

"Our menu?" I asked him.

Walker lifted a dark bottle from the ice bucket. Sparkling water.

My eyes got a little misty as he poured one flute and handed it to me, then another for himself.

"It's water," I told him unnecessarily.

His eyes gentled and he dropped a quick but thorough kiss on my lips, nudging the glass to my mouth. It was cool and bubbly and I sipped at it, blushing.

It was not lost on me in that moment that I had been speculating a scenario like this one to my mother just last night. A fancy restaurant. Public. Limited options for me...

This could've gone bad. I could've either been so nervous to turn down the meal he so obviously called in ahead of time that I ate it regardless of the potential consequences, or I could've turned it away, ruining our night anyway.

But none of those things mattered when our waiter appeared with the first course, then the second and third.

I ate every delicious, completely healthy—Shy approved—bite in silence. My eyes watering so much it was hard to see all the beauty around me, including the gorgeous thoughtful man at my side.

As the last plate was cleared away and we were left in private, Walker tilted my chin up, his thumbs gently smoothing my tears away. "I see you."

I nodded, sniffling. He did. He saw every piece of me.

Walker leaned back, pulling me to his chest so my head was nuzzled under his chin and my legs lay the length of his. We were quiet and it was comfortable. I was so used to his demeanor that I fell into the peacefulness of it with ease. The only noise surrounding us were the crashing waves and the muted voices of the diners who were yards away. We'd never had this type of private opportunity before and deep down there was a swarm of questions *seething* to get out.

I ducked my head down on his chest, my fingers playing with glossy buttons on his shirt as his rough hand ran up and down my spine. "How was your dad?"

He stiffened. It was so slight I may have missed it if my body weren't almost laying on top of his. My belly churned with nerves. There was something going on and, much like he'd been when he found out about my medicine, my mind was likely wandering with far more outlandish possibilities than was really happening.

"Good," he rasped, leaning down to inhale my hair.

I stifled the relief his answer caused. It was no secret he didn't get along with his father. Neither did Jameson. Abandoning them when they were both young and never quite taking the time to repair that relationship when they were adults, it was completely understandable. But Walker had jumped to fly and see him the moment his dad called. That couldn't be for just a visit.

Part of me worried I was dancing too close to a line drawn in the proverbial sand. The other part of me knew I was falling hard and fast for this man, and with that came the undeniable urge to *know* him.

"You left kind of suddenly," I prodded.

He sighed, his chest lifting me a few inches before falling back down. But he didn't talk.

My eyes narrowed and I felt a little coil of apprehension move through me like boiling water. It was painful.

We didn't know much about each other and this was our first date. This was when a couple would learn about each other but, not only did he seem unwilling to open up at all, he never really prodded me either. Not since that day on the bus and when he'd called my mother. We never really got to know each other. I was on the unexperienced side of things, but I knew that wasn't normal when you had strong feelings for each other.

I sat up, drawing my knees up and hugged them to my chest with my dress draped between my thighs. Not the most sophisticated pose in a ridiculously expensive dress in a fancy private dining canopy on a Hawaiian beach. It was a clear position to offer self-comfort and he missed *nothing*.

He sat up, leaning close and turning my chin up. "What's wrong?"

My heart aching, the words bubbled up in my mouth and his intense eyes drew them out like a spew of dejection. "What are we?" I tugged my chin away and scooted back more to face him head on. "I mean, are we like a thing?" Just like my namesake, my words kept coming in a shy, disjointed mess. "We're a couple, right? Or is this just a tour thing? I don't know if I'm thinking too much and feeling too much. I just need clear directives so I know what to expect. My mind can kind of go off in every which way and my feelings can get involved too much or too fast and I don't want to hope for—"

He shushed me with a finger on my lips and an alarmed swirl in his eyes. "Yes. Yes to all of it."

"Huh?"

He moved me up into his lap, giving me no choice but to straddle him. My dress pooled high on my hips. It was indecent for public even if no one could see us, but I was enraptured by the earnest way he looked me in the eyes. "You're mine." A statement, not a question. "I'm yours," he added, forceful, like a demand. "Label it whatever you want, I don't give a fuck as long as I own all your smiles along with every other inch of you."

Relieved and close to bursting with happiness, I said, "Yes. Yes to all of that."

He smirked, but then his eyes darkened. "I got shit going on." No kidding. "Shit, I don't want you involved in."

"Bad shit?"

His jaw tightened. "Stupid fuckin' shit and you're too good for any of it."

"Can it hurt you?" I asked, tentatively.

I knew the guys got threats. They were hounded by the crazies of the world almost as bad as the media. Women who couldn't see through the trees and thought they had every right to touch and claim them when they didn't truly know them. Men who were envious and threatened by their success.

So many people were out there that wanted a piece of them. It was why they needed security with them everywhere they went. Even now, I knew Joe and another man was here, somewhere posted around the restaurant where they could keep an eye out for threats while still giving us privacy. Both armed and ready for anything.

But Walker chuckled, like he was amused. "No, Shy girl. No hurt's coming for me." Then he frowned. "Only you have that power."

I hated and *loved* that answer for so many reasons, but... "So, you're not in danger?"

He shook his head slowly, surely. "No."

My shoulders fell in relief. "Why won't you just tell me?" I grumbled.

His lips lifted ruefully. "Because there are far better things to occupy you with."

"Like what?" An answering smile on my lips.

"Like me," he rumbled against my mouth. "I want all your attention. I'm selfish as fuck."

I fell into his kiss, my body heating all over. His hands smoothed up my bare thighs and I almost let him, but...

"Wait," I pulled away with a gasp. "I have more questions."

"You got thirty seconds," he rapped out, his mouth dropping to my chest and running down the bare skin of my sternum.

My brain short-circuited for a minute as he pulled his hands from mine and dipped under my dress to play at my bare hips. "Color," I gasped. "What's your favorite color?"

Hooded eyes under dark lashes, his teeth flashed deviously and he nosed the silk around my right breast aside and his tongue poked out, flicking my hard nipple. "That pink your pretty silk skin flushes with. I want to see that color everywhere."

I shuddered, my legs spreading wider to drop more firmly onto his lap. Onto the hard-thick arousal of him. He grunted, his hands tightening on my hips. "Anything else?"

His tongue went to free my other nipple and circle it slowly. "I want to know everything about you," I panted out.

He smiled, trapping my nipple in his teeth and giving it a sharp tug. He rolled me over and leaned over me. "Ask and I'll answer," he rasped against my mouth. "But then we're outta here and I'm gonna get a taste of you."

I was totally down with all of that.

At first it was hard to remember everything I wanted to learn about him. There was just so much and he made it nearly impossible to think as he focused on my bared chest.

I was determined to delve into his mind when he was—somewhat—willing to indulge me.

Our surroundings completely fell away and I stopped worrying about who could catch us fooling around, who could see my naked breasts heaving under him as he lapped at them like they were the tastiest thing he'd ever had in his mouth.

Walker cared about me. I knew it in my bones. He wouldn't put me in a position to be embarrassed and so I focused entirely on him and everything he was doing to me.

I asked him everything I could think of.

Where did you grow up? With his uncle, like I'd suspected, in a big town house in New York City. I stayed far away from the subject of his sister.

Favorite movies? Fast cars and horror.

Books? Everything he could find on space and history—cue the wedding bells.

Pets? None, but he always wanted a kitten—again, could I drag him to the nearest courthouse or was that too much?

As I moved down the list, he got more and more frisky with his hands and his answers.

Foods? Shiloh's nipples.

Hobbies? Making Shiloh blush.

For my part, I filled him in on my answers and he did stop teasing me to listen like he was memorizing every answer. Every time I turned it back on him, he seemed more interested in making me squirm than anything else.

"Where do you see yourself in five years?" I asked breathlessly as he growled, finding the thong of my underwear and running his fingers down slowly, tracing it.

"Inside you, woman. I'll be deep inside you."

I nodded, wanting that so very bad now and all the years from now.

My hips punched up and I whimpered as his belt buckle hit me just right. He cursed and stood fluidly, pulling me up, tugging up my dress to cover my chest, and tossing me over his shoulder. "Time to go."

"Okay." My hands roamed down his broad back, my hair shielding our surroundings as he marched with determination to the car. With me slung over his shoulder. He avoided the light, sticking to the shadows and I didn't care one little bit if someone saw us because his hand was big and wide and warm on my thigh.

"Take care of that," he said to someone and I heard Joe grunt, his shoes clipping off the concrete.

"What?" I looked up, moving my hair out of the way and saw Joe redirect the host that had met us when we got here. Joe patted him on the shoulder and handed him something. The man nodded and disappeared.

Walker squeezed my thigh, his fingers just high enough that I trembled, unable to help myself from spreading my thighs a little more.

Walker chuckled darkly and flipped me up and then down, smoothly sliding me into the backseat of the car before he climbed in beside me.

He rapped something out to Joe as he took the driver's seat and then turned to me, taking my mouth indecently as he pulled me across his lap. He breathed out harshly, dropping his head into the crook of my shoulder and his hands dropped to my hips squeezing them tight.

I wasn't sure if I would've had the will power to push him away if he'd went for it in the car, regardless of Joe's presence, but he didn't. His chest rose and fell erratically against mine as Joe drove, his lips dragging up and down my shoulder, his teeth bared as air hissed out between them.

When the car finally stopped, I was out and over his shoulder again so fast my head spun.

"Where are we?" I asked, my voice so thick I didn't even sound like myself.

We weren't at the house. It was dark but there were trees everywhere and a one-story bungalow sitting at the edge of the beach. He stomped over a boarded walkway suspended above the water.

"Somewhere no one can interrupt me," he rumbled and went inside, flipping a switch to light a small elegant room with a giant bed and sitting area, and not much else. At the back was a sliding wall with sheer curtains to reveal the water that rippled under the moon just at the edge of a wooden veranda. We were literally floating on the water.

It was so pretty, somewhere you'd take your new wife on a honeymoon. Walker turned and shut the door behind us, the lock snapping in place with the sound of a bullet.

He walked to the end of the bed and set me down on my bare feet. One fast but deep lick into my mouth and then he was lighting several candles around the room and plunging us back into darkness. Between the candles and the moonlight reflecting off the water, we were cast in an ethereal glow.

He stood a few feet from me, his hands impatiently chucking off his jacket and popping the buttons on his shirt to shed it from his colorful chest.

Anticipation awoke inside me like a dormant beast and I trembled completely, my fingers tingling to touch him all over and explore every one of those tattoos.

"You're mine now," he crooned. The slide of his belt tantalizing. He threw it aside and unbuttoned his pants, leaving them to gape open and reveal that he wasn't wearing a damn thing under them. With determined strides he stalked me, backing me up until my thighs hit the silky sheets on the bed. "You ready for me?"

I nodded, my mouth as dry as a desert. So damn thirsty for the need in his eyes.

He moved slowly, gauging me as he ran his knuckles down my chest to the fabric that stopped him above my belly. He tugged it and me to him, dipping down to take my mouth with his. He licked inside my mouth. There wasn't a thing gentle about it. He was forceful, controlling, indecent in the way his tongue opened my mouth wide to taste every single inch.

I whimpered into his and clutched his shoulders, the warm skin lighting my fingers on fire.

"Touch me," he urged, tugging the hem of my dress up and over my hips. "I want your hands all over me."

I did as he demanded, my hands exploring every dip and valley of his wide chest. Captivated, I sighed into his mouth as they moved around his powerful back, my chest brushing against his.

His hands found my bare bottom, squeezing, and a pleased groan escaped the back of his throat, vibrating against my tongue. "You fuckin' turn me on like nothin' else. You know that?"

The evidence was pressed into my belly.

My legs shook under me as his fingers dipped down like they had earlier, tracing the fabric as it disappeared between my thighs. "I want you naked," he rasped roughly, his teeth scraping my cheek as he moved down to my neck to suck the skin there. "I want to lick and bite *every single* inch of you."

All I could do was touch him back with just as much desperation. Walker wasn't silent. His words for me were addicting. I was drunk on them. Drunk with the need to hear more.

When his fingers dipped farther down they found my arousal. He growled in approval and stood straight, ripping the dress over my head. Naked, except for my soaked panties, I stared at him in wonder. My bare skin shivered in the warm breeze. Air hissed from between his clenched teeth as he looked me over, his eyes wild and mesmerized.

His voice was so low and rough it scraped over me. "Bed."

Every inch of me a live wire, I scooted back, my eyes unable to leave his, and I laid flat on the sheets as they cooled my overheated skin.

He kicked off his pants, watching me take in every single hard inch of him. A needy sound escaped my throat and then he was prowling up my body. No part of me went untouched. From the tips of my toes to the bend behind my knees, his calloused hands scraped up them and I writhed as he stopped to inhale deeply between my legs.

Drowning in the possessive shine of his eyes, my lips parted as he shifted my panties to the side, his finger caressing me slowly. "Open for me, Shy girl." My legs fell open at his command and he licked his lips, taking me in. "This all for me?"

I nodded urgently, anticipating his every move.

He hummed above my skin and my heart punched up with my hips. He made me wait, driving my desperation to unbearable levels.

"You're soaked," he growled darkly, dipping down to draw his tongue top to bottom. My breath hitched and my hands fell to his hair, combing through the locks. He hummed again and I felt every vibration like the spark of a flame.

"Hold on to me," he demanded, and my fingers curled tight into his hair. The next few minutes completely washed every thought from my mind.

He spared me not an ounce of mercy. He licked into me with determination and one goal in mind—to drive me high and send me careening into wild abandon. I writhed under him, his hands an unmovable force on my hips to keep me exactly where he wanted me.

My wails stuttered out of me, his name a choppy chorus on my tongue. His mouth engulfed me, his tongue unforgiving as it lashed against the tight bundle of nerves. I throbbed with every stroke and nip, my fingers yanking at his hair and my body curling up and dropping down erratically to get away and then impossibly closer.

My mouth open to drag in air, I gazed up at the ceiling, seeing nothing but bright light as it ripped through me. Every muscle in my body spasmed as he consumed me. He then brought me back down gently. Lovingly. Caressing me softly. He worshiped my body as I caught my breath, my hands falling away from his hair to my sides.

He hummed again, his eyes watching my chest stutter up and down with avid satisfaction.

"That, that was..."

His eyes smiled and he moved above me, blocking out our surroundings with his body. "Sweet," he rumbled into my mouth. "So damn sweet." I clutched at him as his hands moved around my thighs, dragging them up and around his waist. "I'm gonna take you now."

I nodded, tasting myself on his lips.

His head dropped and he sucked on my aching nipples, soothing them before nipping until they stung. His hand came away and then he was sliding on a condom and then he was *right there*. So long and thick, my entire body tightened and my lips dragged up his neck unable to do more than pant in his ear.

He slid in slowly, his jaw tight. His eyes glittered with hunger as he watched my mouth drop open and my head tip back as he stretched me wide. "Hold tight," he commanded, his voice so rough I felt it all over me.

My arms came around his neck to bury into the slick skin of his back and my thighs tightened around his narrow hips. He pulled back out and then punched back inside, a groan tearing out of him. I watched, captivated as he lost himself inside me. His teeth bared as he watched himself drag in and out. His fists hit the bed on either side of my head. My hands couldn't get enough of the bulging muscles on his arms that were covered in tattoos and the thick veins of his forearms. His pace started to slow and then picked up speed, his head dropping to my chest again while his breath punched out of his lungs.

"*Fuck me,*" he groaned long and low, his lips latching back onto a nipple and sucking deep. My back bowed and my thighs widened for more of him. He sat up then, his hands tightening around my hips as he started to hammer inside me. My bottom on his thighs and my head tipped back to breathe raggedly, I felt every inch of him as he dragged out of me and then smoothed back inside.

"Walker," I panted. "*Please.*"

Air hissed out through his teeth but he kept at me.

My nails clawed at his back, my nipples tightening.

In my desperation, my right hand left him to relieve the pressure between my thighs. He cursed, pulling it away and caging it against my stomach.

"Walker," I pleaded, reaching with the other. He trapped that one too. Holding my wrists together in one fist above my head. My hips jolted with every powerful thrust and my neck strained as it curved away from my spine to dig deeper into the bed. I writhed, my feet curling around his back to clutch him tighter and he hissed again, twisting my arms down and behind my lower back and using his grip there to power me onto him.

I'd never felt anything like him. So determined to drive me out of my mind even as I felt his thighs tighten into rocks to hold back his own climax.

Moans and whimpers clawed out of me, my eyes stinging from the pleasure and pain of having him inside me, wanting it to last forever yet so desperate for the euphoria he held out of reach.

"*Walker,*" I begged. *Begged him.*

He snarled with approval, his thumb dropping to press against me. It was all I needed, I flew apart, my entire body tightening and straining. My breath fled and I shuddered uncontrollably, a hot flush spreading over every inch of me.

He released my hands and dropped down heavily on top of me, throwing my thighs up and wide with a tight grip under my knees as they continued to shudder. I whimpered as he hammered inside, his pace stuttering, and grinding his hips into where little bolts of electricity were exploding between my thighs.

"That's it," he growled, his voice guttural and then he was there with me. "*Fuck yeah.*"

His head dropped heavily to meet mine and he came, his hips jerking erratically as he gazed at me like he'd never seen anything more captivating.

Panting into my mouth, his tongue slicking over mine when he could draw in enough air to do so, he continued to watch me like that. Like he knew I was his all along, but now he *knew*.

22

The rest of the night cemented my feelings for him in stone. It was magical. So much more than I could've ever imagined.

I was irrevocably, undeniably his and he knew it.

After we caught our breath, he poured affection and caring into every inch of my spent body. He lifted me up and carried me out into the night. Both of us were naked under the moonlight. He slid into the ocean first, gently guiding me in after and into his arms. The water was so dark it was a deep pool of mystery, but my eyes were all for him.

He ducked into the water, slicking his hair back when he came up and guided my head back so he could run the salty water through my sweat dampened hair. His hands smoothed over me beneath the water—down my arms and around my chest to flick playfully at my tight nipples, then between my thighs to tenderly wash my arousal away from my sore lady bits. My legs curled around his hips and my chin rested on his shoulder to look out into the ocean. He held me up, his powerful thighs moving firmly through the water.

His voice was low as he whispered in my ear lovingly. I was *beautiful. So sweet* and *sexy,* and *all his.*

He was mine, I'd demanded back and he'd just chuckled, occupying my mouth with his tongue.

After a long swim he carried me back inside, stepping into the warm shower to rinse the salt away and then he dried me with so much care my eyes ached. He let me throw on a silky robe but untied it so he could cup my breasts from behind as I brushed my hair. All my things had been sitting on the counter, every last detail of our night together planned and carried out while we were eating on the beach.

I nervously eyed the little pill container sitting on the counter, knowing he could see it. Either he'd brought it or someone else had, but Walker had made sure I had it.

He rested his chin on my shoulder like I had in the water. His eyes caught mine in the mirror as he dragged the pill box closer with the tip of one finger. He was so large behind me, having to hunch down and around me and I relaxed back against him, knowing this moment would have come eventually.

I must have surprised him when I took the case and opened today's compartment because he stiffened and ducked down further over my shoulder, watching closely as I dumped the pills into my hand and poured a glass of water from the faucet.

I stood there frozen with fear and uncertainty as I debated. He looked so earnest, like he was memorizing what each pill looked like from their shape to color. My lips quivered as I picked up one and quietly, hesitantly, told him what it did for my body.

One by one, I held each of them up and explained their use before I swallowed them.

He was quiet until I finished, letting me swallow the last one down before he took my bare hips under the robe and gently turned me from the mirror to face him. "Scared?" He asked with a thick rasp.

I nodded, my eyes watering. "I don't want to scare you away."

"I have you, Shy." He hugged me and I felt enveloped in his warmth and strength. "*You have me.* Nothing you tell me could scare me away from you."

My mother's voice in my mind, his supportive and warm eyes locked on mine—I told him.

All of it.

Every last embarrassing, nerve-wracking, piece of it. Of Crohn's Disease.

And when I was done explaining how I got diagnosed, what led up to it, all the doctors and the fear of the unknown that followed, I didn't feel unburdened or even afraid. His attentive absorption of my words were too powerful and comforting to feel fear. But I couldn't feel relieved either as I got into my diet, my triggers, the depression and anxiety that fit so unerringly with all of it.

How it wasn't ever going to go away. I would always live with this disease. Some years might be better than others, but it would always be there, always at my back like a haunting shadow reminding me that my life could be thrown off course whenever the monster reared its ugly head.

Crohn's alone was a daunting force that affected me on a level that could be hard to comprehend. Something as simple as changes in season could cause a flare. Accidentally eating something that I either *knew* could make me sick or was completely unaware until one day my body decided it no longer wanted anything to do with it. Sometimes it could be a seasoning on a piece of chicken from a restaurant that I didn't know would be on it, or the oil it was cooked in.

I couldn't just go out to eat like everyone else. Walker had gotten lucky tonight, sticking only to foods he'd seen me eat, but the list was much, much more extensive and I needed complete control of what I put into my mouth at all times. Sickness, a simple cold or flu, could be so, so much worse for me. Bad weeks I could drop weight scary fast and need high calorie shakes to pull me back up, but actually ingesting them when I felt so awful could be harrowing for me.

Medicines that worked for me today might hurt me tomorrow. They could be ever changing, the doses always fluctuating and there was *always* side effects that accompanied them.

But Crohn's was never without its friends.

In itself, it lowered my immune system, leaving me open to more sickness and infections, but paired with medicine that lowered my immune system even worse? It was scary for me to even think about.

Brain fog could be common and I'd suffered from it from some of the medicines I'd been on before we found a better alternative. It starts out unnoticed... Forgot where to put my keys. Or my phone. But then you start to need daily notifications on your phone to take your medicine and a log so you remember you took them a few hours later.

Exhaustion comes from fatigue that can hit you like a brick, but some medications will keep you awake on top of that, and every-thing gets worse when you're so tired that all you want to do is sleep, but you're in so much pain it's impossible. You find your-self in a cycle of deliriousness because you can't do something that seems so simple to other people.

My body fought against me every day and with that comes consequences. It would get better and it would get worse. I had to prepare myself for anything which was impossible when you couldn't see or touch the thing that was threatening you.

I was alone in this fight but I wasn't *alone.*

I had my mother and my father. My steady pillars of strength and support. It was *imperative* that I kept myself surrounded with that energy and people that were gracious enough to gift it to me.

I wanted Walker to be one of those people. I craved it.

But it wasn't my choice. It was his.

I prayed that this disease wouldn't take him from me like it did so many other things.

He stood silently as he absorbed all the information I'd dropped at his feet. My heels ached from standing so long, I left him there in the bathroom and climbed into the bed, pulling the soft banket at the foot over me.

For a long time, he stood in front of the mirror, his eyes locked on the pill case holding this week's medication. I would need to refill it on Sunday. Laying down, I watched him as his head came up and he blinked at the mirror and then at his spread arms like he was confused. He looked over his shoulder and spotted me on the bed, his eyes flaring with relief. Like he'd lost me and then found me.

His naked body still bared to the room, he sat on the edge of the bed and watched me closely. Silently.

When he finally did speak his voice was quiet but it cracked through the room like a whip, startling me. "How are you feeling now?"

I picked at the ties of my robe. "I feel good."

He nodded, rubbing his hand down his face.

"You have to have questions," I said calmly. So damn calm. I was anticipating anything. Preparing.

He swallowed thickly. "I didn't know what to think," he started softly. "I knew something was up but not what." He prowled up the bed and made himself comfortable on his side next to me, curling me against his chest. "I'm relieved it's none of things I was thinking." He shook his head. "But, damn, I don't feel at all *relieved*."

"You can ask me anything you want." It was out there now, I just wanted to get all his worries and questions out in the open.

He inhaled deeply at the top of my head. "I just want to know when you're feeling bad, Shy girl. You'll tell me, won't you? I want to help anyway I can."

My eyes stinging, I nodded.

"*Damn*," he sighed out roughly. "I feel fuckin' useless."

"Why?" I asked, worried.

He growled in frustration. "I don't know about any of this shit and I don't want to fuck it up."

My smile wobbled. "You won't fuck it up."

He looked at me, his frustration and dejection written all over him. "No?"

I burrowed into him. "You're doing everything you need to do right now."

He huffed a grim laugh. "What's that?"

"Just being you," I sighed, content and so in love it filled me up like a balloon.

He squeezed me, his voice thick. "Alright, Shy baby, I'll keep doing that then."

I slept deeply that night. Cocooned in all that was Johnnie Walker Lawson.

He was more restless than usual, fidgeting in his sleep. Leaving the bed to jump into the water and swim laps then coming back dried and restless again. Twice he rolled me to my back and took his disquiet out on my body, both times slow and loving. Thoroughly satisfying me before he jumped up again.

I asked him if he was alright but he just apologized, cursing at himself and kissing me back to sleep.

None of it affected me though. He could wake me up a million times in one night and I would still wake up in the morning well rested and lively just having him near me.

But it still worried me. I knew he worked out a lot to stave off his insomnia, but I didn't know the cause of it, and I wanted to be able to help him.

The next morning, he put it aside and focused entirely on me. Pulling out my cooler and blender and watching me make my smoothie, even trying the green sludge—trying his best to hide his horrified disgust. I snickered, watching him gag and drank it up. After, Joe stopped by with breakfast and he scarfed it down before he pulled me out into the sun and into the water.

All morning we played in the ocean, every touch we shared a mischievous tease. Each of us growing bolder as we explored every dip and curve of the other's body.

But all good things come to an end and we were packing up to go back to the beach house before I knew it, looking back at the magical bungalow we christened our relationship in with melancholy.

The next five days were a dream. One I never wanted to wake from. We spent our days on the private beach, our evenings exploring the night life. I got to know Jameson and Lake in a way I probably never would've had the chance to on tour.

Mavis and I grew closer. I shared my secret with her and listened to all her worries, reassuring her and letting her offer me her comfort and love. Taking it and giving mine in return.

When we really were headed back on tour and not some exotic island, it was bittersweet. I was excited to get back on the tour even though I would miss the bedroom I shared with Walker every night. The privacy we had when he made love to me. I would miss the quiet moments with Walker as well as the loud ones with our friends. I would never forget those six days in Hawaii. I also couldn't wait to experience the future with the man that accepted my every dark fear. Charging through them without hesitation.

I was beginning to feel like he was mine. I felt confident in my position in his life and I wanted to feel that outside our seaside cocoon.

Too bad life had a way of knocking you down just when you started to climb high.

23

S ix weeks later and life looked much different than it had before.

I was in a committed relationship with a rock star. A man that women threw their panties at each night, screaming his name with desperate longing. A man that devoted every free minute of his time to little old me.

We shared a bunk on the bus every night for about a week before Walker lost his cool on Jameson and Lake, grabbing his brother in a headlock after one ill-timed joke about my breathy moans late in the night.

The next night we were in the back room of the bus, the equipment shoved to one side to make room for a full-size bed. A few nights later and all the equipment was cleared out and it became our bedroom. That we shared. Together.

Life was amazing.

I was taking pictures more every day until all my other jobs were taken over by a new intern my uncle hired. A young guy named Cale—Walker *hated* him. Cale had to shadow me for a while at first and didn't hide his interest in me.

The first time Walker caught Cale looking at my butt too long he threatened to, "Rip your dick through your asshole if you don't keep your motherfuckin' eyes off *my* Shy."

Walker then demanded him fired. My uncle found this so hilarious, he lost his breath and had to walk away to catch it after the laughing fit.

Cale wasn't fired but he was also too terrified to look at me at all, and so my uncle and Julie had to take over the rest of his training.

With more time on my hands to dedicate to my photography and a very specific *in* with the band, I followed them around all day —which made Walker very happy. And me.

He wasn't shy for my camera. Most of the photos I took of him— and there were *a lot*—captured him watching me with that ravenous hunger. His relentless need for me making nearly each photo of him too indecent to post. Mostly though, I was just too possessive of him to share those photos with the world. This also made him very happy. It didn't bode well for future shoots. My uncle loved the traction the band was getting online with the more candid look into their everyday lives, my photos artistic and tasteful, and thus a permanent position for me was opened.

I was the band's official social media photographer and was even shooting some group photos for their new upcoming album that

Jameson and Lake were hard at work writing. I didn't know if the label would really sign off on them, but it was fun playing with a few artistic ideas I'd had.

Mavis was still around a lot but as Jameson's interest in her got harder to ignore and way too intense for her, she avoided him whenever she could. And so sometimes me by association. Van noticed Jameson's eye following her every move and though he seemed upset at first, he now hounded her day and night to use it to get him more of a personal audience with the band. She was on edge from their constant fighting and I worried it was all going to reach its culmination and send her running.

I wanted nothing more than for her to leave him, but I also loved having her around. She was my best friend and made tour life that much more exciting and fulfilling. But I wouldn't be so selfish as to persuade her to stay for my own greed. I also didn't want her to go home where I knew her unique personality would be shut away from the world and drowned out by people who didn't understand all the amazing things she had to offer.

Walker and I grew so comfortable with each other that I found myself giving him my worries at the end of every day when we were laying naked in each other's arms. He was *the best* listener. Sometimes he'd listen for hours and offer a suggestion here and there. For the most part, he just listened and that was something I didn't even realize I'd been lacking in my life until he gave it to me.

Someone to just hear you and not try to fix every little thing.

I didn't always need the rusty nail pulled out of the problem, sometimes I just wanted to bitch about the nail, how tarnished and painful it was, how much I hated the stupid nail—and he got that.

But as fantastic as everything with him was and how perfect he treated me, he never opened up. Not why my uncle was always whispering in his ear. Why Julie seemed to grow more and more anxious as the days moved forward.

Something was going on and I wasn't afraid that it would hurt or scare me. I just worried that it was doing that to him and he wasn't letting me help him. I wanted so badly to be all the amazing things for him that he was for me.

I loved him completely. Unbendingly. Irrevocably. He was my every dream come true, wrapped in a sexy, quiet, tattooed sparkly package. So different from what my parents had ever imagined for me but in all the best ways.

The books arrived first. So many books on Crohn's. What it was. How to treat it. What to expect. What your partner can do to support you. It was that last one that filled my heart to bursting. He spent a lot of time reading that one.

He didn't shy away from the challenging aspects. The difficult insights and expectations. He devoured every bit of information he could get his hands on and when something confused him or he had questions, he didn't hesitate to pull me into his arms where he knew I was most comfortable and ask them. So I didn't allow fear to keep me from answering them.

After the books, he took on a more hands-on approach. Making my smoothies perfectly before I even opened my eyes in the morning. Gentle reminders about my medicine, not enough to be condescending or to make me feel like I couldn't handle it on my own but living every piece of it with me.

When I needed him to back off or I needed space from him—because sharing all of it with a person this closely was new for me—he gave me that space. No questions asked. He assured me he wouldn't always be so overbearing, that he just needed time to learn and then we'd find our comfortable space. A place where we both felt confident.

He was my mother's new favorite person. Because no matter how easy he tried to make it all for me, there were the harder things that I balked about discussing with him. The uglier side of the disease. Just how bad things could get. Those things that you never wanted the man you loved to know or deal with. So he turned to her, asking her about them and my mother was more than happy to talk it out with him.

What they shared, I didn't know, but after he called, she would be on the phone with me, gushing about how amazing and caring he was. That he was impressing my father, having their own talks—through phone games of all things. They had a running game of billiards on their phones and a stream of text where neither of them spoke to one another much but my father sent him funny baseball memes in between asking about me and Walker sent my father updates on me. Not about my condition, but about my happiness and life on the road. Just checking in.

It was another way for them to keep an eye on me and though that would've worried me before, worried me that I wasn't as independent as I wanted to be, but Walker was good about that too. He would tell me that my parents loving and caring about me didn't have to be a bad thing. That it didn't make me a burden. It made me their daughter.

I knew it wouldn't always be this amazing. That there would come a time we fought or got on each other's nerves but that was okay too because I knew we would get past those times. I was ready to tackle them head on because I was his and he was mine, and we wouldn't give each other up without a fight.

He didn't say the words and neither did I. I felt them every day and I hoped he felt them from me too. I was still a girl, with nerves and anxiety, and so I couldn't say them first. Not yet.

It was too soon. Too new. We had enough heavy back in that bungalow. I just wanted to enjoy the easy for a while.

♪

WATCHING HIM ON STAGE, SO ABSORBED IN THE MUSIC, I lifted my camera and snapped a photo of him. This one with his arms swung up in the air right before he brought them back down with a slam to create magic to the tune of thunderous excitement of the crowd. His hair was slick with sweat, his body gleaming in the spotlights. His eyes closed as he absorbed every beat, but there was a twist to his lips that was new. It was subtle, nearly undetectable unless you knew what to look for, but I knew, I saw it, and it was all for me. That little bit of amusement,

270

that little spark for me that said, "Yeah, I feel you watching me." It was *all for me.*

And when he stepped off stage and swooped me up in his sweaty arms to devour my mouth with no thought to who would see, no care for the pictures that would be everywhere in a matter of minutes, the world speculating about the girl that caught Johnnie Walker Lawson's eye, I walked away with my own subtle smile. The one that told him "Yeah, I feel you watching me." And it was *all for him.*

Like every other night for the last six weeks, I trembled in anticipation as I took photos of the band with their fans. Waiting for the moment that the last of them would trickle out and he would carry me off to the bus where we could shower together and hide away before the rest of the band found their way there.

The bus was now off limits after shows. No more parties. No more random women.

A teeny, tiny part of me felt guilty on behalf of Lake and Jameson, but when I hesitantly shared this with Walker, he didn't change his mind. His Shy stayed on the bus now and so that was a safe place where I could get a good night's rest beside him and wake up without having to dodge hungover bodies on my way to the bathroom.

Lake seemed to be the one who resisted this new Walker law the most but only briefly because deep down I think he knew things were changing and it wasn't just because of me.

Brooks was restless to get Reese on the road for the last leg of the tour in the states. Without Walker, it was only Lake and

Jameson single, but Jameson was really the catalyst to the change.

He just *stopped* partying. There were no more women that I was aware of. No partners in his bed at night. He still flirted, he was Jameson after all, but he didn't seem as invested anymore.

There were two reasons for this. One, he got really into writing new material for the album and so most of his free time was taken up in his head. When he shut himself away with his guitar and notebook, he barely came up for air. When he did, his eyes were all for Mavis. She seemed to completely enchant the singer and he couldn't pull away. I also suspected his new devotion to the creating and writing was inspired by her.

This thrilled my uncle. The label had been putting the pressure on for new material. It also made his job and so many others easier when the band seemed to slow down on the partying. Less mess. Less cleanup. I think that went a long way to him accepting that his niece was shacking up with the drummer. That and my mother's vocal approval.

Still, something was brewing. I could feel it in the air.

I wanted to discover it. Know it so I could confront it.

I had no idea I was so close to coming face to face with it.

♪

BACKSTAGE, AFTER FINISHING THE LAST FEW SHOTS, I packed my camera away. Walker was eyeing me with intent as he spoke with my uncle, his eyes heating on me and lighting me up. My mouth curved and I decided to rush back to the bus ahead of him. Mavis and I had gone shopping and I wanted to be waiting for him in the new pale pink panties I'd bought for him.

Cale stopped me just outside the door where the fans lined up to scream their love for the band. He looked harried and not at all comfortable enough to be talking to me.

"Shiloh," he panted, keeping his eyes above my head. "There's some guy at security asking for you. Tall, blond hair, wearing a black cap. I tried to send him away. He doesn't have a pass but he's insisting on talking to you."

I didn't know who it could be, hardly anyone ever asked for me, but just that alone made me think it was someone for my uncle. A suit even if he wasn't wearing an actual suit.

I jogged to the security line that held back the fans, smiling at one of the more familiar faces that traveled with us, Frank.

"You know this guy?" he asked me. A man in jeans and a hoodie with a cap covering shaggy blond hair at the temples stood tall beside him. While Frank held up a hand to hold him off, the man watched his surroundings, his face eerily blank, his eyes cold.

He looked familiar but I couldn't place him.

"Can I help you?"

His smile was slow. Dark and ominous. I immediately disliked him.

"Shiloh Green?" he asked me with a bite.

273

I nodded, holding my hand out to be polite. He shook it a little too tight and a little too rough and let it go.

Leaning in, he looked me in the eyes as his darkened into something sinister. "You know who I am?"

A warning went off in the back of my mind, and an internal instinct woke up at the sight of this man. "No."

"You should," he whispered, leaning too far into my personal space. "I know all about *you*." And then he rattled off my parent's names and address perfectly.

My stomach sinking to my toes, I backed away from him, listening to his pleased chuckle.

"You tell Johnnie Walker Lawson, Dane Frederick came by to see his girl." His menacing grin deepened. "That's you, ain't it Shiloh Green? Hard to miss when the two of you are plastered all over the place sucking face."

And with that he spun on his shoes and strolled away with his hands deep in his slacks.

"Shy?" Frank asked me.

"I have to find Walker." I went back inside on trembling legs. I had no idea what that was about or what that man was referring to, but I knew Walker would. That all of *that* had everything to do with what my uncle and Julie had warned me about.

Dazed, I entered the crowded room, searching for him.

He saw me as if he too had been looking for me.

My confusion and worry must have been sitting on my face because his darkened, and he immediately pushed through the crowd to get to me.

"What is it?" he demanded, his arms coming around me. "You feel okay?"

"I just met Dane Frederick."

Walker's face clouded with thunder and then I watched him explode.

24

"Lock him down," my uncle ordered Brooks and Joe.

Jameson stood in front of Walker, his hands up to placate him. "I didn't invite him here, man. Calm down."

Brooks and Joe surrounded Walker and wrapped him in their arms, trying valiantly to keep him from destroying any more of the room.

After Walker flipped the first table and the screams filled the room, Julie and my uncle had ushered everyone out, clearing it as he ravaged everything in sight. Bottles shattered. Chairs were broken.

I'd never seen this side of him and it terrified me. He was *angry*.

"Walk," Brooks urged. "You need to calm down."

"Fuck him," Walker roared back, struggling against the arms that held him against the wall. "The piece of shit came here! He fuckin' *came here* and got to her!"

I trembled as I watched the veins in his neck pop out, his chest heaving with his wrath.

"He didn't touch her, man," Brooks reassured him. "Look, she's fine."

"Get the fuck off me," Walker rapped out, straining and successfully ripping one arm from Brooks' grip.

My uncle, calm as I'd ever seen him, stood beside Jameson. "You'll be personally receiving the bill for this damage."

"Fuck the bill and *fuck you*."

"He's not going to touch her, Walk. He's just taunting you." Jameson stood tall, his voice calm as he tried to reach his brother.

"No!" Walker roared. "You did this shit! You're fuckin' up his goddamn ass again, aren't you?"

"Fuck you."

What was happening? What had this man done to the cool, sweet, drummer I loved so much?

Walker was unreachable though. Mavis had somehow found her way to me and held my hand in hers. "Go to him, Shy."

I gaped at her. Walker was like a bull and I wasn't naïve enough to step in front of him to flag him on.

She rolled her eyes. "He would never hurt you."

I knew that but still. I was trembling with the need to go to him, even though at the same time I was so confused and scared. Something bad was happening and I was completely in the dark.

I was *sick* of it.

She shoved me forward and I came into Walker's line of sight. His chest heaved up and down as Joe wrapped his forearm across his chest, Lake and Brooks both grappling with his arms. His eyes locked on mine and he just froze. Completely stiffened.

Seeing him so still, my feet suddenly moved, carrying me to him.

"Shy," my uncle warned, but I was already in front of Walker, looking up at him as air punched out of his nose, his jaw so tight I could see it pulsating.

From afar, his rage was terrifying but up close I'd never felt safer. I walked straight to him, burrowing into his sweaty chest. Air hissed out from his teeth and the hands holding him back fell away.

Walker didn't shove me out of the way, he picked me clear off my feet. "What did he say to you?"

I swallowed thickly, hearing the pain and shame in his voice. "He knew my name. My address."

My uncle cursed. "Jules, call Stephen."

She nodded and scurried off.

"Who's Stephen?" I asked.

"My father's lawyer," Jameson clipped, angry.

Everyone was quiet, waiting to see Walker's next move. I think he surprised everyone when he lowered his head onto my shoulder and slid down the wall to hold me in his lap. "How did he get back here?" he asked my uncle low. *"It's fuckin' bullshit."*

"What is going on?" I asked for the millionth time.

I was tired of them keeping me in the dark. Hadn't I earned their trust? Didn't I deserve to know?

It wasn't Walker that told me though, it was Jameson.

"Dane Frederick used to date our sister," he said dully.

"And he's been harassing Walker for the last few months," my uncle added dryly.

Jameson rolled his eyes. "Whatever."

I looked up, shocked and angry. "Why?"

Jameson sat against the wall beside us, tipping his head back. "Walker beat the shit out of him after our sister died, he was our dealer."

Walker sat stiffly, his hands smoothing up my back.

"He blames Walker for her death," my uncle added.

Jameson huffed a dry laugh. "He doesn't blame Walk for her death."

My uncle's shoes clipped off the floor as he stood above us. "Yes, he does," he told Jameson. "But that blame is misplaced."

Jameson just shook his head, looking down at his lap. "Won't that shit ever die?"

"What is it?" I asked softly.

My uncle looked over his shoulder, everyone except us four had left the room so quietly I hadn't even noticed.

"It doesn't leave this room," my uncle warned me.

"Quit it," Walker rapped out. "I trust Shy."

Maybe now, but he hadn't weeks ago. He hadn't yesterday. Not until he had no choice but to tell me and that stung more than I wanted to admit.

My uncle still looked wary but he opened his mouth and told me. And I couldn't have been more shocked if a dancing elephant had rolled into the room.

"Jameson was with their sister when she died. But Walker covered for him."

♪

MONEY WAS A POWERFUL FORCE. IF YOU HAD ENOUGH YOU could cover up anything.

The Lawson brother's father may not be close to them. He may not be loving or supportive but he had done something pretty awful when Jameson and Walker were young. He'd thrown his money around to cover up something that was so bad any other person without money or privilege would've had to stand before the world and answer for.

Not Jameson. He may not have shot or stabbed anyone or committed any other crime. But he still had been with their sister when she took those drugs. He'd allowed it to happen, and it had killed her.

I could see how much pain his actions caused him still. The man I thought as carefree was only surface. Deep down he was in a world of pain and guilt.

I didn't know the legal ramifications. It was Dane that had given both him and their sister the drugs, but Jameson had been there and then ran before that could be discovered. He was only sixteen at the time, but he got away without having to pay for his choices.

Not outside of having to live every day for the rest of his life knowing he unwittingly had a hand in ending his fifteen-year-old sister's life.

No, Walker had paid for that.

Young and spoiled, hurting after his mother died and his father abandoned him, Jameson Lawson lost himself in a world that was bigger than himself. He got caught up with the wrong people and found drugs and alcohol to dull the pain.

His sister, young and worshipping her brother, followed behind him.

Living with an uncle that encouraged bad behavior, he didn't have a stable home or someone to lean on. No one but Walker, who was struggling with the death of his mother in his own ways. Jameson tried to dull the pain while Walker chose to face it head on.

Only a year apart in age, I could feel that Walker felt responsible for his sister's death. Not catching onto her relationship with an eighteen-year-old drug dealer. For his brother's part in it and not seeing the drug use when they were younger. So when he found Jameson passed out in a hotel room and lying beside their sister, her body already cold, Walker chose to do something to save his brother. The only sibling he had left. Something awful but born out of love.

He'd held his sister's lifeless body, covered for his brother, took the heat from the police and then lost in a rage, attacked Dane and went to prison for it.

Walker served only three years for putting Dane in a hospital with a broken arm and nose, a concussion and various other injuries and when he got out, it was erased by his father's money and power like it had never happened.

I didn't see how that could be possible. It was always going to be found out. Walker's interrogation and court hearing may have been sealed, but nothing could be hidden away forever. Not if you were in the public eye.

Their father was so consumed with covering up a crime in their name he had failed to realize Walker was protecting his brother. Failed to dig deep enough to find the truth. That not only had Walker not been involved, but it wasn't Jameson that had given their sister the drugs, but in fact, Dane Frederick, her boyfriend.

"Why didn't you tell me?" I asked him later that night in bed. Both of our clothes still on and shoes still on our feet.

Walker sighed. "I don't regret any of it. He's my brother and that fuckin' asshole deserved everything he got."

I didn't understand that kind of loyalty. I didn't have any siblings. I wanted to accept that there were some things of Walker's that weren't mine to have, but I loved this man so completely. I ached for him.

"What are you going to do?"

Dane had shown up for a reason. A threat, a warning, something. My uncle had sent everyone away, stating he'd take care of it.

"We went to see my father," he reminded me. "He's stepping in. Jameson didn't want to believe it. He still feels guilt and he connects with Dane over her death. I don't understand it."

"Why doesn't he hold Dane responsible?"

Walker laughed dryly. "Fuck if I know. His own guilt, he was just a kid. He and Layla both were."

"Is he going to come back?"

Walker shook his head. "I don't know, but I won't let him near you again."

"And Jameson?"

I didn't know Jameson well, but I worried about him. He may not do drugs that I knew of, but he drank an awful lot.

"Fuck James. I lost my shit, Shy," he suddenly bit out. "It won't happen again."

I had a choice here. I could get lost in the thing that was kept from me. Worry that him keeping it a secret meant there could be more. I could get stuck in my own feelings and worries. Or I could move on from them.

Walker had never given me a reason to question his commitment to me. Not really. Anytime I questioned it before was because of my own insecurities.

I loved this man. But loving someone was more than good, easy times. It was loving the hard stuff too.

"I don't want you afraid of me," he rasped, rolling on his side to face me.

"I'm not afraid of you," I told him honestly. "I'm worried about you. About Jameson."

His thumb smoothed over the worry wrinkles lining my forehead.

"This is why you don't sleep well?"

He frowned. "Part of it. I've always struggled with it. My ma said I was like that as a baby too. But I get nightmares sometimes. My sister screamin' for me."

I blinked away a fresh round of tears.

"Will you tell me about her?"

He tugged me closer. "Layla was beautiful, Shy. You'd have loved her."

"If she was anything like you, I know I would have."

He hummed, gazing out the small window.

"Did she like music too?"

"Fuckin' loved it," he grinned. "Could sing like an angel."

I listened to Walker open up to me, curled against his chest. He didn't seem hesitant to talk about her. It was more like he couldn't wait to get it out.

"I didn't know she was dating that guy," he rasped quietly a little while later. "I would have killed that punk if James hadn't pulled me off him." He sighed, tightening his hold on me. "He was a kid too, but he knew it was wrong. All of it. He should've fuckin' told me or stopped it himself."

"Why does Dane think you killed her?"

"Cause he thinks I was with her. It's not that he thinks I killed her, he did that." He closed his eyes tight, as if shutting out bad memories. "He hates me because I didn't save her."

"You couldn't have."

His chest rose with a large breath. "I know it. But I still can't stop thinkin' if I'd just payed more attention. Caught on..."

"Walker."

He shushed me, hiding his face in my shoulder. "I fucked up that night. Lost in my own shit. I should've been there. But I don't regret fuckin' him up. He gave her those drugs. I wished I hadn't stopped until he was dead."

⁂

After almost an hour, he looked down, a question in his eyes as his mouth hovered over mine. I closed the distance between us.

Easy, no thought to it.

Nothing had changed. Life just got a little harder. A little scarier, but I still felt for him today what I did yesterday.

"What are you going to do about Dane?"

"Let V deal with him." He grinned then, but it seemed forced. "You keep me busy, Shy girl. I ain't got time for much else."

I smiled, falling into his heated kiss.

"You still mine?" he asked.

What else could I say? "Always."

I'd found my Superman and I wasn't letting him go.

25

Walker had said he was going to let my uncle deal with Dane.

But it was only a day later that I learned how impossible that was going to be.

I also learned just why my uncle, Julie, and Brooks were so worried about mine and Walker's growing relationship.

It wasn't ever Walker or his past, not exactly, but about the man harassing him.

Dane was not going away quietly.

The night before had heralded a very serious threat. A threat Walker now had no choice but to acknowledge.

He didn't think anything could touch him. That he could keep all of it from me.

But he had been so very wrong.

Dane Frederick spent all his time and attention making it very clear he could get to Walker through me.

He got my phone number, likely the same way he did my address. He called it over and over. The first time I'd answered, completely unaware of the dangerous man on the other side of the line, he had just laughed. Laughed and laughed until I slammed the phone down.

I'd been unsure if I should bring it up to anyone, particularly Walker before the show, but the choice was taken from me as Dane continued to call over and over and over.

I would have turned my phone off if not for needing it to contact my uncle or Julie while running around the venue grounds.

I was with Brooks the tenth and final time he'd called. Brooks had looked down at my phone as it rang and rang in my hand, snatching it from me as he recognized the number.

Without a word, he put it under his boot and smashed it to pieces. "Can't use it anymore," he informed me gruffly, dragging me to my uncle so I could spill it all at his feet.

I was given a new number, worried about having to explain it to my parents, but that choice too was taken away from me.

Not only had my uncle had a long talk with my father, but he had explained to me that it had to be done. The situation was getting too precarious, but I'd quickly found out that they too had been getting strange calls. In the middle of the night, throughout the day.

A man, just breathing. Never saying anything.

My father lost his mind and demanded to speak to Walker. My uncle calmed him down and I never knew if my father ever talked to Walker that day, but my parent's number was changed immediately.

The worst of it was when my uncle had to tell him this Dane freak had my parent's address. That he'd used it to threaten me.

Both Dad and Mom had immediately demanded I come home. It was only my uncle that convinced them otherwise.

The tour was the safest place for me right now. That and I was always surrounded by security.

Everyone had been briefed on the situation.

Everyone knew.

It wasn't long before the media caught wind of it.

It was going to happen eventually. Why it took Dane showing up and threatening me for it to happen I had no clue. But it was out there now.

Walker Lawson had a stalker.

Walker Lawson beat a man when he was eighteen and now that man was harassing the new woman in his life.

Everyone was talking about it.

In a matter of twenty-four hours, everything had changed.

Including Walker.

He was quieter than normal. Broodier. He was also a mix of extremely protective and emotionally distant.

He kept by my side most of the day apart from the show that night, but we barely spoke.

I missed him. I wanted the smiling eyes and rumbling words back. I wanted *him* back.

I got Jameson instead.

Jameson, who on any other day would have been annoying, vulgar, or full of energy, or all of those things, was solemn. He stuck to my side like glue. Well, as close as Walker allowed him. Which wasn't close at all.

Jameson watched me from afar though. Not necessarily *me* but my surroundings. He may not have believed Dane was a threat but that was before last night.

Late that night, I crawled out from beside Walker, his back to me. I could tell he was awake, his legs twitching as if he needed to run or work out, but apart from rolling over to watch me dip into the bathroom he didn't say anything.

I took my time, dreading climbing back into the bed beside the man who would have held me close last night but not tonight. Jameson was leaning against the wall when I finally walked out.

I looked from him to the bedroom I shared with his brother.

"He's watching, but I need to talk to you."

Surprised, I followed Jameson to the small dinette, peeking into the bedroom. Walker sat on the end of the bed, hunched over, watching me closely.

I sat down gingerly, my attention torn between the brothers.

Jameson fell into the seat, his head in his hands. "I'm sorry, Shy."

I blinked, focusing on him. "For what?"

"I knew he was callin' Walk and V. He called me too but I swear I never answered except that first time a few months back. He was fuckin' cryin', losin' his mind about Layla. It's been years, but I still feel her as if she were here yesterday, you know?" He seemed to curl into himself. "I miss her. I fuckin' miss the shit out of her. It felt good to share that pain with him. Until it didn't. I knew somethin' was up with him. That he was this worked up over her all these years later. I was her brother and though they were datin' I never thought it was serious. The more I think about it. The more I can't help but think it's not healthy to still be that fucked over a girl you only dated a few months. For me and Walk, it's okay. She deserves that from us. But not him." He leaned into me. "He ain't right in the head. But I couldn't see past Layla. I didn't think he'd go this far."

He sat back, sighing and scrubbing his face.

"I, uhm, it's okay. I don't blame you or anything," was all I could think to say, just kind of stunned he'd spewed all that out to me.

He shook his head. "No. You should blame me. All this is my fault. Layla. Walk goin' to prison. Now this? I should have stopped all of it. Should never got mixed up with him when I was kid. I was fuckin' stupid."

Hesitantly, I reached across the table for his hand. He flinched but let me touch it. "It's okay, Jameson. I can't begin to understand how it feels to lose your mom. To let that loss fuel your choices. And I hope I never do. You all were young."

He clutched my hand tight. "I don't know why he's doin' this. If he really is workin' up to somethin', but you gotta know we won't let him near you again. Walk would kill him before that happened."

"I'm not worried," I told him honestly. I never had been. I was worried about them. About Walker. Now, strangely, for Jameson too. "It's going to be okay."

He seemed to doubt my words but his smile came a little easier than it had lately. "Big bro seems to think you're somethin' special."

My cheeks flushed and I sat back, pulling my hand away. "Yeah, well..."

"Sorry I've been an ass," he told me somberly but that grin was still there. "If I'm bein' a prick just call me out on it, all right?"

"Every single time?" I shook my head. "I'm not sure your ego could handle it."

He huffed a laugh, slapping the table. "Good talk. I'm gonna hit the sack."

I watched him go, a little astonished that he'd spoken to me at all, let alone so seriously. About something so sensitive.

I believed him that he'd only spoken to Dane that once and I couldn't begin to imagine the pain that had driven that conversation. And I didn't know if there was any truth or not to him using again. It didn't seem like it, but I didn't have much experience with drugs or people that took them.

But I was happy to have talked a little of it out with him.

Now if only I could get his brother to break his silence.

Unfortunately, I was in for a long wait.

⚜

THINGS WITH DANE ONLY GOT WORSE. WHEN HE COULDN'T call me, he started sending care packages. Little notes that were mailed with flowers or stuffed bears. Strange, cryptic warnings about something coming.

The police got involved pretty quickly. If they hadn't been already.

I stopped receiving my own mail, my uncle taking that over.

Dane was missing. The police couldn't find him.

The threat seemed minor right now, but Walker and my uncle weren't taking any chances. I was never to be alone and that topic of me leaving the tour had come up on more than one occasion.

Most surprisingly of all, it was Walker that brought it up. Over and over and over.

He wanted to send me off somewhere. Somewhere private. Where I couldn't be photographed or seen with him.

Walker seemed to do a complete one-eighty on me. We still slept in the same bed. He was still everywhere I was, but he was so emotionally distant he might as well have been on another planet.

He hadn't initiated a single intimate touch between us. It was always me reaching for him and him gently rebuffing me.

A week of this and I finally reached my breaking point.

"You weren't worried before," I told him as he paced on the bus. We were headed somewhere new.

City names and roads blended together. I didn't even know where we were anymore. Everything looked the same now.

I was exhausted. My stress levels at an all-time high. And I was worried. Not about Dane and whatever stupid vindictive vendetta he had.

I was worried about Walker. The state of our relationship.

"That was before," he barked back, his temper flaring with me for the first time.

But I knew this man. Loved him. He would never hurt me. I stood up, catching myself against the table as the bus swayed. Even then he stalked over to stabilize me, even as he scowled. He still stopped whatever he was doing to physically watch over me.

"You told me yourself," I reminded him. "He's nothing. He doesn't matter. You're not in danger, remember?"

"Not me, Shy. You," he rumbled. "I'm fuckin' worried about *you!*"

"Then you should have never touched me in the first place!"

"Guys," Brooks called from the bunks, his worried eyes peeking from his curtain.

"No I shouldn't have," Walker shouted over him.

I blinked, taken back. "So what? You're breaking up with me now?"

"Yes. No, I don't fuckin' know."

I pressed my palm against my chest as if I could hold my heart inside as it throbbed to break out. "I don't care about him."

"It's not the right time, Shy," he softly told me.

My eyes immediately watered, a ball of dread thickening in my throat. "I don't care about him," I told him again.

"It was fuckin' dumb. Draggin' you into this."

"Don't do this," I begged, fucking *begged*. "I don't' care about Dane. Please don't do this."

"I won't let him hurt you," he told me, reaching for me.

I backed away, a sob ripping from my throat. "Don't send me away."

"It won't be for long," he whispered achingly tender. "Just until we find him. He wants me, Shy."

"Walker," Jameson called from the bunks. He, Lake, and Brooks, all stood there, watching this fight. "Won't it be better if she's here where we can watch her?"

"I'll hire a security team. He won't get close to her. There's too many people here, I can't risk him finding a way inside."

"How fuckin' bad is it?" Brooks asked, angry now.

Walker sighed. "He sends her letters. Outright threatening to come here for her."

"That escalated quickly," Brooks muttered.

"Why Shy?" Lake asked.

Walker growled, kicking the couch. "I don't fuckin' know what's in that psycho's head. But I won't risk it."

"He wants to take what you took from him," Lake said, watching me closely.

"He didn't have Layla," Jameson barked. "Don't fuckin' say shit like that again."

Lake held up his hands backing away.

"Let him come then," I told him. "Uncle V has Joe on me all the time. He'll catch him and this will all be over."

"Shy," Walker whispered. "I can't risk you."

"And if he never shows his face?"

The answer was written all over his stiff stance. Then we were done. If only to keep Dane from having a reason to come after me. Even if it were ten years from now.

I hunched over, holding my stomach as I choked on my own pain. Sobs wracked my chest.

"Shy baby," Walker whispered, picking me up to cradle me. "Don't cry."

"Don't send me away," I choked out.

He shoved past the guys, laying me down on our bed and curling around me. "Don't cry, baby. Please. I can't fuckin' take it."

I hid my face in the pillow, my entire body shaking with the pain of losing him.

"Come here," he tugged me over, pulling me to him and holding my face against his chest. I grabbed onto him, my fingers curling into his shirt with the intent to never let go. "If I'd known this would have happened I never would have touched you."

Just the very idea of him never touching me was so abhorrent, I sat up, shaking him off and crawling off the bed.

Angry now, I stood, meeting his eyes as he sat up. "I love you."

I said it angry. Not at all how you should tell your entire world how vital they were to you.

He eyes filled with something beautiful and tender and I looked away, slapping the tears from my face. "If you send me away, fine. But know that I love you and I'll be waiting for you."

With that I stomped out of the room, slamming our bedroom door shut and locking myself in the bathroom where I could stare at the floor and cry out my pain in peace. Where I could wallow in self-pity all the while loving him for wanting to protect me. Loving him for sending me away even as I hated him for it.

"When do you leave?" Mavis asked the next day, sulking along with me as we tossed breadcrumbs to the ducks in the lake.

I'd begged Joe to take me away from that night's venue. Walker was busy with sound check and I needed the space from him. Uncle V had agreed to let me go, already having heard Walker's plans—plans he was now apparently on board with. Something must have happened with Dane for him to change his mind.

My uncle thought it best for me to take some space and come to terms with their decision. And I had Joe, Frank, and two other security with me.

"Tomorrow morning."

Walker wasn't wasting any time. I didn't know where I was going. One of his friend's places.

Stone Belvore was his name. He was ex-military and had grown up with Walker. Walker told me he didn't trust anyone on the planet more with my life.

He still hadn't told me he loved me.

It bothered me to know how much I'd been waiting for the returned sentiment.

"Want some company?" She asked me, angrily tearing at a hunk of bread.

I glanced at her. "You want to?"

"Is my best friend going to be there?"

"Yes?"

She nudged her shoulder with mine. "Then that's where I want to be."

"Thank you," I told her, my throat closing up. But I was out of tears. I'd cried them all out last night.

"How are the 'rents handling all this?"

I sighed, already wary about the dozens of missed calls. I wasn't ignoring them. The opposite. I talked to them several times today already. They were happy about me leaving the tour. They already had plans to meet me at this undisclosed location. They didn't blame Walker, but my dad certainly wasn't happy with him either.

I felt like I'd taken one giant step back on my path to independence. I wasn't sure how I was going to regain it.

"They keep calling." All day long. She shot me a pitying smile and I groaned. "I'm so mad at him."

"I get that," she nodded. "But I also get him."

"You're supposed to be on my side," I reminded her.

She chuckled. "I am. Always. But if he and V are this worried about this guy, maybe you should heed it."

"I'm in stupid, careless love," I sighed wistfully. "I'm not worried at all about my own safety."

She leaned her head against mine. "Good thing you have a big strapping rock star to worry for you then."

Yeah, good thing. It still felt like the end of my whole world.

♪

IT STARTED WITH A STOMACHACHE. JUST A LITTLE ONE. A little nauseous, nothing serious.

I was so consumed with leaving Walker that I barely had time to pay it any attention.

But steadily throughout the day it got worse.

Sharp little pains that had me bending over, cradling it.

Panic kicked in pretty quickly then and pretty soon it was *all* I could focus on.

I located the nearest bathroom with not a second to spare. Then I spent most of the show locked away in the bathroom, angrily fighting tears as I fought back the pain. Every time I thought I would be okay, I was doubled over, cradling my stomach. Back and forth to the toilet.

From here, I knew from experience, it was only bound to get worse.

And it was at the worst possible time.

Exhaustion hit me pretty fast. During a flare-up, the symptoms could come on slowly or all at once. When they came on fast like this, I knew it was going to be a bad one.

Anything could have started it. But it was likely the stress of the last few days that did me in this time.

Joe sat outside the door, occasionally knocking to check on me and that only made the entire ordeal that much worse. I had a spectator to my pain. Even if I could have made it to the bus, it was the last place I wanted to be so close to the end of the show. I did not want to be anywhere Walker was going to be.

So I sat there, refusing to move until I was sure my stomach had calmed.

Unfortunately, that turned out to be a *long* time.

Walker found me instead.

My quiet, murmured, *I'm fine's,* did nothing to reassure him. He burst through the door, thankfully as I was sitting on the floor rather than the toilet.

Seeing him there, looking down on me so damn *worried,* broke me.

I just completely lost it. It was like an explosion of emotion. Nothing I said made any sense as I babbled through my sobbing wreck of an explanation.

He crouched down, his hands smoothing my damp hair away from my face. Likely, the smell of my vomit and other things assaulting his senses, but he didn't show it. But I knew. *I knew* and I was *mortified*.

"Just go away," I sobbed, curling away from him.

"Shy," he rasped. "Come here, baby. Let me take care of you."

"I d-don't want y-you to."

He ignored me, picking me up carefully and cradling me as he stalked from the bathroom. "There ain't a damn thing for you to be embarrassed about," he whispered quietly in my ear. "Not with me."

I hid my face in his neck, shutting out Mavis and Julie's concern. I hadn't realized they were waiting out there with Joe.

"What do you need?" he asked, walking at a clipped pace. "Heating pad? I got it in the room. You need meds? Water? Tell me."

"I just want to lay down," I choked out. Alone. Where he couldn't witness my pain. I didn't want our last night together to be full of this.

But once again, my body didn't care what my mind wanted. It had its own battle to fight.

♪

THE REST OF THE NIGHT WAS SPENT WITH HIM HOVERING AT my side, fretting over me in a way I *loathed*.

All I could do was wait it out, call my doctors, discuss a new dose of medication and pray it calmed the inflammation instead of needing something stronger.

I had my normal rituals during moments like this. Mostly sleep, heating pad, and lots and lots of water. Then there was a cream to prevent sores. I hated that the most because I knew Walker was just outside the door, listening just in case I needed him.

I did *not*. I wanted to be alone.

It could have been something I ate. Coupled with stress. Hopefully just an irritated bowel. But it could also be more than that. But whatever it was, Walker got his first taste of what life would be like with me that night, but only just a small experience in the grand scheme of things. He wouldn't be around the next day. He wouldn't be there for the doctors or tests, if I needed them. He wouldn't be there if it all blew over as nothing more than a bad night.

He would only see *this*. He would remember me *this way*.

I was terrified it would be a lasting impression.

We had the bus to ourselves. I wasn't sure where everyone else hid, but I was grateful I didn't have any more spectators.

I barely caught a wink of sleep even though that's all I wanted to do, I couldn't. I hurt all over and I made regular trips to the bathroom. Sleep was out of the question.

Early morning, my uncle came to check on me. Only an hour before I was supposed to be on a flight.

I think it was then that it was really hammered home how exhausted I was. Just how unable I was to get on a plane. My stomach had thankfully calmed a little by then but I needed sleep badly. I could barely get out of bed, and Walker took a beat before demanding I not move the rest of the day.

I wasn't even capable of feeling justified about the change of plans. I just wanted to feel good. Better. But all I could do was curl up in a ball and doze fitfully.

"I'm sorry," I told him groggily sometime later that day. I wasn't even sure of the time.

"Don't you dare apologize," he told me, smoothing my hair back. "You'll go when you're feeling better."

And so nothing had changed. I was still leaving. If anything, this only cemented in his mind the need for it. He wanted me somewhere safer but now also calmer. Somewhere I could rest and get better.

"Will you miss me?" A small broken part of me asked him late that same night.

"You fuckin' know I will, baby," he whispered back, holding me tight. "There's nowhere I want you but with me."

"Then keep me with you."

"When it's safe," he told me gruffly. "When that fucker is locked up."

"I hope they catch him," I bit out vehemently.

"So vicious," he teased, humming against my throat.

I was angry. Vicious, sure. But Dane was fucking everything up for me. My love life. My personal life. My work life. My health, I even blamed on him. He was taking everything from me and I hated him for it.

♪

THREE DAYS LATER, MY STOMACH WAS CALMER. THE MEDS doing their job.

And I was preparing to get on a plane.

Joe was taking me after the show. Me and Mavis. We were catching the red-eye. I was not looking forward to it. I sulked the entire time I packed.

Walker watched me from the bed, his eyes heated on me but he didn't reach for me. And if I weren't suffering from my period, I would have questioned if that was because he might think me gross now.

Stupid, ridiculous insecurity, but it was there all the same.

I was a little crampy. A little tired, but whether from my Crohn's or mother nature, it was manageable. Much more than it had been three days ago.

We left the bus together. Not touching in case a picture was caught somewhere. Walker was taking every precaution not to insight Dane's anger. Photographers and fans weren't allowed backstage but that didn't mean there weren't crew. Both the band's and the arena's. They weren't concerned with a psycho so I couldn't blame them for snapping a photo on their phone—other than it being a little rude. But Walker was a man you couldn't *not* snap a picture of when the moment presented itself. Hell, I did it all the time. But the outside world came with the territory.

I could tell it was wearing on him. We hadn't been the same since Dane showed his face. Our easy comfort was missing and that wasn't like the man I knew and fell in love with. He was in my space all the time before. Touching me whenever he wanted. And I returned the favor. Not so much now.

"You're going to call me when you land?" He asked again.

"I'm going to call you all the time," I teased.

He winked at me. "You bet your sweet ass."

"You're going to get sick of me," I warned him.

His eyes dancing, he scoffed. "Never."

"I hope so," I whispered back.

Stopping outside the dressing room doors, he turned to me. "This'll get worked out, baby. I won't let it go on forever."

"And if you can't fix it?" I couldn't help but ask. Irrationally scared Dane would hide forever, threatening from afar for the rest of our lives.

"You trust me?" he asked, his face filling with intent.

My eyes aching, I nodded. "You know I do."

"Then you know nothing will keep me from you."

I wiped at my eyes with my sleeve. "You better not find any more shy girls while I'm gone."

He smirked, briefly tugging at the shirt on my belly. "You're my only girl, Shy. I don't want to find another one."

"I want to kiss you," I whispered, aware of the people walking through the hall.

His eyes heated and he tugged me around a corner, ducking down to whisper his lips across mind. "Who do you belong to?"

"Johnnie Walker Lawson," I breathily answered.

He grinned, grabbing my jaw as he licked inside my mouth with a pleased growl. "And who do I belong to?"

"Me," I sighed into his mouth.

"That's right, baby. You. I belong to my sweet, sexy, shy girl."

I hugged him tight, burrowing into his chest. "I'm going to miss you."

He wrapped me up, holding me in his protective embrace. "I like to hear that."

"You're supposed to say you'll miss me too," I told him with a smile.

He chuckled. "I'll miss you, Shiloh Green."

I frowned, pulling away from him. "Will I see you after the show?"

He sighed, briefly touching his thumb to my bottom lip before we walked back to the dressing room. "Probably not. Joe will be takin' you to the airport about that time."

♪

But the end of the show rolled around and I wasn't on my way to the airport.

I was locked away in the dressing room.

With Dane Frederick staring at me with a wild look in his eyes and a gun pointed straight at me.

27

I know you're expecting some harrowing fight for my life.

Maybe some badass encore where I regain my independence with a blockbuster worthy battle yell.

Or maybe for Johnnie Walker Lawson to roll in like a knight in shining armor, prepared to battle his foe and to win the forever love of his damsel in distress.

But there were a few problems with those expectations.

One, and mainly, this was the most important one, Walker had already won my forever love. He'd coaxed it from me for a while. Then when my resistance proved to be wavering, he struck hard and true and stole it. Once in the palm of his hand, he nurtured it, watched it flourish and returned his own. Even if he still had yet to say the words. It was there. I could feel it. See it. Savor it.

So I didn't need him to prove his commitment by risking his life.

I also wasn't down for throwing myself into the fray. I wasn't a violent person. No matter if that person deserved it. I was soft in all the places that mattered and strong in all the ones that fell short. Violence wasn't always the answer. It was necessary sometimes but there were times, like this one, where a softer approach worked just as well, if not better.

Which led me to my battle for independence.

I didn't need Dane Frederick to reach some milestone in my search for an independent life.

All of this. This entire journey was me finding my way. Me crawling out of my protective shell and taking risks. Those risks were with Walker, a lot of them were.

But they were also with Mavis. Finding a friend that had always been fated to enter my life and latching on, forcing myself to be *more* than a girl that hid away in her bedroom all throughout her childhood, always wanting to go outside and play with the other kids on the playground but was too sensitive or nervous to take the risk.

It was also Brooks. It was Lake. And Jameson. It was opening myself up to people not normally in my wheelhouse. People that I would not have necessarily found myself befriending in other circumstances.

It was finding them and growing as a person, as a friend.

It was the tour in its entirety. Taking a chance on something a little crazy. A little exciting and a whole lot frightening.

It was a party with a rock band.

It was dancing in a club.

Singing in a bar.

A romantic night on a beach in Hawaii.

It was taking that first step out from under the loving umbrella of my parents and experiencing the pain and joy of my own mistakes.

I had gained my independence but I was also still searching for it. I likely always would be. I had a lot of life left to experience and I would always change and grow. My wants and needs growing with me.

But ultimately, finding my independence was standing there with a man holding a gun that was very clearly full of pain and guilt and staring my own precarious life in the face and deciding to reach out rather than run away.

His hand shook, his entire body trembled.

"Dane," Joe warned, holding his hands up in a placating gesture. "How did you get back here?"

"The roof," he strangely stuttered, his eyes glassy. "No one stopped me."

"Put the gun down, Dane. You don't want to do this."

Dane cackled a crazed laugh, tears falling from his eyes. "You have no idea what I want."

"I look like her, don't I?" I asked Dane.

He froze. His entire body stiffening as he turned his attention back to me. "What?"

"Layla. I look like Layla."

"Shiloh," Joe warned me from the other side of the room. I ignored him.

Dane blinked, looking me over. "Yeah," his voice broke with a sob. "You look just like her."

I nodded. I had suspected. Jameson's strange aversion to me at first. Walker's immediate attention.

I hadn't looked her up at first, not when Lake had said Dane didn't want Walker to have me, but the thought had been a whisper in the back of my mind for a while.

The calls started when I came on tour. They may have been coming before, but I knew they picked up a lot since then. Then he showed up, his eyes on me like they were familiar. His obsession had started nearly the time Walker's had I suspected. Then the gifts. Flowers. A teddy bear.

"Why are you here Dane?" I asked him softly, rooting my feet to the floor even as I was terrified.

"He can't have you," Dane whispered back. "He already let you die once."

"She's not Layla man," Joe barked.

"SHUT UP!" Dane suddenly screamed and I jumped, startled.

"Walker didn't let Layla die," I whispered. "You know he didn't."

"He did, he did," Dane chanted, waving the gun around. "He didn't do anything to save you."

"He tried to save her," I told him, waving Joe's warning away. "He loved her. Just like you did."

He nodded. "No one believes me. But I loved her," he choked out. "I loved you so much, Layla."

"You don't want to kill me," I told him, watching shadows creep under the door behind him. It was then real fear kicked in. If someone burst in, there was no telling what Dane would do. Cornered. Out of his mind. He would just react.

"No," he choked. "I want you back. I didn't mean it. I didn't mean to give you the drugs. I told you no." He took a step forward. "Don't you remember? I told you no, but you took them anyway."

"I thought she got them from Jameson." My mind was whirling.

"No." A sob and then a laugh and then another sob. "Jameson never gave you anything. He wouldn't do that to you."

"Jameson thinks he did," I told him.

"He was high. Drunk. He doesn't remember shit!" His arm swung wide and Joe and I both ducked. "You stole them from me! I told you no!" He then took a sudden step toward me. "We fought. Don't you remember?"

I shook my head. So confused. "No."

"You told me to leave! You were crying, upset about your dead mom, so I did what you said! I left you!"

I backed away, bumping into a table as he took several more erratic steps toward me. "You're scaring me, Dane."

He stopped, as if suddenly taking himself and me both in. His eyes flew to the gun. "I-I don't want to scare you."

"Then put the gun down," I coaxed. "Put the gun down and talk to me."

He choked back another sob. "I can't do that. I want Walker to pay. He deserves to pay!"

"Walker loved her too, Dane. He loved her so much. But she loved him too. You don't want to hurt someone she loved," I urged him. He shook his head. "You don't want to hurt someone I love."

He blinked, looking up at me through sweat-soaked hair. "You love him?"

"So much," I whispered, fear and emotion coating the words.

"Layla loved him too," he brokenly whispered back. "You're not Layla are you?"

I shook my head, my chest bursting open as the gun lowered minutely. "I'm not Layla."

"You don't have her eyes," he told me, stepping closer, I held my breath as he lifted a piece of my hair to run through his fingers. "You have her hair though." He tapped my nose. "You look so much like her."

I nodded, my eyes watering. "I'm so sorry, Dane. But I'm not her."

Shock rooting me to the floor, he dropped his head to my shoulder, the gun clattering to the floor. "I miss her."

I nodded, my stomach dropping as Joe dove for the gun but Dane didn't so much as flinch. He wrapped his body around mine, crying into my shoulder as he held me tight, his entire body shaking with the effort. "I'm sorry," he sobbed. "I'm so sorry."

Those three words rang in my ear as Joe tackled him to the ground. "I got him!"

Only then did my knight burst through the door.

But I hadn't needed him. I had a feeling he'd needed me a lot more than I ever needed him all along.

EPILOGUE

The last show in the states was the best one.

The crowd was the biggest. The loudest.

The music fueling them into a frenzy and the band ate every bit of it up and delivered the best show of the tour.

It was also the scariest.

I didn't know how my uncle held my parents back. How he convinced them I was okay and mentally capable of staying on tour. How Walker convinced them to give him a chance rather than drag me back home.

Even though Walker didn't hide anything from me, he also didn't feed me the details. The calls came less and less until they eventually only came once a day. Just a quick check-in to tell me they loved me.

For Walker's part, he was mostly back to normal. He slept a little more. A little deeper. He was still restless but it wasn't as much as before.

Jameson battled with what Dane had revealed the most. All this time thinking he'd given his sister the drugs that had killed her only to find out it hadn't been him at all. She'd gotten them herself.

The most uncomfortable conversation had been about my appearance. That Dane had been triggered seeing me in pictures after I joined the tour.

I looked like her. A lot like her. But there were differences. Subtle ones. Ones that came more pronounced after you got to know me.

I had her hair, even its length. Her button nose. Even the divot in her chin. But my eyes were my own, as was the dimple in my left cheek.

Our personalities were starkly different.

Layla was outgoing. A social butterfly. She loved to sing—music her passion. She wasn't shy or quiet. If anything, she had a lot more in common with Mavis.

Still, I would be lying if I said I wasn't self-conscious about Walker's interest in me.

That feeling didn't last long. After I brought it up, this look had come over his face. This horrified, disgusted look and then he had just shaken his head like he thought I was nuts.

"You look like her, shy baby, but not *that* much. I never wanted to fuck my sister."

Relieved, but still upset it had been kept from me, I remained distant the first few days.

It was Jameson that broke through to me.

"It may have caught his attention," he told me. "But once you opened your mouth or even smiled, you look nothing like her."

"But Dane was convinced I was her." He lost his mind with it.

"Dane was fuckin' nuts," Jameson told me. He felt not an ounce of sympathy for him after he had held me at gunpoint. Jameson may have understood Dane's pain and guilt at one point, but not anymore.

So it took a while, but after staring at her old pictures for hours, I was able to look past the small similarities.

It took some time, but we eventually found our way back to normal.

Well, rock-stars-on-tour normal.

But...

Walker Lawson *still* hadn't told me he loved me. So I was holding back just a little.

THE MORNING AFTER THE SHOW, FOUR HOURS BEFORE WE were to board a plane to Australia, Uncle V held a press conference.

Walker sat beside his brother as he told the world about the last year. About their sister. How she'd died, even though it was public knowledge already, they went into detail about Dane's part in it. It was newsworthy on its own, especially when just that morning Dane had been committed into a psych facility. Hopefully one where he could get the help he needed. But the media flame flared when they discussed me. How Dane had broken through a skylight on the arena roof, scaling the building like ninja. How I'd talked him down and Joe physically took him down.

I couldn't escape the attention. The media and fan frenzy.

We didn't know how the rest of the tour would go. Uncle V was preparing for anything and refused to allow anyone to avoid any of it. He wanted all questions answered as quickly as possible so it could eventually die down. The tour was still on, and beside it would be interview after interview. Public appearances.

Even my own. Walker hated every minute of it but it was Jameson who surprisingly bolstered me for every interview and appearance.

A little sister to him in a lot of ways—but none that had anything to do with the little similarities I had to his sister—and he a big brother to me. It was weird but only if I allowed myself to focus too heavily on Layla. If I put our very small similar appearances aside, then all I felt was warmth.

I had his back, there was nothing else I'd rather do. He was a completely different man than I had met in that limo all those months ago.

On the plane ride over he sat behind Mavis, his eyes stalking her as she steadfastly ignored him.

I sat with Walker, both of us curled up on the seats of the private jet and listening to a new song he and the band had recorded on the bus the night before.

It was dark. Sad. All of Jameson's pain poured into three minutes and forty-eight seconds.

It was one of the best songs he'd ever written.

Once we touched down on Australian soil, we booked into the hotel, exhausted.

Walker dumped all my bags by the door and had me up and on the bed, coming down to tear my leggings from me before I could even gasp his name in surprise.

My shirt shoved up to my neck so he could tear down my bra, his lips latched onto my nipple and sucked deep.

Overwhelmed from the emotional days past and long journey, my eyes fluttered and my back bowed, feeling every touch like he was drawing my attention to him with the force of a freight train.

His hand dropped to tear open his pants as I struggled with his shirt, getting it up and over his head as I growled impatiently.

He chuckled, ducking out of it and latching onto the other nipple. My panties went next and then he was right there, panting into my mouth. "You love me?"

Shocked from the words and the force he used to ground them out between his teeth. Scared out of my mind I nodded, unable to hide it.

"You're supposed to say you love me," I shot back.

His eyes gleamed with approval and he licked into my mouth just as he shoved forward and slid inside me. "You haven't been paying attention, shy baby," he teased.

"Yes I have," I panted. "And I've noted you haven't said it back."

He hummed, his hips pulling back to slowly sink inside me again. "You need the words from me?"

I nodded fast, so close already it was embarrassing. Just the anticipation of hearing them was going to send me over the edge.

He chuckled into my mouth. "Shy girl," he teased. "You know I love you."

I did, I so did.

He came at me fast, his thumb dropping to take me there. I flew apart immediately, his words a chant in my mind and he fell right behind me.

Sometime after, my eyes fluttering sleepily, he drew circles on my bottom, one arm under his head.

"Not tired?" I asked groggily.

"No, baby," he whispered. "I'm just gonna hold you a while."

"Mom wants to fly out to see you play," I managed to say.

He hummed. "Good. She and your dad can come to the show in London."

"Why that one?"

He ducked down to take my mouth in a soft kiss. "So they can watch me marry you."

My eyes flew open, *wide awake.*

THE END.

EPILOGUE 2

The phone ringing woke me. It was nearly four in the morning and I was supposed to be on my honeymoon.

After the best party and even better private after-party, I was spent. And so was Walker. He had nearly slept the entire night before my phone started blaring.

I groaned, burrowing into his warm side and he chuckled groggily, reaching around me to grab the phone off the nightstand.

"It's Mavis," he told me, rubbing his eyes.

I yawned. "I'll call her back in the morning."

Her and Van had gotten into a fight at our reception. I could tell she had been embarrassed, trying to discreetly escort his drunken ass from the party but he was belligerent, shouting at her.

There had been a moment when I thought Jameson would've caused a scene. His body had vibrated with need to intervene but Mavis had made it *very* clear he was to stay out of her private life.

And the singer was turning over a new leaf in light of his every word and move being cataloged by her even though she'd never ever admit it.

Then there was Walker who had warned him if he ruined our wedding reception he was going to "Beat the piss" out of him.

Lovingly of course.

Besides, Van was making a fool of himself all on his own. We didn't need to do it for him.

We left before her, but I did receive a million apology texts from her.

It was coming. I could feel it. She was starting to find the courage to fight back with him. I couldn't *wait* for her to dump him. Neither could Uncle V. He was ready to kick Van's entire band off the tour.

I honestly didn't know what held him back.

Walker smoothed his hand up my bare thigh, rolling me to my back.

I whined with exhaustion. "Tired," I groaned, burying my face into his arm.

He pressed his naked chest to mine, catching my face and forcing me to look at him. "You don't got anything for your husband?"

That word.

I shivered, waking up to focus on him and the hunger building in his eyes.

Her smiled wickedly and bent to take my mouth...and my phone rang. Again.

Walker groaned and dropped his mouth to my chest to lap at my nipple even as he handed me my phone.

My breath hitched as I answered it, my back bowing to get closer to his mouth. "Hello?"

"Shy," she said in my ear. Her voice broken and terrified.

I rolled away from Walker, sitting up on the side of the bed. "Mavis?"

"I need you," she sobbed into my ear.

My eyes shot to my husband's and he frowned.

"What's wrong?"

"Van," she sobbed. "I think I need to go to the hospital."

I was up and running for the door before she finished speaking.

Jameson: Chains and Dames Book 2 Coming Winter 2021

PLAYLIST

Inside the Fire- Disturbed
So Far Away- Staind
A Warrior's Call- Volbeat
lovefool- twocolors
Burning Man- Dierks Bentley (Feat. Brothers Osborne)
Slow Dance- AJ Mitchell (Feat .Ava Max)
Chocolate- 1975
Hangover Cure- Machine Gun Kelly
Oh My God- Alec Benjamin
Better Days-Goo Goo Dolls
I Fall Apart- Post Malone
comethru- Jeremy Zucker
Nothing Inside- Machine Gun Kelly

THANK YOU

Thank you for reading Walker!
Please take a moment to leave a review.
They help so much!

ACKNOWLEDGMENTS

I started this story back in June when quarantine blues were really starting to kick in. It's completely out of my usual wheelhouse but I love it all the more for that reason alone. It is dedicated to my mother who has suffered from Crohn's most of her life and whom I worried and still worry a great deal about with covid running rampant. She is one of many people that are at a far greater risk to covid.

Crohn's is a hard disease that takes a lot out of a person and those that love them. The illness looks different for everyone who suffers from it and often comes with many other complications. This book was written inspired by my mother's experiences and my own.

Please wear your mask and social distance for those like my mother and the people that love them.

Here's to finding your own special Superman like my mother found in my father and I have in my husband. May he or she be caring, understanding, and supportive in all ways that matter.

Wishing you good health and safety and love,

Erin.

BOOKS BY ERIN RAEGAN

Galactic Order Series

Pythen: Galactic Order Book One

Home World: Galactic Order Book Two

War For Earth: Galactic Order Book Three

Juldo Made: Galactic Order Book Four

The New King: Galactic Order Book Five

Pythen Blessing: Galactic Order Book Six

Shadow Assassin: Galactic Order Book Seven

Galactic Order Novellas

A Not So Lonely Christmas

Kilbus Lord Series

Playing Cards with Aliens

Flying in Spaceships with Aliens

Hunting Aliens with Humans (TBD)

Space Warrior Adventures

Battle Won: Book One

War Torn: Book Two (March 2021)

ABOUT THE AUTHOR

Erin Raegan is an obsessed reader, a dedicated writer, and a lover of all things fantastically impossible. When she's not plotting her next project, she spends hours on her Kindle, though nothing beats a real book in her hands. She can be found at home in Connecticut with her Chihuahua, Minnie, and her German shepherd, Odin, waiting with her six-year-old son for her active duty husband to come home.

For more information about Erin Raegan and her books, visit:

www.erinraegan.com

Facebook:

https://www.facebook.com/ErinRaeganAuthor/

Instagram:

https://www.instagram.com/author.erinraegan/

BookBub:

https://www.bookbub.com/authors/erin-raegan

Goodreads:

https://www.goodreads.com/erinraegan

Subscribe to her Newsletter:

http://eepurl.com/dIv6n1

Email:

author.erinraegan@gmail.com

Printed in Great Britain
by Amazon

61899502R00210